I0665762

Death at Rosewood Manor

Louise Penfold Mysteries
Book 1

Eva Bernhard

EB Press

Books by Eva Bernhard

Louise Penfold Mystery Series

Death at Rosewood Manor – Book 1

Death at Eagle Roost – Book 2

Agnes Taylor Mystery Series

Absent Beauty - Short Read Prequel

Silent Sands – Book 1

Writer's Death – Book 2

Snowbound – A Holiday Mystery – Book 3

Stormy Night – Book 4

ISBN 978-1-997787-02-0 (Standard Font Paperback)

ISBN 978-1-997787-03-7 (Standard Font Hardcover)

ISBN 978-1-997787-00-6 (Large Print Paperback)

ISBN 978-1-997787-01-3 (Large Print Hardcover)

ISBN 978-1-0688740-5-5 (eBook)

Editorial Services by Pam Clinton at pccProofreading

Cover design by EB Press with an AI generated cover image, using various AI models and Photoshop edits.

Though there are many lovely small towns in the Canadian province of Ontario, Cascade, its environs, businesses, and people are purely fictitious and a product of the author's imagination. Any resemblance to existing entities, characters, etc., would be coincidental.

Shadow, however, strongly resembles the author's much-loved pooch by the same name who shared her life many years ago. The kitty, albeit changed in appearance, is uncannily similar to the writer's more recently departed rescue.

 Formatted with Vellum

Don't miss the next
Louise Penfold Mystery

Death
at Eagle Roost

**Behind the grandeur of Eagle Roost
lurks a household at war with itself.**

To all the dogs and cats I loved before
and to present furry company.

Chapter One

With a shiver of unease, Louise Penfold frowned at the black-framed postcard among the junk mail. The famous sketch of praying hands—skin aged and veins protruding, cut off at the cuffs—stared back at her. Below the drawing, the legend read, *In Deepest Sympathy*.

Bemused, Louise turned the card over and read the message.

In the midst of life, death awaits.
Thinking of you.

'How weird,' she thought. 'Who sends a condolence postcard?' Her mouth twitched in distaste.

She glanced at the address portion, printed in sloppy letters.

To The Resident, 49 Charlotte's Lane.

The town and postal code were hard to decipher.

It couldn't be meant for her. She'd only moved in two days earlier. Maybe the previous owners suffered bereavement. Was that why they moved? She had no information on the sellers of the house. The deal had gone through digitally while she and her dog licked their post-divorce wounds on a trip to the Canadian Maritimes. Her lawyer and realtor dealt with the listing agent and the paperwork.

Of its own accord, Louise's hand crunched up the card. She let it drop and wrapped her wooly cardigan tighter around her torso. The evening had turned chilly.

No point in letting the odd missive mar her contentment. Her hand reached for the wine glass on the table next to her armchair.

Glass raised, she proposed a toast. "To fresh beginnings, Shadow. May our new home bring us nothing but happiness."

The pooch eyed her dolefully from below. From the very first, he'd been suspicious of the place. No one could blame him, considering how neglected and, yes, one had to admit, smelly the house had been.

Her contractor had worked wonders at record speed. Now, even a discerning canine like Shadow shouldn't scrunch up his nose at their spruced-up abode. She'd seen the potential of the 1930s one-and-a-half story, clad in cedar siding, despite the sad state it was in when she viewed it with her realtor.

With a contented *ahh*, Louise sat back in the armchair and glanced at her prized possessions. Favorite books breathed freely in the built-in shelving that took up an entire wall of the living room. They exuded the familiar scent of well-loved books.

The window wall her chair faced looked out onto the sloping, forested property. For a moment, the racing clouds revealed an almost full moon. In its eerie light, the branches of the sugar maples waved silvery-black in the wind.

Louise smiled to herself. What a setting for one of the mysteries she was planning. She'd switched to freelance editing and a home office to carve out time for writing. After years of working in the city and tired of Toronto's ever-increasing traffic, she'd moved to Cascade. Sedate small-town life, she thought, would be a tonic after a messy divorce. Just the place to begin life anew at fifty-two. Only me and my Shadow, she vowed.

At Louise's chuckle, her canine best friend cocked his head. Since nothing happened, he rested his beautiful black snout on his paws and closed his eyes, leaving Louise to her idle musings.

Spring came late in south-central Ontario. She might haul in some firewood for the woodstove tomorrow. More for ambience than from necessity in early May. The electric heat pump worked well this time of year. Next winter would be the actual test. She'd need some handy person to prepare firewood and help around the yard. Maybe plant some herbs and vegetables in raised beds.

A scream, muffled by the closed windows, broke into her thoughts and shattered the silence of the cozy room. At her feet, Shadow sprang to his haunches. Floppy ears pricked forward, his nose quivered. No bark came. Just a fretful whimper.

Maybe the little tyke next door woke up and requested his parents' attention, Louise thought. The kid was a bit of a screamer she'd noticed already since she moved in.

Yet her pooch clearly was not at ease.

"Shadow, what kind of watchdog are you?" Louise regarded her best friend with a mixture of indulgence and bemusement. If he could talk, he'd tell her neither his Labrador dad nor his Irish Setter mom had sported such genes. His specialty was spotting game and splashing through water. Leave guard duty to the Dobermans and Rotties of this world. Louise smiled at the image of a speaking canine. Oh boy, would they ever talk back!

Another shriek cut off her fanciful thoughts and sent Shadow—tail tucked firmly between his hind legs—scrambling for cover under her chair. Only his head fit. The gleaming black back wriggled in a vain attempt to follow.

"Now, don't turn coward on me," Louise admonished him as she got up and moved resolutely to the patio door. Though cautious in certain situations, Shadow had shown no signs of timidity before they moved here. At two, he wasn't a baby by canine standards. Still telling her dog not to worry, she opened the door and poked her head out, all the better to hear.

Prepared as she was for the next volley when an inhuman screech rose above the wind, Louise jumped back.

"Who's the coward here?" she muttered, exasperated at her reflex reaction. Cautiously, she ventured onto the deck. It ran the full width of the house's rear, suspended about eight feet above the sloping ground of the ravine lot. Its wooden structure was a mere six or seven feet deep, just enough for a small patio table.

With a growing suspicion of where the screecher was hiding, Louise crossed to the outer railing. Her loose cardigan billowed in the wind, sending a chill through the cotton top she was wearing underneath. Back turned to the ravine, her eyes scanned the roofline above the living room windows. All the while, her lips formed soft *pss–pss* sounds.

Suddenly, two yellow glowing dots appeared above the eavestrough. They contrasted sharply against the black of the shingles. A mournful meow rewarded her cat calls.

"What in the world are you doing up there, kitty?" Louise asked, aware of the pointlessness of her question. "If you've made it onto my roof, surely you might come down that way. No need for a midnight racket to wake the dead."

The disdain in the cat's answering mewing told her egress by the same route was not an option. Nor was the feline inclined to take a plunge onto the deck. Though the disembodied yellow eyes leaned precariously over the gutter. An arched back materialized as an errant moon ray penetrated the clouds. The cat remained aloft.

"Well, there's nothing for it," Louise said. "Stay put. Don't do anything silly."

Not a cat person, Louise wasn't sure if a jump would hurt the animal and shorten its nine lives by one. Of course, if she or he had forfeited some of the allotted number by similar stunts before, who knew what the score was now? Since the kitty seemed disinclined to take the risk, Louise bowed to the feline's better judgment.

Back inside, her canine awaited her, tail wagging in uncertain spurts as if unsure where he stood with his person after his cowardly retreat. She patted his head reassuringly.

"Males," she said, thinking more of her Ex than her devoted quadruped. "Desert you at the slightest provocation."

Shadow took her tone as 'all is forgiven' and wagged with vigor. Strangely, he made no move for the door to investigate the cause of their disturbance. She could feel the warmth of his body close to her leg as he followed her to the galley kitchen. Head tilted to one side, he watched her remove a ladder from the broom closet.

"Sit and wait," she ordered before opening the patio door anew.

It took much careful maneuvering to confer the ladder onto the porch and install it close to the wall without spooking the cat through a noisy clatter. Her whispered cooing probably didn't reach the kitty over the wind's whoosh. 'It's the thought that counts,' Louise told herself. Yet, from above, the glowing globes moved back and forth, watching her every step.

"Now, hang on tight," Louise said and mounted the rungs. Would the cat scratch her? Jump into her face when they came eye to eye?

The entire operation seemed foolhardy, she thought. She hadn't even stopped to trade her clogs for sensible footwear or changed the flapping cardigan for something less likely to snag on a roof nail.

"I guess we both are rather unprepared for our late-night adventure, kitty. Do me a favor and come quietly."

Up on the ladder as far as she dared go without increasing the danger of toppling it, Louise stretched out a cautious hand. If dogs preferred to sniff a new acquaintance before getting physical, so might cats.

This one apparently didn't stand on ceremony but rubbed a toothy cheek against the offered hand. A soft purr set the whiskers vibrating against Louise's skin. Emboldened, she let go of the ladder and reached with her left hand, her lips making little smacking sounds.

"There's a good kitty," she whispered. "Easy does it." Her fingers gently stroked the cat's head and glided down the sleek back.

After another minute of meet and greet, Louise lifted the cat off the roof. It hung limp in her arms as if this was their daily routine. Kitty cradled against her shoulder held with one arm, they descended to the safety of the deck.

"We'll leave the ladder where it is. You're free to go home. There are

5

the stairs." She deposited the uninvited visitor on the top step leading down to the backyard.

The kitty watched her make for the patio door. With one giant leap, the animal was inside as soon as Louise opened it.

"Oh, my!" Louise hastened after the intruder, more worried about damage to her beloved pooch than the cat. Shadow, she knew, acted rather goofy in encounters of the feline kind.

She needn't have hurried. Enthroned on the table for two in front of the window, the black cat eyed her.

About to shout, 'Get off my table,' Louise met the inscrutable yellow gaze and relinquished what she'd hoped to become her favorite breakfast and afternoon tea spot. She'd fondly imagined herself watching birds and squirrels scamper on the porch railing or twitter and chirp in the maple trees. The ravine lot would look gorgeous in any season.

Well, the cat would be gone again in the blink of an eye. Let her take the high road for the moment.

As if penetrating her every thought, the amber-yellow eyes, bright in reflected light, observed her—unblinking. Shadow sat bolt upright in front of the armchair across from the intruder. Considering canines beneath her, which he literally was, the cat ignored him and yawned. The little head rose, nose up in the air, revealing a loony-size white patch under the jaw.

'That'll help in ID'ing the kitty if need be,' Louise thought. At present, it didn't look as if the cat was ready to leave. Worst-case scenario, she'd have to canvas the neighborhood in the morning. Someone might know where it belonged.

"You'll have to donate a can of your salmon, buddy," Louise told Shadow and received a low whimpering in answer.

Though she knew he reacted to her tone and to the unwanted disturbance of their domestic peace, she said, "Don't be inhospitable. I'm afraid he or she is here to stay. Just for one night."

The cat raised a paw, turned it over, and licked the rosy pads thoughtfully.

Driven by an uncanny sense of the cat understanding every word, Louise retreated to the kitchen to prepare a welcome snack. Shadow stuck close to her side as she dropped a generous serving of salmon onto a saucer and filled a dessert bowl with water. She placed the meal within easy reach on the little table and grabbed a soft cushion for a makeshift bed on a chair. The cat might find it more comfortable than the wooden tabletop.

Then it hit her. "You'll need a litter box. We can't leave the door open." The windows had screens. Too chilly and windy to leave them ajar, anyway.

A plastic container would do. There was a bag of sand out front, she remembered. Left over from winter sanding, most likely. Louise smiled wryly, amused at her eagerness of playing hostess to the uninvited guest.

———

It was long after midnight by the time she'd let out Shadow and he'd settled in his dog bed. Up in her loft bedroom that spanned the width of the house, Louise sank wearily into her pillows and gazed at the sloping roof.

She turned off her bedside lamp and let her mind wander. The last weeks, nay months, had been exhausting. Divorce tired enough but sorting and packing up one's household while scouting and then renovating another took its toll. It drained one's physical, emotional, and financial resources.

'You can do it,' her drifting mind cajoled her. 'You have the strength, determination, and the skill set to succeed.' The freelancing editor gigs brought a steady income to get by on.

As she slipped toward sleep, the black frame of a condolence card floated by her mind's eye. Like a vague, ominous threat, it seemed in the inkiness of the night. She'd never checked the postmark. Who would send such a nasty missive? And to whom?

Chapter Two

The next morning, Louise woke with a heavy heart. Or so it seemed to her as her mind struggled to full consciousness.

Her lids felt gooey from sleep. She forced her muscles to wrench them wide.

And met the unblinking stare of her night-time visitor, firmly established on her chest.

Two paws kneaded Louise's flannel nightgown. Afraid claws might play a role in the exercise, Louise freed her hands from the fluffy blue and white comforter and reached for her bedfellow.

"My dear kitty, this is going too far," she said. "You're not the queen or king of the castle here."

The tiny mouth twitched as if in derision. But the sleek body went limp when Louise got the cat off her chest and rolled onto her side. They eyed each other while Louise's fingers stroked from the ridge of the kitty's nose to the cranium. Shadow liked the facial massage. So did this feline.

"Enough TLC. We'd better get up and find your home. Your people must worry where you are."

Jumping off the bed, the cat took command. The little body strode proudly to the stairs, back slightly arched, tail swishing. When Louise remained in bed, the cat uttered impatient meows.

Reluctant to leave the comfort of her pillows, Louise's glance traveled over the freshly renovated loft room. The satiny white paint worked perfectly as a backdrop for her collection of art prints and paintings. She loved serene country scenes in pastels just as much as abstracts in vivid colors. Many a summer, she'd spent scouring country fairs and local art exhibitions in search of treasures. When things got rough while still living in the city, the art in the sanctum of her study provided solace and a daily dose of imagined rural peace.

Light birch and ash Scandinavian furniture, with a treasured antique piece here and there, complimented the summary ambience. At the far end of the room, she'd created another favorite retreat in front of a south-facing window. Her work as an editor involved so much reading there just couldn't be enough cozy spaces to complete the work. 'Thank heavens for laptops,' she thought. Brain labor on the go meant freedom these days.

A much louder meow called her to order.

"Coming in a minute," Louise said.

She dressed swiftly in gray slacks and a roomy azure-blue sweater. The combination pleased her and gave a nod to her eye color. Her fingers reached to fluff her sleep-flattened hair. After the pandemic, she'd gone back to a no-nonsense short style, cut by a good stylist in Toronto. A small indulgence, just like the occasional spa treatment she splurged on. Lately, the hairdresser had suggested a coloring job. But Louise loved the tiny silver strands mottling her auburn hair.

The cat came back and wound its sleek body around Louise's calves.

"Alright, kitty. I get your point." They descended the rather steep stairs together.

Shadow stood waiting below. Louise lowered herself into a knee-creaking crouch and ruffled his floppy ears. The feathered tail thumped the floor in appreciation.

She slipped into wellingtons and opened the front door. The yard lay shrouded in dense morning mist despite the sunny day forecast.

Nose to the dew-covered ground, her pooch certainly delighted in the moist, earthy scents. He scampered ahead, intent on important doggy business.

With a deep inhale, Louise strolled along the graveled drive. She hugged herself in anticipation of her new life in this peaceful enclave.

Her step slowed. Too early for knocking on doors in quest of the kitty's folks. The thought of the midnight rescue made her smile. A mental flash of a black-rimmed, ominous postcard quenched any amusement. Impatiently, she brushed it aside.

As she neared the limits of her property, aware now of sweet chirping birds in the trees' canopy, a harsh voice cut through the mist like a whipping cord.

"You pay up, chum, or else we make you."

It stopped Louise in her tracks. The murmur of a second, younger-sounding male voice was too low for her to make out.

The first rose a notch. "Cut the BS. We mean business."

Before she could retreat, the younger male shushed in more confident tones. "Keep it down, man. Give me a couple of weeks." Then truculent, "Hell, I only missed one payment. You'll get your money."

Attracted by the noise, Shadow bounded up to Louise. She grabbed his collar and felt his throat vibrate in a low growl.

Embarrassed at the prospect of the men catching her eavesdropping, she retreated softly, pulling the pooch along.

Yet, the first man's hissed threat, "Three days. Or else..." rang in her ears.

For the next few hours, Louise concentrated on her editing labor, comfortably enthroned at her favorite spot by the living room window. With Shadow napping at her feet and the kitty up on the table across from the laptop, alternatingly gazing at the birds perched in the trees of the ravine and at Louise typing away, it felt like domestic bliss.

Still, a niggling sense of unease pervaded whenever her thought strayed to what she'd overheard.

By mid-morning, she stretched her aching back. Time for the neighborhood inquiry into the cat's home and a brisk dog walk. A scenic route down to the river trail from the end of Charlotte's Lane would bring them to the village and its attractive café.

Louise donned sensible shoes and a windbreaker and attached Shadow's leash. Resolutely, she pushed aside the lingering awkwardness at the thought of meeting the next-door neighbor after witnessing the money lender's visit. No reason for her to feel shamefaced.

Gone was the gray morning mist. Glorious sunshine revealed a transformed world. Bluebells and crocuses peeked out among a thick layer of last fall's leaves. The natural forest ambience of the property, with its fieldstone borders along the drive and flagstone walkway, resonated with her desire for countrified living.

When they stepped onto the lane, she glanced over her shoulder at her new abode. Dappled in sunshine, it felt magically secluded from the harsher realities of city life.

As if divining her intentions, Shadow aimed for their neighbor's place, hidden by giant spruce and pine trees. Much bigger than her one-bedroom, the white clapboard with decorative black shutters was typical for 19th-century Ontarian houses. Though no blooming plants enlivened the window boxes, here too, early spring flowers sprouted in the equally leafy ground.

With Shadow sitting expectantly at her side, Louise straightened her shoulders and grabbed the cast iron doorknocker to announce her presence.

Just then, voices drifted through an open window, causing Louise to yank back the knocker before it hit the steel plate. Should she retreat yet again? Too late. Someone might see her walk off.

A female voice grew louder, its tone impatient. "But it's on sale now. And we need it."

"I told you we can't afford it. 500 bucks isn't cheap either." The same voice as this morning, but it sounded exasperated now. Given what she caught about his money trouble, Louise could sympathize with the unknown man.

"We can so! If we get the money—"

Intensely uncomfortable with what felt like snooping, Louise let go of the iron clacker. Its clank echoed metallically. The voices ceased.

The door opened so suddenly, Shadow jumped to a stand, ears at attention, tail raised. Louise laid a gentle hand on his head, and he subsided into a sit.

A man's head poked around the door. Barely thirty, at a guess, flashed through Louise's mind.

"Oh no, you don't," he said. His knee appeared, clad in sweatpants, blocking the gap to the doorframe.

Taken aback and feeling guilty, Louise said, "I'm so sorry. I didn't mean to intrude. It's just..."

The man reached behind him. "God, no. Not you." Which disconcerted Louise even more. Had he caught her eavesdropping this morning?

"This little monster here tries to escape," he said, pointing downward with his chin.

At knee level, a tousled shock of red hair bounced back and forth in a private peek-a-boo game. Tiny hands gripped the door, vainly attempting to wrestle it open.

"Oh, goodness me." Relief flooded her. "I can come back later if more convenient."

"No, no. Hang on a sec." Masculine fingers reached for the child's hands and pried them loose quite tenderly.

A moment later, the door fully opened. The man stood, cradling the red-headed toddler, who squirmed in his arms.

"Doggie," the kid shrieked, both arms stretched toward an unimpressed pooch.

"You can pet Shadow when he's made friends with you," Louise assured him. "I'm Louise Penfold," she told the father. "Your next-door neighbor."

The little guy stuck two fingers into his mouth and sucked them with vigor while regarding her.

"Say hi to the nice lady," the man urged, whereupon the tyke buried his face in the father's sweatshirt.

"Again, I'm sorry for interrupting your morning," Louise said.

"Not to worry. I'm Trevor, by the way. And this is Holy Terror. Ah, unofficially," he laughed at Louise's incredulous expression. "On paper, he's called Daniel."

Behind Trevor, a young woman swathed in a flowing, ankle-length indigo dress emerged from an inner room.

"Here's Zoe. My wife. Meet our new neighbors. Louise and Shadow."

Like Trevor, in her early thirties, Louise guessed, Zoe's handsome face looked pinched from stress or the domestic squabble. The smile, as she stretched out her hand in greeting, appeared forced.

"Won't you come in?" Zoe's wavering glance belied the sincerity of the polite gesture.

"Maybe another time. I won't keep you but wanted to ask if someone around here misses a black cat with a white spot below the chin."

While she spoke, the young couple stiffened. Zoe's eyes widened and then veered to meet her spouse's. With a kid's radar for tension, Daniel hugged his dad tightly.

Trevor slid the toddler down along his legs to the floor and said, "You go play with your tractor, buddy. Daddy and Mom got to talk grown-up stuff. Too boring for you, bud."

Only when Zoe added encouragement did Daniel retreat slowly, his backward glances speaking volumes for his reluctance.

"Sorry to keep you standing at the door here," Trevor said. "We've got to get Daniel ready for his playgroup. Plus, I've a virtual meeting coming up."

Zoe interrupted Louise's renewed apologies, saying, "It's us who need to apologize. The cat is our auntie's. She ran off again last night."

Into Louise's astonished, "Oh?" Trevor grinned sheepishly. "No, not my aunt. The cat ran off." His face grew serious. "My aunt passed away recently, and her cat keeps returning to her place. Sorry, I mean, it's your place now."

"I see," Louise said. "I've heard people say cats feel more attached to their home than to their people."

"I think Magic is, or was, deeply attached to Auntie *and* to her home." Zoe's soft voice trembled. "So sorry she bothered you. We try hard to keep her inside."

"Ah, the kitty's a girl." Louise smiled. "And she's your cat now?"

"Sort of," Trevor said. "We need to find her a good home."

"Don't think us mean." Zoe wrung her skinny hands. "We tried. Magic doesn't like it here. She meows all day. I'm so worried she'll scratch Daniel."

"And no wonder if he pulls her tail," Trevor said. He crossed his arms over his chest. "I'm not sure it's such a bright idea to get the puppy."

Zoe's face scrunched up, and she turned on Trevor. "Daniel's still a baby. He'll learn. The puppy is good for all of us."

A head taller than Zoe and two inches above Louise's 5'9", Trevor rolled his eyes at Louise. "Fifteen hundred bucks for a pup. Never mind the vet bills."

No wonder anxiety lurked behind the young man's affable tone, she thought. Didn't his wife realize their financial difficulties?

But the young woman's fretful head shaking that set her long hair flying spoke of obstinance. She looked tempted to stamp her small feet on the wooden plank floor of the foyer cum mudroom.

"It's Magic who causes trouble around here," she cried. Dark eyes ablaze, the voice shook. "I know we promised Auntie to look after the cat. We never said we'd adopt her."

Her agonized expression pleaded with Louise. "I'm sorry Magic is such a bother. We hate to surrender her to the Humane Society. But if that cat stays with us, she'll find a way back home."

To her dismay, Louise saw tears course down Zoe's cheeks.

Trevor bent to lean his chin on his wife's head and slung his arms around her. "Don't cry, honey. We'll find someone soon. Won't be long."

Louise coughed gently. "Would it help if I were to foster Kitty? I mean, Magic. My, what an apt name for my midnight visitor. She's quite a character, isn't she?" Aware she was babbling to cover the evident embarrassment all around, Louise glanced down at Shadow's patient face. "Mind you," she said, "I'm not a cat person. Still, I think Shadow and I could manage for a little while with our feline guest."

On hearing his name, Shadow rose from daydreaming and nudged her leg with his snout. She fondled his ears. Her offer astonished her even more than it seemed to surprise the young couple. With a high-maintenance toddler, a puppy in the offing, and serious financial difficulties, these two had enough to cope with. How they hoped to afford a sizable house like this at their age was a mystery. Or did the parents pay for it?

In any case, Louise figured, a demanding cat who, indeed, had something magical about her might be a tad too much.

Trevor and Zoe outdid each other in their thanks and assurances of finding a permanent home for Magic as soon as possible.

Zoe was on her knees making friends with Shadow, who licked the salty tears off her cheeks, which brought on girly giggles interrupted by tiny sobs. Canine gentleman from glossy nose to feathered tail, he submitted to Zoe's hugs with grace.

Trevor and Louise were amid arranging a time for him to drop off Magic's belongings when a piercing scream came from the bowels of the house.

"Omigod!" Zoe sprang to her feet and swooshed inside.

Startled, Shadow sprang up against Louise, a habit he'd shaken already in his puppyhood.

"Down, there's a good boy," Louise murmured.

"No worries," the experienced father assured her. "Daniel is fond of exercising his lungs. Has a brilliant career as saxophonist ahead of him."

"Well, I'd better let you go, Trevor. I'm so glad to have met you and your family. We'll chat another time at more leisure."

"Our pleasure, Louise. I can't tell you how much your generous offer means to us. Life's a bit tough lately. What with my aunt's passing and everything."

"My sincere condolences on your loss."

Howls from inside cut off any further talk.

When Louise strolled down the lane a moment later, the ever-patient

Shadow right by her side, she shuddered at the thought of listening to the screamer's racket day in, day out. Enough to put anyone on edge.

The child, she pondered, might be the least of their problems. Was the young woman blissfully unaware of their dire financial difficulties? If Trevor got himself into the claws of threat-uttering loan sharks, the young couple was in over their heads.

But Trevor only asked for a two-week reprieve. Did he expect to inherit from his recently deceased aunt?

Chapter Three

Three-quarters of an hour later, Louise and Shadow reached the village by a circuitous route along the river path. The roller coaster up and down of this stretch of the famous Bruce Trail proved more strenuous than Louise had expected. If she was to keep up with her sure-footed companion, she must invest in proper hiking boots.

With much practice, she and Shadow might tackle other sections of the Bruce that snaked for over 500 miles through Ontario, from Niagara to Tobermory at the tip of the Bruce Peninsular on Lake Huron. The thought made her smile. Their morning hike covered not even two miles of the scenic trail. But wasn't there a proverb, 'a thousand-mile journey begins with a single step?' She'd made giant strides by that standard.

Down the village street, Louise spied the dangling sign of the local café sporting, as she knew from driving by, a witch riding a broom with the word 'Brew' entwined in the moon shape of the logo. Fatigued from her walk, Louise sauntered on, sparing many admiring glances at the picturesque houses along the village's main street.

When she'd first seen Cascade a year ago, tucked away in a corner of Ontario's rolling hills, she could hardly believe such a gem could still exist within a two-hour drive of the megapolis, Toronto.

Victorian beauties sat sedately in their well-tended yards next to modest clapboard or board-and-batten-sided homes. One or two original log cottages, much weathered after centuries of exposure to the tough Ontarian climate, caught her eye. White picket fences bordering the front yards were a nostalgic delight. Everywhere, early spring blossoms bloomed shyly as if distrustful of the balmy day.

A tug on the leash interrupted Louise's fanciful musings. Her prosaic canine aimed straight for the water bowl set out at the café for four-footed guests. A clean strip of outdoor rug provided a comfortable resting place. How thoughtful of the café owners to think of dogs-in-waiting.

Such an attractive place, Louise had already thought every time when driving by. Now, her glance lingered on its midnight blue façade. Tall flower containers, spilling spring flowers, flanked the entrance. Above the awning that was still tucked into its casing, Witch's Brew was emblazoned on a flat board with the broom-riding witch logo in an artistic rendition. The hanging sign she'd seen from afar proved to be black metal.

Too early in the year for the outdoor seating that drew her attention to the place last summer when she passed on the way to a country fair. The vision of families, hikers, bikers, and cyclists relaxing at umbrella-studded tables or on planter benches marking the patio's limits caused her to include Cascade in her house-hunting endeavor. She'd pounced when her realtor announced the new listing on Charlotte's Lane. The rest, as they say, was history. She smiled to herself.

Shadow nudged her jacket pocket. His tail beat a tattoo on the patio floor when she obediently unearthed his yak milk bone. "Right you are," she said, looping the leash through a cast iron ring on the wall. His favorite snack would keep him busy outside while she indulged in her own late-morning treat.

With a last check of the water bowl and a rub along Shadow's glossy back, Louise ventured inside the café. After the bright sunshine, her pupils took a moment to adjust to the soft indoor lighting. The narrow, latticed windows faced west and would illuminate the place in the afternoon. An assortment of cozily arranged mismatched cane and painted wooden chairs, round or square tables, dotted the room.

Fewer than ten customers enjoyed a morning break. In the back, a row of bookcases stood packed with books of all shapes and sizes. An elderly couple sat there in armchairs at a low coffee table, engrossed in their reading. Three women in hiking outfits, the trekking poles resting under their chairs, engaged in animated chat. Their table was loaded with food and drink as if they fortified for a major trek.

From behind the glass-fronted counter came a man's greeting. "Good day to you. What's your poison, then?"

"Never scare away new customers, Owen," said a woman and leaned back in a cane chair that creaked in protest. Clad in an old-fashioned, or perhaps timeless, mauve twinset and a nondescript gray-green skirt that clung to hip rolls and fleshy thighs, the woman regarded Louise over the rim of a coffee mug.

"Not to worry," Louise said and, after a perfunctory smile at the woman, turned to the counter. "I'm not easily scared. I'll have a cappuccino and a little something to go with it." Her gaze traveled over the sumptuous offerings displayed behind the curved glass.

"Hearty or sweet, I've got you covered," said the man. He leaned forward, pointing at trays full of small Danish-style squares. "Mushroom and sundried tomatoes, spinach feta, bacon, ham and cheese, you name it, I've got it."

If the laughter lines around his eyes and mouth were anything to go by, he must be her own age, she guessed. From the trim figure, muscular arms, and weathered skin, she pegged him as an exercise and outdoor enthusiast. He wore a short-sleeved white shirt over blue jeans. His proprietorial air fit an owner or manager rather than serving staff.

"Thanks. I'll have one of each. Oh, and add a cherry Danish for dessert. They look delicious." She hesitated. "Owen, isn't it?" When he smiled, she told him, "Your café looks so inviting. I'm Louise, by the way. Bet you'll see me and my Shadow quite often after our walks. We just moved here."

"Ah, yes," Owen said, already busy loading a plate. "'Tis' the lady of Charlotte."

His quick glance at her astonished face told her he aimed for effect.

"News must travel fast in Cascade." Louise's mouth twitched wryly. "I take it Camelot is just downriver from my place. Pray there's no curse involved." She certainly wouldn't want to float dead in a boat like Tennyson's Lady of Shallot.

Her neck prickled from a sense of being the center of attention. As if to decide on a table, she glanced around and met the furtive stare of a man hunched on a high stool by a window. When their gaze connected, his eyes shifted to his mug. A bar-like ledge, mounted along two outer walls, extended almost back to the book corner. Several such bentwood stools were available, but only this grubby-looking fellow in torn jeans and a tattered plaid shirt had opted for a window seat.

Behind the counter, the espresso machine hissed and spit. The scent of exquisite coffee had Louise's nose quiver.

Owen asked, "No marks for brilliant deduction, then?"

It took a second for her mind to recollect and to muster an amused smile. "How did you guess I live on Charlotte's Lane?"

"Elementary. You said you moved just now. Carol's place is the only one that sold recently. You lucked out. Hardly any houses come on the market here and are snapped up before you can say presto. You've beat the competition." An exaggerated widening of his eyelids made his pupils sparkle as he jutted his chin toward the twinset lady, who'd disappeared behind a broadsheet newspaper.

Louise heard her mutter, "I hear you, Owen."

The proprietor grinned at Louise.

"Hah, I might be renting a place." Louise continued the game.

"Not on your life, dear lady. You'd be hard-pressed to find anything but overpriced Airbnbs in this area. Now, would you call that 'moving?' I'd be doubting it."

"True," Louise admitted. "It sounds like you knew Carol. Her passing must have saddened her friends."

"We all mourn Carol." Owen's quiet words and sweeping gesture took in not only the woman veiled by the paper, but the man at the window and the elderly couple too absorbed in a bookish world to pay heed.

"Carol and Kendra," Owen tilted his head toward the twitching broadsheet, "were thick as thieves."

The newspaper gave a sharp crackle, and the woman's nose poked over its rim. Narrowed, ice-blue eyes aimed to pierce Owen with their unblinking stare. "Another of your ill-chosen cliches, Owen. In poor taste when speaking of the dear departed. Or of me, for that matter."

'Then why draw attention to it?' Louise wondered.

Far from contrite, Owen chuckled and addressed Louise in a stage whisper. "Kendra owns Precious Treasures, the antique shop down the road here. You might've gone by it, Louise."

He deposited her cappuccino and a plate with five pasties on the counter. "Make yourself comfortable. I'll top up your doggie's water and slip him a biscuit if I may." His fingers dove into a giant cookie jar labeled Dogs Only, and below a cartoonish grinning pup, Mutt's Special.

"Fresh from our local pastry chefs. Just like all the baked goods I offer. Jeremy and Jessie at Petit Four You supply us daily."

"My goodness. I'll pack on the pounds in no time." Louise sighed with anticipated delight at such treats.

Owen's cheerful laugh increased the lines on his skinny face. How did the man stay so slim among his delectable wares? Shaking her head at the mystery, Louise took her cup and plate to a nearby table within speaking distance of the antique dealer, Kendra. Eager to explore her chosen community, the allure of an antique shop decided her. A good relationship with local proprietors paid dividends. Healthy neighborhood and community relations mattered in villages.

At the first bite of the flaky pastry, a tiny, pleasurable moan escaped her. Ham and bacon melted into gruyere cheese and rich buttery puffed dough sent her taste buds into ecstasy. And cholesterol levels into alarm mode, Louise's voice of reason commented. Just today, she appeased her conscience as she munched the equally mouth-watering cremini squares studded with tomato morsels.

When she raised her cup, she encountered her neighbor's stare. Framed by more strawberry than blond wavy hair, Kendra's chubby cheeks protruded when she smiled. It turned the earlier stern expression into a homey, good-natured countenance.

"Go down a treat, don't they?"

"Divine. Best I've had in a long time." Louise closed her eyes in gourmand delight.

"We're all addicted to Jeremy's heavenly creations. As you can see." The lady hooted and patted her bulging stomach.

"So rare for a village to have a bakery at all these days," Louise said.

"Did I hear bakery?" Owen's voice cut in. He'd returned unnoticed. "Patisserie, I have you know. They're a cut or two above your average bakery if such things still exist. No assembly line frozen dough at Petit Four You."

He passed between their tables on his way to the counter. "Your Shadow is a wonderful fellow, Louise. Licked my nose in thanks for the treat."

"My, the pooch must like you a lot. He can be a little stand-offish," said Louise. "Thanks, Owen, for caring about canine guests. You certainly impressed Shadow, it seems."

"My dog whispering charmed him and won his heart." Owen's features wrinkled into a broad grin.

"The treat didn't hurt either," Kendra remarked dryly.

"Join you in a tic. Folks will come soon for lunch. My chance for a quick break." Owen's glance scanned the room, apparently making sure none of the guests wanted refills.

Louise had barely time to ask the antique lady about grocery stores in the vicinity before Owen returned with a plain white mug holding black coffee.

"Do you work the floor all by yourself?" Louise asked him. "I've noticed in passing how busy the place gets in summer. It's still your slow season now, isn't it?"

"Business is steady at lunch and teatime. My employees' shifts vary. The servers come on in half an hour. Kitchen staff's prepping already." He waved in the direction of a door near the espresso machine. Louise had noticed it but assumed it was the delivery entrance.

"So, how do you like your leafy tree house on Charlotte?" Owen asked. "Hope you don't find it too spooky at night."

Chapter Four

Louise laughed at Owen's remark about her new abode. "It has its spooky moments, alright," she said, thinking of her midnight visitor. "Such a lovely little cottage. Quite bewitching," she added, ready to launch into a dramatic recital of the cat rescue mission but missed her chance.

"I hear you've already increased your menage. Terrific of you to take in the cat. Not everyone would."

"People are ridiculously superstitious," Kendra said with a snort. "Nothing unlucky or witchery about black cats."

"Oh?" Louise frowned. "How do you know?"

Though she'd meant Owen, the antique dealer raised a scornful brow and took her to task. "What? You dabble in the occult?"

"Hey, black Magic," tee-heed Owen.

Despite the merriment, a vision of the disembodied amber eyes against the dark night sent a shiver over Louise's arms. She rubbed them crosswise. "I meant, how did you find out so quickly about me fostering Magic?" Again, it sounded ambiguous to her own ears.

"No witchery involved," Owen said. "Trevor stopped by after dropping off the howler at playschool down by the church. He grabs coffees for him and Zoe."

He downed his own coffee and looked straight at Louise. "Don't get me wrong. We all dote on Daniel, the terror. But he sure is a handful. The much-plagued parents are thoroughly grateful to you for riding to the rescue."

"Inexperienced parents. Overindulgent, if you ask me." Kendra's lips puckered in a moue of disapproval. "No child of mine ever got away with tantrums."

Louise could well believe it. To change topics, she remarked, "Illness is a challenge for seniors living alone. What a solace and help for Trevor's aunt having him and Zoe next door."

A barely suppressed snort from Kendra. The woman's features, however, remained affable. Maybe she suffered from congestion.

"Too late. Rather sad." Owen shook his head in regret. "Not much they could do for Carol. By the time they moved back from Europe, Carol had transferred to Rosewood."

"I'd no idea," Louise said. "Somehow, I'd assumed they'd lived here for a while."

"Bad timing," Owen continued the tale. "Yep, they'd bought the house to be close to his aunt. Trevor convinced his bosses to recall him to head office in Toronto. Works from a home office anyway and can manage the overseas portfolio from anywhere. A few days before the closing date on their house, Carol took a bad turn. Was lucky Kendra found her and called 911. Saved her, Kendra did."

Owen nodded at the antique dealer, who gave a deprecating head-shake, saying, "If I hadn't, old Simpson would've called them."

Out of the corner of her eye, Louise noticed a movement and caught the gruffy guy watching them. As he hunched forward, strands of greasy hair escaped the rubber-banded ponytail and covered his hawklike features to the tip of his nose.

Distracted, she said, "What luck, indeed. Did Carol pass away in hospital then?" Surely, a listing agent would've disclosed a recent death on the premises if the elderly lady died at home.

"No. They kept her for a few days," Owen said. "She passed away at Rosewood. They could accommodate her on short notice. Carol had reserved a place for the future but assumed she had years before the need arose."

"Overly optimistic at her age," muttered Kendra.

"Sorry, I don't quite follow," Louise said.

"My bad. Should have explained properly." Owen leaned back as if to launch into a good yarn. "Rosewood Manor is a local assisted living and nursing facility. They admitted Carol to the nursing wing of the residence. She'd hoped to spend a good many years in one of their suites." When Louise's eyebrows shot up, he said, "Hey, nothing grand. Nicely done up place and popular around here." He nodded toward the guy by the window, who'd turned his back on them again.

"So sad it didn't work out for her." Aware it sounded inadequate, Louise groped for empathetic words. But a vision of the strange missile she'd found in her mailbox intruded. Might the Canada Post carrier have filed it in the wrong compartment of the community mail station at the end of Charlotte's Lane? Was the condolence postcard intended for Carol's nephew and niece next door? No. Carol's, or rather her own, house number showed in the address line, didn't it? She'd need to check later.

"Carol wouldn't have enjoyed life in a nursing home," Kendra put in, which caused the gruff guy to sneer over his shoulder.

"You can't know that," Owen said rather sharply.

'Do they vie for who was a closer friend of the departed?' Louise wondered. Earlier, Owen appeared to include the loner at the window among the grieving friends. Yet, no one spoke to the man or he to them.

As if closing the topic, the antique lady asked Louise affably, "How did the renovations turn out? I'd love to see what you've done to the adorable place."

'Is she inviting herself on such short acquaintance?' mused Louise. Her brief hesitation relieved her of a need to respond because Owen jumped into the breach. "Kendra is dying with curiosity. She'd hoped to buy it directly from Carol and primp it for a money-spinning Airbnb or flip it. Isn't that so, Kendra?"

"Don't exaggerate. They hardly are goldmines." She gave a tug at the hem of her twinset and pointedly addressed Louise. "The intention was to save a non-designated heritage home from the wrecking ball. Carol abhorred the thought of its destruction. I promised to keep it safe and am so pleased you did so for me. Wherever she is now, Carol will smile on you."

"Kind of you to say so. The little place has good bones and was worth renovating. I'm afraid I can't lay claim to loftier motives. Though, I never considered tearing it down. Much too expensive to rebuild from scratch."

"No hidden treasures unearthed in the process?" Kendra chortled at her own joke.

"Yeah," Owen chipped in and sang a line about being a miner for a pot of gold, which Louise dimly associated with a Neil Young tune.

"I'm afraid no stunning revelations are in the offing." Louise smiled. "An interesting thought, though. Would it be finders keepers? Or would a treasure retroactively become part of the estate and go to the heirs? The young couple might appreciate such a find."

"I doubt they're the immediate heirs," Owen said. He sounded quite somber. "Carol's son, Dennis, must be her heir. Trevor's only a great-nephew. They just call her aunt. Always thought there's some history there," he ended vaguely.

"Oh, I see," Louise said, though she didn't quite. "Does the son live in town, too?"

"Nope, only here for a visit, Dennis is. Wraps up Carol's legal affairs and hops back on a plane for Australia, I assume." Owen mimicked a flight taking off.

The antique dealer's nostrils twitched in a sniff. "He's never been much help to dear Carol in her lifetime." Her plump features puckered as if biting into a particular sour lime. "Curious how relatives swarm when you're about to take your last breath."

Louise wondered if Kendra worried about her own offsprings' grabbing nature. At the most in her mid-fifties, she'd not be in danger of imminent demise. Yet, acquisitiveness of loved ones could materialize in other unpleasant fashions. Enough to jade anyone.

"Come, come, now," soothed Owen. "No cattishness."

'Oh, my,' thought Louise, and aimed for lightheartedness. "Well, in any event, no secret hiding places surfaced. My contractor didn't exactly gut

26

the walls. But it would be a slim pot of gold fitting between the studs." She laughed at the mental image.

"Ah, there's always the basement." Owen mirrored her joking tone.

"No luck," she shot back. "It's crawlspace only, with an ancient dirt floor."

"All the better for hiding bodies." He chuckled, his eyes sparkling at her.

"Really, Owen. That's not funny," Kendra admonished him. "It's disrespectful to Carol."

"You sure are on your high horse today, Kendra. What's ailing you? Carol died in her bed at Rosewood. She'd be the first to laugh at my little joke."

He swiveled back toward Louise. "I'm sorry. Should've thought of you living there. Just ignore my flight of fancy, Louise."

"No harm done, Owen. Oh, look at the time. I really need to get going. Shadow's been patient for so long. And work awaits me. Let me settle my bill, and I'm off."

"Heck no. Today's on the house. Our standard welcome to Cascade." A wide grin split his features. "Devious plot to tempt newcomers back."

"How sweet—and hearty—of you." She found herself smiling at him with more warmth than seemed warranted. He was a likable chap.

As Louise made for the exit, accompanied by the solicitous proprietor, the antique lady shrouded herself again behind the discarded newspaper. From its shelter, she called, "Be sure to visit Precious Treasures. I'd love to show you around."

At the door, Owen said to Louise, "Come again soon. You and your pooch are always most welcome. Oh, and if you need help, we're only a buzz away. Eh, Alfred?" He pointed to the grubby guy on the barstool, who gave them a vacant stare. Hard to tell if he was their contemporary or merely an unwashed 40. Dirt exaggerated the skin creases, turning them into furrows.

"Alfred here," continued Owen, unfazed by the lack of response, "might be induced to continue as gardener and handyman. He did for Carol."

Though he must have heard, the man didn't react but buried his hawk nose deeper in the mug that must have been empty by now.

Louise said with studied politeness, "I'll keep it in mind." Then, warmly to Owen, "Thanks so much for the hearty welcome. I enjoyed our chat and feel already a connection to this beautiful community."

"Any time, Louise. We're glad you joined us." He waved his farewell and disappeared inside the café when she untied Shadow's leash.

Louise saw a couple of cars pulling into the parking spots. Owen's lunchtime customers were about to descend.

When she glanced back at the Witch's Brew, a movement behind the window caught her eye. Was it her imagination, or did Alfred scowl at her from behind the glass?

"Time to head home, Shadow." His dark brown, velvety glance regarded her dolefully as she wrapped his rather drooly yak bone in a plastic bag she carried for the purpose.

"You've been a wonderful and patient boy." Ruffling his neck and ears, she said, "Home, we go. Magic is waiting."

She could have sworn Shadow groaned at the mention of the kitty's name. Or did he expect magic of a different kind?

Chapter Five

Rather than retracing her steps along the scenic river path, Louise took the short route home along the village streets and lanes. Still, lots to sniff for a keen canine nose.

She stopped at the mailboxes but found neither letters nor postcards, offensive or otherwise. The watercolor header image of a laminated flyer tacked to the community notice board next to the mail station caught her attention. Set in a picture-perfect spring garden, a stately gothic revival home sported steep gables and a wraparound porch adorned with hanging plants and trailing vines. Two blue old-fashioned rocking chairs invited the viewer to rest a while.

The caption read:

Rosewood Manor — We Care for You

That must be the nursing home where Carol spent her last days, Louise deduced.

The primary purpose of the flyer appeared not to be an advertisement for their services but soliciting for volunteer readers. 'An hour of your time brings immeasurable pleasure to our residents,' it said.

Louise could well imagine that many seniors would prefer the company of a flesh and blood reader to a lonesome consumption of audiobooks, no matter how professionally done. Worth considering volunteering as an excellent way of giving back to her chosen community.

She captured the flyer and contact info with her phone's camera. "Who knows?" she told Shadow, who listened, head tilted to one side. "They might appreciate a therapy dog, too. I'm sure I do." He licked her nose in agreement when she bent for a hug.

Back in their new abode, Magic greeted them at the door, weaving her sleek black body around Louise's calves and letting Shadow sniff her rear end without swatting his snout.

Pleased with this progress in animal relations, Louise offered them a salmon snack, bowls several yards apart. She'd proved Shadow as a young pup against food and toy protectiveness, a vital precaution in case he'd mouth something unwholesome or hazardous. Yet, she didn't wish to risk a claw encounter lest he felt duty-bound to clean the cat's bowl.

Dog at her feet and cat at eye level, Louise settled for a few hours editing at the table overlooking the ravine. Over years of collaboration, the client relationship with the true crime writer, Odette, morphed into friendship. For this manuscript, they'd completed fact-checking and in-line editing over the past weeks. Nitty gritty proofreading in this final editing round required Louise's closest attention. After glancing at Magic, whose scrutinizing gaze didn't waver, Louise became completely absorbed in the editing task.

By mid-afternoon, Louise felt stiff and bleary-eyed from staring at the screen. Time for a short dog walk before Trevor would deliver Magic's belongings.

When she'd viewed the house with her realtor during the annual snowmelt, the property was covered ankle-deep in slush and mud. They'd inspected only the area around the house, but she'd looked at aerial maps and Google satellite images to get a sense of what she was buying into.

Perhaps she and Shadow could venture farther out today. The sunny weather invited adventure, and the blackfly season hadn't started yet. Within the next weeks, the back part of her overgrown property, which sloped towards the cascades the town was named for, would become infested with the little bloodsuckers.

Equipped with rubber boots, denim pants, and a sturdy jacket, she felt armored against brambles and pesky insects. She pocketed a small pair of clippers in case Shadow got snared in the undergrowth. He cavorted around her, sensing an off-leash romp was on the cards.

"Back in a while, crocodile," she told Magic, who observed their every move, a paw raised thoughtfully to black lips. Rosy tongue protruding between white fangs, the kitty replied with a pointed meow. Louise suspected the feline understood humans all too well. The oval pupils didn't miss a thing.

The moment she opened the patio door and gave the go-ahead, her exuberant canine bounced down the porch steps at a gallop. In her clumsy wellingtons, Louise padded after him at a sedate pace. Shadow aimed for a breach among the tall evergreens. She hadn't noticed the decaying wood fence separating her lot from her unknown neighbors' on that side.

"Good boy." Louise praised Shadow's ingenuity of discovering the most accessible route.

The fencing panels and posts were a few inches taller than her 5'9" but leaned increasingly towards her side. Ten yards down the slope, they ended abruptly in a tangled heap of underbrush and pruning debris piled haphazardly. Difficult to tell if the decaying twigs and branches stemmed from Carol's or the neighbor's amateur arborist efforts. No professional, Louise assumed, would leave such a mess.

A sharp bark interrupted her musings. Feathered tail raised high at its root, Shadow stood frozen.

From behind the final section of the fence came a wheezy cackle. A wizened visage, hallowed by yellowish-white hair, poked around the precariously tilted post that must once have anchored the fencing panel.

"The hound of Baskerville." The quavering voice stumbled over the last word into a phlegmy cough.

Louise stepped forward and grabbed Shadow's collar, though her trusted canine was not prone to attack. From that angle, she perceived a remarkable figure whose back curved in a permanent stoop, causing the skull to jerk forward in a bird-like fashion. Clad in an ancient tweed jacket of indeterminate color at least two sizes too large for the sparse frame and sagging pinstriped trousers stuck in rubber boots of a disproportionally large size, he peered up at her. Was he her neighbor or a gardener well-advanced in age and of uncertain temperament? For the claw-like hands thrust vicious-looking hedge shears, blades gaping wide open, in Shadow's direction.

In case the man felt tempted to jab at innocent pets, Louise said in an affable, soothing tone, "How do you do? A fine afternoon, isn't it?"

The shears swung and jabbed in quick, upward stabs as if aiming for her head. Louise thanked heavens for the ten feet separating her from the apparition.

"Come to live here? Took over Carol's dumpy place, haven't you?" His voice seemed hoarse from disuse. Maybe he was just a lonely, socially disconnected senior and unaware of his threatening stance.

She mustered a stiff smile. "I moved in a few days ago. Glad to meet you, Mr. ..." She raised the pitch to turn the last bit into a question. "I'm Louise."

"Rhymes with geese, *hee hee.*" The merriment culminated abruptly in another hacking cough that made her step back involuntarily. "Simpson, Simpson is the name."

For a moment, Louise wondered if it was a double-barreled surname but rejected the notion as unlikely. The man's respiratory issues made her hanker after the masks of yore. Pandemic habits had their advantages in social discourse.

"Well, Mr. Simpson. A pleasure, I'm sure. Shadow, here, and I are out for a little jaunt around my backyard," she said. "We'll let you get on with your yard work."

He wasn't finished with her, though. "No cat, I hope?" The shears jabbed again toward her dog. "Can't bear the creepy creatures." His rheumy eyes darted as if one might lurk in the bushes.

Before Louise could admit to fostering Magic, the man hissed, "The evil beast. Carol let it roam free. Attacked dear Peek-a-boo, the Lord rest his poor soul."

"Who attacked whom?" Louise asked, thoroughly puzzled.

"The beast," Simpson cried. "My lovely Peek. Dead."

"Oh, my God. You don't mean Magic, er, Carol's cat, killed yours?" Visions of neighborhood catfights and her midnight visitor revealing a Jekyll and Hyde personality unsettled her.

The watery eyes narrowed into slits. "You know that witch cat?" Suspicion dripped from every word.

"*Know* might put it too strongly." Louise dissembled. 'Truth be told,' she thought, 'it would take a lot to know the enigmatic feline.' Opting for diplomacy, she inquired, "What breed was yours, then?"

"Just told you, lady. A Peek."

"Oh. A Pekingese dog." Not a cat at all. "Ah, they're sweet." She covered her confusion. Surely, Magic couldn't kill a dog. Weren't some Peeks aggressive? Of course, so were some other dogs if ill-trained. When walking Shadow on the Toronto lakeshore trail, small-breed dogs often yapped and snapped at him, mostly in fear aggression. Yet, she'd better hear the worst about her foster fur baby now.

"Did your, er, Peek-a-boo, was that his name? Did he get into a fight with Carol's cat? Was it cat scratch fever that took him?" To be on the safe side, she'd get Magic checked out by a vet in case the kitty carried the bacteria causing the fever.

"My lovely Peek was fifteen when he passed last May. I lit a candle on the anniversary."

"I'm so sorry," Louise said. "A ripe old age for your little pooch. Elderly dogs are so much less mobile. They can't run from a cat."

"It wasn't a cat's scratch killed him." Simpson rose to his full height of almost five feet. He thrust the tip of his shears against the fence post. The clang made Shadow jump.

Spittle spewed from the withered mouth. The words came in a venomous hiss. "She poisoned him."

Chapter Six

Bemused, Louise trotted after Shadow, who scampered ahead through the tangled vines dangling from the tall maples. Every so often, he darted into the underbrush for a quick sniff. When a chipmunk or squirrel shot up a tree, he stopped dead, a front paw raised.

Whatever had her shear-brandishing neighbor meant by his ominous parting shot? No answer came when she asked. He'd raised two dirty fingers and brushed them over his quivering lips in a ludicrous zipping motion. Without another word, he'd snapped the shears shut and disappeared behind the fence.

She'd watched his hunched figure clambering up the slope to his house. Even without a white beard and pointed red hat, he'd reminded her of garden gnomes.

'How uncharitable,' she scolded herself now. Yet, an aspiring writer's imagination had a mind of its own and lived by vivid imagery. If Mr. Simpson were six feet, rather than barely five, his blade-wielding would have frightened her. The man couldn't seriously believe Carol had poisoned his Pekingese, could he? She must ask Trevor or Zoe about the incident.

Increased light made her look up. The dense growth gave way to open space. Freed of any constraint, leash or brush alike, Shadow barreled ahead. It took a moment for Louise's mind to process the visual clues. There was nothing at the far end of the sloping field. A void. Or, at least, a sharp drop to the unknown.

"Stop!" Her shout brought her pooch to a cartoon-like halt. Comical if her heart wasn't pounding so.

With no further risk of her best friend going over the edge, Louise took in the lay of the land. About 500 yards across from them rose the opposite side of the river ravine, studded with stunted trees precariously perched on rock outcrops in the granite cliff face. A few villas dotted the forest at the top, lawns sprawling to the edge.

Of course, she'd known her property was near the cataracts, the cascading river section. Neither the Google satellite image nor the survey made her suspect the lot dropped off sharply. If she'd thought of it at all, she'd have pictured a gentle slope and water meadows.

Time to investigate. With Shadow called to heel, Louise ventured out into the wilted grass, flattened by months of snow and rain. Some hardier weeds and limp stalks of rotting goldenrod stuck in tufts. Molehills the size of dwarfed melons pockmarked the ground.

Off to one side of the field, she noticed a large pile of detritus. Discarded junk, half-hidden by weeds and more pruning debris. How annoying not to have walked the property during the pre-closing inspection. She could have asked for the junk to be removed at the seller's expense, she thought. Now, it would cost her.

First things first. "Sit and wait," she ordered Shadow when they were ten yards from the edge. As she proceeded cautiously, she heard him yip and whine. Later, she wasn't sure what made her do it. She crouched, stretched out on her stomach, and inched forward. Her senses, she assumed, must have signaled she ought to see a slope now. If there were one.

Head thrust forward, she gasped. There was nothing immediately below where she lay. About a hundred feet down, the raging waters of the river, swollen from the spring melt and rainstorms, cascaded over rocks and boulders. A mesmerizing sight.

Mouth dry and limbs contracting in timorous spasms, Louise crept backward. Only when she'd put several yards between herself and the ledge suspended over the void did she dare rise to her feet. By now, Shadow was keening but kept to his assigned post. She crouched close to him for a hug.

"You sensed something was amiss. Foolish human that I am, I didn't listen." The tremor subsided slowly. "Heights are not my thing," she said as if that had caused her fear and trembling. A relentless battering of the elements must have undermined the outcrop where she'd lain face down moments ago.

From a safe distance, the view over the valley was stunning. An ideal spot for a gazebo with a wrap-around porch. Her mind pictured it. A writer's bower.

"A folly, they used to call it," she said aloud. A lick on the nose was Shadow's enthusiastic response.

"First, we need someone to remove the junk. It's an eyesore." Once spring had sprung, she'd seed wildflowers. Her imagination raced ahead, conjuring vivid images of her reclining on a chaise, laptop on her knees, best friend by her side. She might churn out mystery after mystery, her gaze lingering over the vista, courting the muses.

Her pragmatic mind kicked in. "Enough fanciful meanderings, Shadow. Let's check this garbage pile."

With her companion prancing ahead, all worry forgotten, Louise approached the unsightly heap. On closer inspection, she recognized rusty farm equipment. A lidded milking can caught her eye. Spruced up, it would make an attractive umbrella stand or vase for bullrushes and dried flowers. She tugged at its handle and freed it from the stranglehold of weeds. Empty of anything but spiderwebs, loose grit, and rust, it didn't feel too heavy to carry back home.

Some farm implements, like a seed spreader, a wooden plow mounted to a single steel wheel, and various tools might make interesting lawn ornaments. She'd need someone's help sorting the 'worth keeping' from the 'haul to the dump.' Might ask the antique dealer...

"Time to head back," she told Shadow, who nosed the grass for enticing scents. "Trevor's due in a short while. We've stayed out far longer than planned."

By the time they'd clambered through the woods and were within sight of the house, Louise hauling the milk can, she felt a little breathless from the exertion. Vigorous exercise must move up on her bucket list if she wanted to get in shape for the Bruce Trail.

She almost stumbled over her pooch when he stopped. Ears pricked and tail wagging furiously, he pointed a paw. Louise wiped the sweat from her brow and followed his gaze.

A little procession came marching down her graveled drive. Zoe strode several steps ahead, dark hair cascading onto the back of her indigo maxi dress. Her arms hugged a large bag, which Louise assumed to be the cat food. In her wake followed Trevor, swinging a plastic cat crate from one hand and a cloth shopping tote from the other. Daniel formed the rear guard. His tiny feet tripped over the cat bed he dragged by his side.

Trevor glanced over his shoulder and scolded. "Lift it higher. You get it all dirty."

A gurgling laugh was the kid's only answer.

"Daniel!" The dad's voice rose.

Conscious of witnessing what might not be intended for her ears, Louise yoo-hooed and waved. A joyful woof did the rest. All eyes swiveled their way. Shadow raced ahead to greet his newfound friend while Louise ambled after him. Zoe dropped the bag and crouched to envelop the pooch in a hug.

"Hey, Louise," said Trevor and lifted the tote and crate a fraction instead of a wave.

"So good of you to come," Louise said, still breathless from the climb. "Let's bring it all inside."

"Hi, Louise." Zoe smiled, arms holding Shadow, who nosed her hair. "Did you find that in the woods?" The oval chin pointed at the milking can.

"Not exactly," Louise said. "There's a junk pile in a clearing at the bottom of my lot. It'll need sorting."

"Oh, Trevor can help." Zoe volunteered her spouse.

A slight frown passed over Trevor's face. His "sure, no problem" showed no sign of dissent.

Daniel watched curiously from below, thumb in his mouth, the other grubby fist clutching the fleece of the pink cat bed. When Louise smiled at him, he dropped it and plopped bum-first into the soft nest, gurgling what sounded like, "Kiddy, kiddy."

"Daniel," Trevor admonished him sharply. "Get up!"

"No harm done," Louise said and kneeled in front of the giggling child to speak at eye level. "Let's go see the kitty. My, she'll be so happy you brought her pretty things." She stretched out her hands to hoist Daniel up.

His green eyes sparkled with mischief below the thatch of red curls. He removed a drooly thumb from his mouth and pointed his fingers at her. Before she could prevent it, he bounced up, slung his arms around her neck, and nuzzled his wet lips against her shoulder.

Louise struggled to her feet, holding on to the warm little body with one arm while steadying herself with her other hand.

"Really, Daniel," said Trevor.

Zoe's soft voice murmured, "Sorry, Louise. Here, I'll take him."

"Oh, it's quite alright. The sweet chap is no burden at all." She led the way to the front door. "Try the handle, Zoe. It should be unlocked." In her eagerness to get out, she'd entirely forgotten to secure either front or back door.

Chapter Seven

As Zoe held the front door open for her, Louise glimpsed a black shape streaking toward the living room. Magic must have waited at the entry but changed her mind.

"Drop the kitty's stuff here. I'll store it later. Would you like some tea? I'm parched. So is Shadow." Louise laughed as the pooch made a beeline for his water bowl and slurped noisily. Daniel squirmed in her arms. When she lowered him to the floor, he wriggled his outstretched fingers and tottered over to the dog.

"No, sweetie." The young mother sounded alarmed. "Don't touch the doggie when it eats or drinks."

Though Shadow hadn't a possessive bone in his body, teaching the child caution before their puppy arrived was wise.

Trevor came back in with a domed litter box and bag, cat bed squished under his arm. "Gotta take Daniel to swim school. Sorry to rush off," he said when Louise invited them to the living room. With a playful growl, he reached for his son. "C'mon, monster. Mommy needs a break." He swung the kid onto his shoulders.

Daniel's screech bubbled into sweet, gurgly laughter.

"Say bye-bye Auntie Louise." Trevor waved with a free hand, whereupon Daniel let go of his dad's ears and punched two tiny fists into the air.

As she blew him a kiss, Louise discovered an unsuspected fondness for the tyke.

The kid's mother stood motionless, watching their exit with an anxious expression. Concerned, Louise suggested, "A perfect chance for a restful cuppa. Come help me get it ready."

The young woman could do with a respite from domestic duties. Let the spouse deal with readying their child for swim class.

"You're so kind, Louise," Zoe said and followed into the kitchen.

While she filled the electric kettle, Louise instructed Zoe where to find teacups and biscuits. "I'm so delighted to hear of a genuine bakery, pardon me, patisserie, in town," she said and amused the young woman with a droll tale of this morning's roller-coaster hike and village stroll.

They settled at her favorite window spot overlooking the ravine. Shadow unearthed his yak milk bone and settled by Zoe's feet. They smiled at the crunching and scraping.

Louise's glance strayed to the window. Now that she knew it was there, she recognized the weathered fence panels that blended with the gray-green tones of lichen-covered tree bark. The property line to Mr. Simpson's lot was so much closer to her house than Trevor's and Zoe's on the other side.

"Delicious," Zoe mumbled while nibbling a cookie with small white teeth.

"Mass-produced, I'm afraid. Next time, we'll have scones with jam and real cream," Louise promised. She wondered where Magic was hiding. Probably in bed upstairs. What double-standard, she thought. Her strict bedroom policy always had been no dogs allowed. The kitty was a law onto herself. Louise sent the pooch an apologetic smile.

As her visitor gazed at the budding maples weaving in a breeze, the stronger light marked the strain on the young features. The lids were puffy and red-rimmed like from recent tears.

On an impulse, Louise said, "Are you alright, Zoe? Is something worrying you?"

41

A barely stifled sob, covered up by sniffling. Zoe's hand fluttered to her trembling lip. "It's nothing. Really."

The whispered words didn't reassure Louise. Yet she hated to pry.

"I met our neighbor," she said, briskly changing topics. "Mr. Simpson seems a unique character. Doesn't he?" The man's claim about Magic's ferociousness might distract Zoe from whatever ailed her. No need to share his enigmatic parting shot, but no harm in talking about the cat.

"Is it true?" she continued, "Did Magic ever attack his Pekingese?"

Zoe glanced up from contemplating the crumbled chocolate digestives on her dessert plate. At least the question animated her. A slight flush crept into the pale cheeks.

"That dog was vicious. Auntie said so last summer. A nasty little beast." The vehemence grew with every word, and the dark eyes flashed. "He chased cats, and the old man let him! People with cats hate him."

"Goodness. Is that so?" Louise gave a tiny headshake in commiseration. In humorous exaggeration, she added, "Well, I'm glad Magic isn't a dangerous tiger. My, I feared for Shadow's safety."

"What? This big guy isn't afraid of cats." With a smile, Zoe bent to scratch Shadow's ears.

"I wonder, were Mr. Simpson and your aunt on bad terms after the incident? Is he a difficult neighbor, do you think?" Better forewarned than sorry.

Zoe let go of the dog's ears and sat straight. "We've hardly met him." She leaned toward Louise as if to confide, though only the pooch and maybe the lurking kitty were near to hear. "He and Auntie used to be an item."

Louise couldn't hide a smile at the somewhat incongruous wording. "You mean in their younger days?"

"Trev says they split about ten years ago." Her earnest gaze sought Louise's. "He thinks the old guy never forgave Auntie for dumping him. I don't get what she ever saw in him. He's so...you know, not handsome or anything." The skinny fingers reached to twirl her long hair. "Auntie was beautiful when she was young. I've seen pictures of her in her twenties driving a sports car. She liked fast cars until her arthritis got bad."

Beauty and the Beast came to mind. The young woman seemed to be impressed by the aunt, Louise mused. "Sounds like Carol was an enterprising woman. I wish I'd met her."

When Zoe's face puckered, and a tear rolled down her cheek, Louise wished she hadn't spoken.

"I'm so sorry. The loss must still leave you feeling raw, dear." She reached and patted her guest's hand that gripped the edge of the table so tightly the knuckles showed bluish-white.

"Sorry. I'm such a mess," Zoe mumbled, staring down at her plate. "And I've made a mess of the cookies, too," she added in a brave attempt at humor.

"No worries." Louise matched the lighter tone. "There are more in the roll where those came from." She pointed at the empty cup. "Care for a refill?"

"Thanks, but I'd better get back." The young woman regarded her as if uncertain. She took a deep breath. "There's something I ought to tell you, Louise."

"Go on," Louise encouraged her softly when Zoe hesitated.

"Aunt Carol's passing is now considered a suspicious death."

Chapter Eight

The next morning, Louise woke from a fitful sleep. Vivid dreams of gravediggers unearthing a rotten coffin in an overgrown gothic cemetery morphed into stony-cold morgue scenes with a shear-wielding diminutive pathologist whose bulging back strained a blood-spattered lab coat.

In the light of day, and with a warm kitty curled in the crock of her arm, the origins of these alps were obvious. A mistake to ponder the implications of Zoe's disturbing announcement at bedtime. The police didn't share details of why they launched an investigation weeks after Carol's death but requested an interview with Trevor and Zoe for today.

Did they suspect neglect at the nursing home? Or something more sinister? Horrible accounts of neglect in long-term care facilities hit the news during the pandemic. Surely, Carol's friends would have noticed anything amiss, Louise thought.

Well, she was about to see the place for herself. Upon a surprisingly prompt reply from Matron Juniper last evening, expressing their keen interest in her volunteering as a reader, Louise had arranged to meet Matron at Rosewood Manor around 11:30 this morning.

"Okay, Kitty," Louise said with fresh determination. "Enough of this slouch. We've got work to do before heading out."

The yellow irises, pale against the white sheet, gazed at her, unwavering.

Ready to set out for Rosewood shortly after 11, Louise cast a quick look at the bathroom mirror. The black slacks, light blue blouse, and navy cardigan conveyed a no-nonsense, tidy impression, Louise figured as she fluffed up her short auburn hair.

When she donned slip-on shoes and grabbed a shoulder bag, Shadow watched from afar. With an unerring instinct, he always seemed to know if he would be invited along. A matter of her choice of clothing and shoes, Louise felt sure.

"Be a good boy, and leave the kitty in peace," she said unnecessarily to judge by his expression. "If you could roll your eyes and talk," Louise smiled, "you would say, what do you take me for? Some cat stalker?"

The pooch shook himself in answer.

The morning fog had burned off, and another sunny day awaited. As Louise strolled down Charlotte's Lane towards the village, she glanced at Mr. Simpson's driveway. The house, barely visible among evergreens, appeared drab and neglected. A 1960s bungalow, she guessed.

Several other houses of various styles, age, and condition flanked the lane on both sides. Some showed picture-perfect front yards, while others retained the forest ambience. At the corner of Charlotte's Lane and the street leading to the village sat another one-and-a-half story in much worse shape than hers had been before renovating. The vinyl siding must have been white in its youth but now was greenish with algae. Its curled, moss-covered roof shingles stood in urgent need of repair. In the front yard, crates, oil drums, and metal debris surrounded a dismantled motorbike.

Every time she passed, Louise wondered if none of the tidy neighbors complained. Live and let live was her own attitude. Yet, others might worry an eyesore would affect property values.

The 20-minute walk to Rosewood led her through the prettiest village streets. Most of the houses and yards looked well-tended and showed clear signs of spring. Lawn chairs, benches, and rockers had emerged from hibernation in sheds and basements. A pleasant, earthy smell scented the air.

Louise exchanged greetings with some people pottering in their yards. The sun put smiles on winter-weary faces. Spring fever gripped Cascade and filled Louise with renewed zest for life. If she could, she'd have embraced the whole village.

Rosewood Manor looked just like the flyer image promised, rocking chairs and picket fence included. Here, too, an air of spring cleaning pervaded. Flower beds, still damp with freshly turned soil, showcased crocuses, tulips, and daffodils.

The elaborate off-white frill work of the lancet arches over the entrance and gables appeared recently painted. Built from light ochre sandstone, the Gothic revival mansion, with its pointed windows and crested stone chimneys, stood timeless and solid. A large box bay window, kept in the same off-white as the trims, added to its charm.

When Louise entered the foyer, the warmth inside struck her as excessive. It intensified a slight whiff of institutional cleaning agents. The reception area wasn't spacious. A young receptionist greeted Louise from behind the glass enclosure of a fake mahogany counter.

"Good morning. Welcome to Rosewood Manor. Did you book a tour of our facilities?"

The question took Louise aback. Did she look particularly old today? Usually, people complimented her on how well she kept, which always made her feel like a carton of milk.

"I'm not there yet," she said. "But I have an appointment with Mrs. Juniper. Louise Penfold is my name."

"It's never too early to plan ahead," the young woman said unabashedly. "Our waiting list fills years in advance. But I'll let Matron know you are here, Mrs. Penfold."

"Ms.," said Louise. Stands to reason there would be long waiting times for placing. Someone would have to die to make room. The thought sobered her.

"This way, please, Ms. Penfold." The receptionist led the way past

46

several doors. Louise glimpsed a formal parlor in Laura Ashley style wall-paper. The bay window she'd noticed from outside held an upholstered window seat. No one sat in the armchairs and stiff-looking settees.

"Here we are," her guide said, and knuckle rapped on a door labeled, 'Mrs. Juniper. Matron — Please knock.'

"Come in," a melodious female voice called.

"Ms. Penfold for you, Matron," the receptionist announced, peeking around the doorjamb before opening it wider to let Louise enter.

"Ah, so good of you to make time for us, Ms. Penfold." A woman got up behind a desk loaded with file folders, papers, and a desktop computer. She wore a colorful tunic over a beige skirt. Of ample proportions, glowing brown skin, a profusion of wiry black curls highlighted by natural streaks of white and silver, the woman appeared ageless. Not least because of the radiant smile that enveloped Louise. Together with the mellow voice, it made one want to sigh with content.

"It's Louise. So pleased to meet you, Matron."

Mrs. Juniper motioned Louise to a comfortable settee off to the side of her desk and asked, "Would you care for a cup of mocha? Freshly brewed."

"Yes, please. I'd love some. It smells divine." Louise's nostrils twitched appreciatively. She'd noticed the aroma of a quality coffee already.

Once ensconced comfortably, Mrs. Juniper offered a tin of cookies studded with dried fruit and nuts.

"You don't have allergies, by any chance?" she asked. "Loaded with allergens, I am afraid. I can offer you a plain gluten-free variety I keep on hand."

"Thankfully, no allergies," Louise said and chose two cookies. She bit off a piece. "My, these are delicious. Are they home-baked?"

Matron chuckled. "Almost. We get them from the local bakery. Our residents rave about treats and breads from Petit Four You."

"Oh, I've heard of the patisserie already from Owen at the Witch's Brew."

"You know your way around town, I see." Mrs. Juniper smiled and sipped her coffee. "Ah, I needed that." She rested her cup on the saucer.

Louise felt the woman's gaze assessing her.

"We are so grateful to you, Louise. One of our volunteers has relocated, and dear Mrs. Norton misses her dreadfully. Your voice actually sounds quite similar. Nora Norton will be so pleased."

"Entirely my pleasure. It's great to form connections in the new community. Mind you, I'm inexperienced in reading to others. As an editor, I routinely read passages out loud to check the flow. But that's different."

"A fascinating occupation. I'm sure you are an accomplished reader with a feel for the story. Our residents are appreciative and always supportive of our volunteers." Mrs. Juniper hesitated for a moment and took another sip from her cup.

Louise followed suit. The mocha was rich and smooth. She'd come back just for that. She smiled to herself. A glance at the other woman's beautiful features let her sense the matron's difficulty.

"You will need some references, I assume," Louise said briskly. It must be awkward to ask for that when people offered their help. Yet, the residents were vulnerable and needed protection. "I can supply whatever is needed."

"Good of you to think of it." The matron's brilliant smile returned. "I'll give you a form to fill out. It states what we need."

She rose and reached for a sheet from her desk. "Here you go. If you—"

A tentative knock on the door caused Mrs. Juniper to shift her attention.

This time, she merely said, "Yes?" in a questioning voice.

It wasn't the receptionist but a timid girl in lilac-colored scrubs and long black hair tightly braided. Her entire posture expressed regret at the intrusion.

"Yes, Uma?" Mrs. Juniper sounded severe.

"There's someone to see you, Matron." The girl's voice came softly.

"Do they have an appointment? I'm busy." Glancing at a day planner on her desk, she said. "No one is scheduled until this afternoon. Can't it wait?"

"They say it's important to see you." The girl, Uma, seemed awfully embarrassed to Louise.

"Who is it?" Mrs. Juniper smiled apologetically at Louise, saying, "Sorry about that."

"Police!" Desperation rang in Uma's cry.

"Goodness," the matron said. "Whatever for? Well, never mind. Tell them I'll see them in a few minutes."

As the girl retreated, closing the door with exaggerated care, Louise got up. "I won't keep you, Mrs. Juniper. And I'll drop off the form by tomorrow. We can text or email."

"Thank you so much, Louise. I do apologize. Please, call me Haydee. Once I've given Nora the good news, we can arrange a mutually agreeable time for the first reading session."

Matron Juniper walked Louise into the hallway and waved in parting.

When Louise entered the reception area, she noticed a man in his 30s whose eyes scanned the surrounding area without obviously staring. Despite wearing slacks and a lightweight blouson, something about him said cop, or so Louise believed as their eyes met.

Uma stood by, wringing her hands. Seeing Louise, she blushed and said to the fellow, "Er, I think Matron will see you now, Inspector."

A smile cracked the man's rugged features and made him almost good-looking. He brushed five fingers through his sandy hair and turned to a woman by the noticeboard next to the parlor entrance.

"Ready, Serg?" he asked.

The woman, probably closer to 40 than 30, swiveled on her heels and walked ahead in the direction of the hallway.

When Uma hastened to show them the way, the young inspector said, "No worries. You take care of the lady." With a polite "ma'am" to Louise, he strode after the woman.

Louise stared at his back, certain the police came calling about Carol Benson. A suspicious death, they considered it. Where better to begin the investigation than at the scene—of the crime?

"Uma. What're you standing around for?" A male voice preceded its owner. "You're supposed to—sorry, ma'am."

The man, who entered through a door on the other side of the still unoccupied reception desk, took Louise by surprise.

Though he now wore pale blue scrubs, and appeared clean, hair hidden under a matching cap, there was no doubt in her mind. The gruff, hawk-nosed guy whom Owen wanted to foist on her as a gardener. What was his name again?

"Can't you tell, Alfred?" Uma's pert rejoinder answered Louise's unspoken question. "I am filling in for Sarah. She's on lunch break."

"All I know, we've got work to do. Make it snappy." With a perfunctory "Sorry again" to Louise, he left the way he'd come.

Well, that is one for the books, Louise thought. Curious and eager to test her assumption, she said to the now pouting Uma, "Is the young man—Alfred, did you say?—employed here as a nurse?" He'd hardly wear scrubs as a gardener.

"Yeah, that's our Alfred, all right," Uma said with evident dislike. "He's the head nurse." Something like fear flickered in the girl's eyes.

"Quite bossy, perhaps?" Louise let the pitch rise to make it an open question.

The girl's face shuttered like she'd donned a veil. "He's popular with the old—with our residents. Is there anything else?" The question was a dismissal.

"I'm good, thanks. Have a nice day, Uma. We are bound to meet again."

Fear flashed over the features yet again, widening the young nurse's eyes. "What?"

"Sorry, I thought you knew," Louse said, surprised at the girl's skittishness. "I'm the new volunteer reader for Mrs. Norton. So, I'll be around off and on."

"Oh, that. Great to hear." Relief animated Uma's words. "See you."

When Louise opened the entrance to let herself out, the receptionist rushed in from outside, murmuring breathlessly, "Excuse me," as they almost collided.

"No harm done," said Louise. But the young woman wasn't listening.

From behind her, Louise heard Uma's voice rising. "Where have you been? Alfred's throwing a hissy fit."

"Just chill, won't you?" said the tardy colleague.

Louise closed the door and stepped out into the sunshine. Only when she strolled toward the antique lady's shop did she realize she hadn't seen a single inhabitant of Rosewood Manor. Where did they hide the residents?

Chapter Nine

A carved totem pole greeted Louise at the entrance to Precious Treasures on Main Street. Striped wings spread horizontally, it conveyed either a warm embrace or an attempt to bar the way, depending on how one interpreted the faded features staring right through the beholder.

The store's aged awning remained retracted. Behind a none-too-clean shop window, a dusty collection of vintage signs advertising everything from soup to motor oil kept company with dolls, ill-assorted porcelain, knickknacks, and plastic kitsch.

When Louise entered, an ancient bell tinkled above her head. It immediately set the mood of stepping back in time. The interior seemed a wild jumble. Cast-offs she'd expect at a garage sale stood carelessly atop genuine antique cupboards and polished tables, mixed with attractive vintage pieces and collector items of all shapes and various sizes. Some were in mint condition, others cracked, chipped, and worn to the point of exhausting their usefulness.

An artfully arranged chaos. Casual browsers would gleefully assume precious treasures lay hidden among the junk, unsuspected by an ignorant shop owner. Antique aficionados like her recognized the method in the mad display. A curious smell of beeswax, potpourri, musty fabrics, and rusting metal accosted her nostrils.

From behind an Upper Canada pine armoire floated the proprietor's distinctive voice. "Let me know if you need help."

No sales pressure. Another smart move, Louise acknowledged, as her eyes scanned a shelf of cookware and other miscellaneous copper items, like a lidded bedpan and an interesting contraption with protruding pipes reminiscent of bootleggers of the days of yore. Verdigris, the bluish-green deposit on neglected copper, showed or mimicked age. A box of vintage tools on a lower shelf was of more interest. She flipped over some price tags. If woodworking stuff fetched a decent price, she thought, the agricultural detritus pile in her field might not be garbage.

She cleared her throat in a gentle heads-up before approaching the antique lady.

The woman raised her glance from a glossy catalog spread atop letters and bill-sized papers. An open MacBook sat on a pile of magazines. No recognition dawned on the woman's face. The store's dim lighting and a brief acquaintance would account for that, Louise thought.

"Hello again," she said. "We met at Owen's yesterday. I'm Louise. Just was passing by and have time for a quick peek."

Garbed in the mauve twinset, this time over synthetic trousers, covered with pilling as from a severe measle attack, Kendra removed her gold-rimmed reading glasses and peered at Louise.

A smile transfigured her face as she rose. "Of course. Lovely of you to pop in. Were you looking for something in particular?"

"Just browsing today. I was in town, anyway, for a quick meet and greet with Matron Juniper at Rosewood."

"Oh?" The shop owner's brows shot up.

'Doesn't take me for old enough to need care,' Louise concluded with satisfaction. Her mouth twitched, amused when saying, "Not what it sounds like. I'm volunteering as a reader."

Or did Kendra hear already of the police investigation, she wondered, and took her for a ghoul who rushes to the scene?

The woman's face relaxed in an affable smile. "How kind of you. I call it public-spirited to jump in the breach the moment you move here. Recommendable."

Embarrassed by such praise before she'd even had her first session with Mrs. Norton, Louise hastened to change topics. "You've got a nice set of woodworking tools out there," she said.

"Are you into the craft?" Kendra asked. "I can let you have them at cost. Discount for newcomers." A throaty chuckle accompanied the offer.

"Sorry. Thanks, but no thanks. They caught my eye for a different reason. Yesterday, I discovered a pile of discarded farm equipment on my property. You know, seed spreaders, hoes, and a few hand tools. The tools over there made me question if it's indeed worthless or salvageable."

Louise felt a little breathless after her excessive explanation. But Kendra's keen glance told her it hadn't been wasted.

The hooded eyes regained a bland expression when the dealer's vein took the reins. "Yes. Much of what people find in old dump sites has no commercial value. Cleaned up, some of it can make for fun decorative pieces. Purely sentimental value. If you want, I'll drop by sometime and have a look." The tone implied scant interest.

"Do you happen to know someone who might help shift it?" Louise asked. "Garbage heaps on private land are environmentally irresponsible, I find."

"I can check with my guys," Kendra said. "They're rather busy in spring. If not hauling merchandise to shows and markets, they're into junk removal."

"Thanks. I'd appreciate it."

"There's always Alfred, of course." Disdain showed plainly in Kendra's raised upper lip and colored her tone.

"Funny you mention him. I was much surprised to run into the man this morning."

"Why? He lives on your road. You're bound to see much of him. The man's always tinkering with his bike."

Wheels chucked over in Louise's brain. The pieces fell into place. "Do you mean he lives in the little white house at the corner of Charlotte's Lane? With the motorcycle out front and all the—the stuff?"

Kendra laughed. "The junk. Let's call a spade a spade. Yes, exactly. Was Alfred at it again this morning?"

"Oh, no. I saw him at Rosewood. He's the head nurse there, I hear. Quite a versatile fellow, isn't he? Owen recommended him as a gardener. Now, he's also handy with motors and liked as a nurse by the seniors, I'm told." Louise regretted yesterday's snap judgment of the man, based superficially on appearance. Yet, both Uma and Kendra seemed to dislike Alfred.

A derisive snort confirmed the impression. "He has his way with the old folks when he wants to."

"Carol must have thought well enough of Alfred if she employed him as a gardener," Louise said.

"Weaseled his way in, if you ask me."

Louise returned to the topic of most interest to herself. "Speaking of Carol, you were her good friend." Though she noticed a shrewd expression flickering over the woman's pudgy features, she continued, "Did she mention an incident between her cat and Mr. Simpson's Pekingese?" Better to feel her way first before alluding to the poisoning accusation, Louise judged.

It merely caused the other to frown. "What incident?"

"From what I could gather, Magic, the cat, attacked Peek-a-boo. What a name," she said in an aside. "Boggles the imagination picturing Mr. Simpson shouting for his Peek by name. Sorry, I digress." But Kendra laughed appreciatively. Sobering, Louise added, "The dog died."

"A nasty brute. Just like its owner. Carol's cat didn't kill the beastly thing. Or any other dog." A flush crimsoned the antique dealer's cheeks. "Did the odious man claim that?"

"No, not really." Louise hesitated. Yet, she must find out the truth about what happened. Mr. Simpson might still retaliate. Magic was now her responsibility until the kitty moved to a forever home. An unexpected wave of sadness swept over her at the latter thought.

She shook it off and said, "His claim was much worse. He implied Carol poisoned his dog."

There. It was out.

Kendra didn't appear shocked but venomous when she hissed, "If there was any poisoning, the old dwarf did it."

Chapter Ten

Out in the street again, Louise shivered in the building's shade. It was horrible enough to think she might have bought a dead poisoner's home. Much worse, contemplating a live poisoner lurked next door.

Surely, Kendra's vicious remark made little sense. Mr. Simpson had loved his Peek. She'd said as much to the antique lady. The woman merely rolled her eyes and shuffled some papers, saying airily, "I'm not one to gossip," and proffering a business card, almost shooed Louise out.

Determined to get to the bottom of this, one way or another, Louise walked on. She crossed the street to the sunny side. At noon, the sun's radiance warmed the asphalt. It exuded a tarry smell, a whiff of summer heat yet to come.

Farther down the street, she saw the shop sign she'd been looking for. A white baker's hat dangled from an ornate cast iron wall bracket. The legend became visible as she drew close, Petit Four You. 'Patisserie' inscribed along the crest of the hat.

The shop windows sparkled. Freshly washed white clapboard siding and blue window trims gleamed just as much as the red entrance that completed the French flag color theme. Lacy drapes covered the lower part of the window. The upper portion yielded a clear view of the wooden counter and racks holding baskets loaded with baked goods.

What could be more inviting? Louise smiled in happy anticipation.

Divine baking scents met her when she stepped inside. A contented 'aah' escaped her. It drew the attention of three or four customers, who turned around, smiling their understanding.

"Smells lovely, doesn't it?" one woman said.

"And it's as good as it looks," another customer added.

The rotund woman behind the counter beamed. "Go on with you. Let the lady find out for herself." She reached for a plate and arranged bite-size samples on it. "Here, pass it on," she said, handing it to the person first in line. "The proof's always in the pudding. That's what I say."

Everyone waited expectantly for Louise to taste test and pronounce the samples delicious. As if they had been holding their breath, the customers resumed chatting and shopping.

While she waited patiently in line, Louise glanced around. Iron racks contained wicker baskets lined with red and white checkered paper loaded with brioches, baguettes, buns, and croissants. Rustic bread types set on horizontal shelving.

Rotating glass vitrines displayed sumptuous petit fours. Cream-layered chocolate and glazed fruit squares sat aligned at precise angles to round cream puffs and eclairs. Marzipan-coated morsels crowned by striped white, pink, or chocolate icing reclined in their crinoline paper cups.

The sights mesmerized the gourmand in Louise. She detected assorted Danish squares of the kind she'd sampled at Owen's in flat baskets on the counter. Not even scones and Scottish oatcakes were missing.

When it was her turn to be served, Louise complimented the woman on the wonderful display and selection. The wattage of the answering smile increased with every word.

"Och, we do what we can."

Obviously not of French derivation, Louise deduced and asked, "Are you Jessie?" The woman nodded, beaming away. "Owen at the café mentioned your patisserie. The Danishes I had there convinced me to come looking for you. You have a well-deserved reputation around here. Matron Juniper sang your praises when I spoke to her this morning."

"Get on with you. You make an old woman blush." Indeed, the round cheeks were rosy. "You're new in town, then, by the sound of it? I've got a good memory for faces and don't recall serving you before."

"Oh, yes. I am Louise. Pleased to meet you, Jessie."

"Likewise, likewise, dearie. You're not living at the manor, are you? Much too young, I'd say."

Pleased, Louise said, "I just moved into my little place on Charlotte's Lane. Such a scenic spot. After living in the city for decades, I love the sedate village pace."

"Och, aye. You are the lady on Charlotte. Jeremy and me were wondering who bought Carol's place."

"My. It seems everyone in town knows the house sold." Louise smiled.

"Word gets around." Jessie's chin wobbled as she nodded. "Stands to reason in a wee town like Cascade. We keep tabs on property prices. Everyone does these days." The pebble-like brown irises sparkled in their fleshy folds. "What brought you to Rosewood, then? Got relatives living there?"

Curiosity, of course, was the number one entertainment in any village, Louise realized. She'd caught the bug long before she ever moved here. You've got to give if you want to get, she thought.

"The flyer caught my attention. So, I volunteered as a reader," she said.

"Oh, yes." Jessie pointed to a corkboard hanging behind Louise by the entrance. The Rosewood flyer stuck prominently in the middle, surrounded by business cards with easily recognizable real estate logos and sheets advertising items for sale and services for hire.

While Louise selected a loaf of bread, a few scones, petit fours for afternoon tea, and a selection of mutt's special dog biscuits, she said, "Everyone seems to have known Carol. Was she active in the community?"

"Not so much the last year. She was getting on, wasn't she? Mind you, still came for her bread and pastries until the last month. Then Jeremy popped by her place with the orders. She was that fond of his petit fours. He is the baker, my Jeremy."

"They do look delicious. I'm bound to develop Carol's predilection for them." Louise laughed.

"Loved them to the last. So sad. She passed away the night after her birthday, you know. Everyone came by that day to pick up treats for her. Was enough to feed the whole lot of them at the manor." Jessie's face wrinkled, visibly pleased with the popularity of her husband's baking skills yet saddened by a customer's demise.

"Was she well enough then to have a little birthday celebration?" Louise asked, glad to think the unknown Carol enjoyed visitors to the very end.

"Och, aye. We were so pleased to hear she was getting better. But you never know at that age. 86 Carol was. Next thing we heard, she passed away after a relapse that night. Hit me and Jeremy real hard. We'd sent a miniature cake along with Owen. Just like them little squares with the absinthe cream. He put the cutest wee candle atop—my Jeremy did." Jessie pointed to the green glazed squares in the vitrine and wiped her moist eyes with a chubby hand, reddened perhaps from too frequent washing.

Behind Louise, the shop door opened, and two newcomers called a greeting.

"I'd better let you go, Jessie," Louise said and tapped her credit card on the machine handed to her. "Expect to see me often. I'm addicted already," she joked.

"Happy to see you anytime, dearie. And our best wishes for your new home." Jessie reached behind and passed Louise a bar of handcrafted chocolate in cellophane wrapping with artfully tied golden ribbons. "A special treat for you. Enjoy."

Conscious of curious eyes watching her, Louise thanked Jessie and bid everyone a nice day.

Small-town living took some getting used to. But she'd master the art soon enough. Louise smiled to herself as she strolled home.

Chapter Eleven

The sun was about to set when Louise took Shadow for an after-dinner walk on the trail at the dead end of the lane. She felt exhausted after a long day, not least from child-minding Daniel while his parents went for their interview with the police. Zoe had sounded desperate and close to tears when she asked for the favor. Though planning a solid afternoon of editing and fearing the child might scream his head off once left behind, Louise hadn't the heart to say no.

The little fellow, however, proved trusting and quite delightful at closer acquaintance. It gave her a warm fuzzy feeling to recall him cuddling in her arms when he tired of throwing balls for the dog and digging with Louise in the flowerbed as their sandbox.

Too bad she couldn't ask Trevor how things went at the station. Her questioning gaze received no response when he picked up the sleeping child.

'Oh well, maybe tomorrow,' Louise thought and walked on.

Twilight descended as she and the pooch returned home. In the drive-way, Shadow strained at the leash. Floppy ears at attention and nose to the ground, he'd picked up a scent. The portico lights revealed no visitors.

"Easy does it. Don't pull me," Louise said. "Calm down. Just a rabbit or squirrel."

Shadow paid no heed and dragged her toward the back of the house, yipping and growling softly in turn.

Not like Shadow at all. Louise frowned. Then she remembered the sighting of her odd neighbor. Did Mr. Simpson prowl around her home? How dare he? She would give him a piece of her mind.

Determined, she shortened the leash and followed the pooch's nose. When they rounded the corner, the ruff on Shadow's neck rose. With the low growl, he yanked her toward the door to the crawlspace, awkwardly accessible under the back porch.

It wasn't even a proper door but a siding-clad entry, only four-and-a-half feet high. She'd entered it two or three times. Except for some old gardening tools and potting equipment, it held nothing of interest.

Now, the entrance flap was ajar. Did some animal get in? A raccoon or a fox? She would hate to close the door and trap the poor creature inside. Odd. She felt sure the bolt on the closure was shot when she last saw it.

Surely, her neighbor wouldn't sneak in here? He was small enough to stand upright in the low, windowless space her mind supplied unbidden.

Shadow snarled. "Heel," she told him. He obeyed under protest.

Pulse beating furiously in her throat, she pushed the trapdoor with sudden force and stood back. Shadow used her momentary inattention to plunge into the darkness. Losing her balance, Louise let go of the leash.

"Nice doggie. No! Stay away!" yelped a man's voice in a ludicrous mix of entreaty and fear.

Braced against the door jamb, Louise groped for the switch. The weak light of a naked bulb dangling from the exposed floor joist illuminated a male bent over in an awkward stoop. Definitely not Mr. Simpson. Attired in casual clothes more at home on a golf course than in the bowels of her home, he blinked at her.

"What are you doing in my basement?" Annoyance overrode fear.

"Please! Call off your dog," the stranger whined, then cleared his throat as if aware of sounding pathetic. With an uneasy laugh, he added, "I'm not a burglar."

Nothing to burgle down here, Louise figured. Though her heart thudded, she forced a calm tone but refused to stoop, literally, to join an unknown individual in the damp underground. "Well, come out then."

Her voice soothed Shadow, whose growl softened into a rumble in his barrel chest. She backed up from under the porch and gave a tug on the leash. The man followed but stopped to secure the latch on the entrance flap.

"Let's talk where I can see you." Shadow at heel, Louise kept the intruder in front as she steered him to the narrow flagstone patio next to the portico.

The lantern lights flanking the front door confirmed her earlier impression. About six feet two, the intruder wore chinos, a light polo shirt, and a dark windcheater. Gray around the temples, his mousy hair was well-trimmed. She judged him to be in his early sixties. Not a house breaker type.

The clean-shaven features expressed amusement when he spoke with a slightly nasal drawl. "You caught me in an awkward position. I'm sorry to have given you a scare, Ms. Penfold. It wasn't my intention, believe me." His eyes veered over to the front door. "My mother used to live here. I'm Dennis Benson."

He stretched out his right hand but stuffed it into his jacket pocket when she made no move to shake it.

"That does not explain finding you inside the crawlspace."

His left arm shot up, palm facing her. "Hold on. Let me finish. Sorry, it's a long tale."

"Well, hopefully not a tall one," she said, a trifle sarcastic.

He chuckled. "Ha, no. The honest truth. My mother's affairs brought me to the area, and I thought I'd stop by to see the old place and meet you." He bowed his head to her.

When she remained silent, he continued with increased speed. "The lights were on, but no one answered. I took the liberty to check the back. I heard some noise and noticed the door to the crawlspace was open. Thinking you might be inside, I hollered, but again, no answer."

Louise hoped her exaggerated frown told him what she thought of the likelihood of this story.

It didn't stop him. "I thought I'd have a quick peek and went in," he said.

"Without switching on the light?"

"I used my phone's flashlight. Anyway, I looked around to make sure no animal got inside. That's when your hound launched his attack."

He smiled at the dog from a safe six-feet distance.

Louise glanced at Shadow, who had placed himself right in front of her. His body alert, he was ready to interfere at the least provocation.

"Well, thanks for sharing," she said. Relenting, she added in a softer voice, "I'm very sorry about your mother's passing. My condolences."

As he mumbled an acknowledgment, the strange condolence card flashed into her memory. Maybe the sender intended it for Dennis but didn't know his name. Too unlikely.

She seized the opportunity to question him. "You're visiting from Australia, aren't you? My neighbors said... I guess they must be your cousins?" She pointed toward the young couple's place.

"Once removed," he corrected her. "Trevor is the son of my cousin. His dad is the black sheep of the family." He chuckled as if it was a joke, but his eyes narrowed.

'An odd tidbit to share with a stranger. No love lost between the cousins of whatever degree removed,' Louise thought.

"But, yes, I live in Christurn."

"Ah, I see. Did you have a pleasant visit with Trevor and Zoe?" Though his frown deepened, she kept talking. "They are such a nice couple. And the little one is adorable."

Surely, Dennis Benson would be the first police talked to while investigating his mother's death. Nothing about his bearing suggested grief or concern. Not everyone showed emotions openly, she told herself.

"It's so comforting for families to be close in times of bereavement or trouble," she added the conventional sentiment to avoid seeming inquisitive.

"Er. No. Not exactly." His glance shifted from her to the tall evergreens separating her property from the young couple's. "I leave communication to the lawyers."

"Oh? I'm sorry." Why, things must be very much amiss if he sought legal advice.

He gazed at her. Speculative, as if trying to penetrate her thoughts. "You know Trevor and his little wife already, do you?"

"Yes, indeed. In fact, Daniel spent the afternoon with me today when his parents—were busy," she amended, not wishing to be the first to mention the police.

"Did you now? Doesn't surprise me one bit they roped you in. Fast work. You've only lived here a few days." The suave tone disappeared as the twang increased.

Louise felt offended on Zoe and Trevor's behalf. Unsmiling, she said, "It was entirely my doing. I offered to help and enjoyed every moment of the sweet tyke's company. I look forward to many more occasions."

He took a step toward her but retreated when Shadow rose with a deep growl.

"Well, before you get too cozy with that lot," he said, his voice vibrating with anger. "Let me tell you one thing. That house the young blighters are in ought to be mine. I was born in the place and was to inherit it. The nice young couple, as you call them, sponged on my mother until she sold it to them. Loaned them the down payment to boot. I'll see them in hell before they get another penny."

With that, he strode off. From several yards away, he hollered, "No offense, lady. Good day."

Before she went up to bed that night, Louise double-checked the door locks. For a moment, she considered getting a motion detection camera installed.

"Bah. This is not the city or a hotbed for muggers and burglars," she said to Shadow, who followed close beside her. "I've got my alarm system right here." Her hand patted his head, and she crouched to give him a good-night chest rub. The brown eyes regarded her earnestly before he abandoned himself to pure enjoyment.

Magic watched from the stairs and darted ahead to the loft when Louise came up with a book and a glass of water.

While she undressed, Louise pondered the strange encounter with Dennis Benson. His explanation might be true. Essentially, it mirrored her own reason for checking the crawlspace. Many people would hate to think an animal might be trapped down there. Somehow, the man didn't look the type to care.

'That's stereotyping and prejudice,' she told herself.

A scratching sound distracted her.

"Magic! Don't do that." Louise softened her tone as the kitty's head swiveled to glance at her. "You have your scratch post downstairs. No need to sharpen your claws on the wall."

Raised on hind legs, the cat remained poised against the wall under the eaves. It reminded Louise of her contractor's plan to convert the useless lower space between the sloping ceiling and the floor into custom-made drawer units and an accessible cubby space. Apparently, it was a popular way of increasing storage.

She sighed. There were so many little things they'd planned originally. But the contractor's time was limited. In fairness, she had wanted to move in as soon as possible.

"Okay, kitty. I'll buy a scratch mat and hang it there if it's your favorite spot. Let's get some sleep now." Too tired to read, she sank into the pillows.

Magic leaped onto the bed and snuggled close, the huge amber irises staring at Louise.

"There's something of a sphinx about you, kitty cat," Louise said.

Magic yawned contagiously.

"Who'd have thought small-town life was so exhausting?"

Chapter Twelve

The next morning, Louise rose early and took Shadow for a brisk walk. She'd arranged Magic's appointment at the vet's for 11:30 a.m. and hoped to squeeze in a couple of hours of proofreading before heading out. A dank mist shrouded the evergreens and lilac bushes. Water beads pearled on Shadow's furry coat and Louise's rain jacket as she headed back, entering Charlotte's Lane from the village street.

Now that she knew who owned it, the shabby house at the corner invariably caught her attention. The fog and dripping trees increased its dismal appearance. In weather like this junk piles looked so much worse. Even the motorcycle, mounted on the stand, shared the abandoned air.

Someone was lying next to it.

"My God," she murmured and moved closer.

Her relief at seeing the arms of the reclined person reach up to the engine was chased by horror as the massive bike leaned sideways and toppled over.

"Oh, no!" she yelled, dropping the leash and hastening into the yard.

A volley of swearing answered. Louise grabbed the handlebar with one hand. Her other hand gripping the saddle, she eased the heavy machine off the man caught underneath.

"Are you hurt?" she asked.

But he already rolled sideways and wriggled to his feet.

"Alfred, isn't it?"

He nodded and relieved her of the weight straining her muscles. Though he might not admit it, his features, grubby with motor oil or dirt, twisted in pain.

"Thanks, ma'am," he said. The glance from under the damp thatch of hair wasn't grateful. It softened when Shadow pushed between them, rubbing his snout on the man's grimy sweatpants.

Alfred crouched and stretched out his palms. "Hey, handsome," Louise heard him murmur.

Astounded, she observed her cautious canine's attempt to lick the proffered hands.

"Hey, no. Motor oil's not good for you, fellow," Alfred said and wiped his fingers on his pants. His face leaned forward far enough for the pooch to lick his nose. The gruff man's features crinkled in a genuine smile. It lasted when he got up and faced Louise.

"You sure you're alright, Alfred? Can I help in any way? I'm Louise," she said. Then, she recognized the irony of it. "Ha, you are far better off doctoring yourself than letting an amateur like me administer to your wounds."

An answering grin lit up his craggy features. "You're a great help, Louise. The d—dratted beast weighs 500 pounds. Lucky it didn't crush me." Louise noticed the handlebar had hit a rock, which stopped the machine from falling flat.

"If you ever need someone to walk this guy, give me a shout," he said.

"Thanks for the offer. I'll keep it in mind." Though she doubted ever asking him for such a favor. "Well, I'd better get home."

"See ya," he said, looking at the dog. "And thanks again."

Louise bid him a nice day and strolled along the lane to her own place. She'd barely gone a few yards when her phone dinged. A text from Zoe asking if it was okay to drop in around 10. Of course, it was, Louise replied. In fact, she was eager to hear about the police interview. If her young neighbor would share.

As she unlocked her entrance door, another SMS popped up. Matron Juniper inquired which afternoon would suit for meeting Mrs. Norton, who was free any day from today until the weekend. Curious about her role as a reader and about Rosewood, the place that proved fatal for Carol, Louise confirmed her availability for this afternoon.

Neglectful of her, she admitted to herself, to take more time off. But her true crime client was at a US conference and unlikely to check over proofs for another week. A couple of other clients were yet to send the next installments of their work. No need to feel guilty for slacking a day or two. She would work for an hour and put in additional time tonight.

Immersed in proofreading, Louise lost track of time. The pooch's sudden yip startled her. As Shadow scrambled to his feet, Magic jumped off the table with a thud and streaked to the loft stairs. Louise rested her reading glasses on the laptop's keyboard and followed Shadow, who already stood tail wagging at the entrance.

"Good morning, Zoe. Come on in." Louise held the door wide.

"Hi, Louise. Hi, Shadow." The young woman held a cup tray and a paper bag. "I brought you a cappuccino. Owen says you like it." The voice sounded far from certain.

"Lovely of you, Zoe. Thanks." When Louise accepted the proffered tray, her visitor crouched to pat the tongue-lolling pooch.

"Shall we sit by the window?" Louise asked, leading the way to the living room. "If you don't mind the reminder of the dismal weather."

"Oh, it's so cozy in here. I love this room. It's like an enchanted library," Zoe said.

The mellow light from the shaded floor and table lamps Louise had turned on to ward off the foggy morning indeed created an atmosphere of comfort and ease, Louise thought as she took in the comfy seating in front of the bookshelves. By the window wall, the little table appeared like another island of rest. She'd ordered a sectional sofa lounger that would add to the relaxed ambiance.

As Zoe ripped one side of the paper bag, Louise removed her laptop to safety. "Should I get us plates?"

"Not on my account," said Zoe, and distributed paper napkins from the bag. "We've got chocolate zucchini and carrot loaf, and banana bread." She pointed to each pair. "I hope you like them."

"Wonderful." Louise smiled and removed the lid from the cappuccino. "What a treat." She reached for a slice of the zucchini loaf and broke off a piece. The rich chocolate flavor and smooth texture pleased her taste buds.

Across from her, Zoe picked at a corner of banana bread. Hair combed back in a tight ponytail, the young woman's features were taut. The black hoodie she wore over skinny blue jeans increased the paleness and dark under-eye circles. At a guess, Zoe hadn't slept well, Louise deduced.

"How's the little fellow?" Louise asked to put the young mother at ease. "My, Daniel is such an adorable child. I hope you'll let me enjoy his company often."

A timid smile transformed the drawn features. "He tried to say your name last night. I said, it's Auntie Louise. I hope that's okay." Zoe glanced at her and continued, "He kept on saying 'ant loose' or something."

Louise laughed. "Whatever he makes of my name is fine with me." She didn't want to raise any concerns about the toddler's language proficiency. The parents presumably were more than aware of it. They had enough to worry about, Louise thought.

"Time with you and Shadow was so good for him." Zoe reached down and stroked Shadow's head. He lay on his side, stretched out between them. "I can't thank you enough for looking after him."

"Not at all. My pleasure," Louise said and wondered whether to ask about the police or wait if Zoe volunteered. Then she remembered. "The oddest thing happened last night. We had a strange visitor." Was it her imagination, or did fear flash into the dark eyes? She hastened on. "Oh, just the circumstances made for strangeness. When Shadow and I returned from our evening walk, we found your cousin Dennis in the crawlspace below."

"You what?" Zoe looked panicked.

"Oh, no. I'm not putting this well. Shadow sniffed around and led me straight to the back of the house. The crawlspace door wasn't closed, and when I checked, there was this man. It turned out to be Dennis. He said he'd been looking for me and heard some noise. Like me, he checked it out."

Though Zoe's face relaxed somewhat, she seemed as unconvinced as Louise.

"He's a creep. Don't trust him, Louise." The fragile face puckered in a frown. "What would he want down there? It's empty, isn't it? Or did you store anything in it when you moved in?"

"Far too damp for storage," Louise said. "I can only assume he actually heard a noise." She regarded Zoe for a moment. "From what he said, I gather you aren't on friendly terms with him?"

The sound Zoe made seemed a cross between a snort and a mirthless laugh, Louise thought wryly.

"Like I said, he's a creep. Dennis hates us. Just because Aunt Carol was kind to Trevor and me." The young woman's eyes blazed. "You know what he did? He got his lawyer to stop the payout of Auntie's investments. She made us the beneficiaries, so the money won't go into the estate." A bony forefinger stabbed the center of the banana bread as if aiming for a bull's eye.

"I see," Louise said in soothing tones. "Not a nice thing to do among relatives."

A furious glance answered that commonplace. 'Oh, dear,' thought Louise.

"And now he tells police we tricked Auntie into lending us money. That's so untrue. She offered to sell us her house and help with the down payment and a second mortgage. Much better than renting it out and paying for the upkeep, she said." Tears spilled from angry eyes.

Dismayed at so much distress paired with barely suppressed rage, Louise tut-tutted. "There now. Don't get all upset. I'm sure it will work out."

"No, it won't."

Shadow jumped to his feet and turned his head from side to side between Zoe and Louise.

Zoe's anger crumbled. "I'm so sorry. You're so nice to me, and I go all mean."

"Not to worry," Louise said. "My remark trivialized things." She reached across the table and touched Zoe's clenched fist lightly. It relaxed at the contact. "Why not talk about it sensibly? I realize the situation is complex. If it helps to get a clearer perspective, use me as a sounding board. Some of my friends claim it helps them."

Zoe smiled timidly. "I'm so confused. I don't know where to start. Trevor is so angry he won't talk. He always does that with personal stuff. He's a great problem solver at work. But when it's us, he clams up."

"I think it's a common trait," Louise said, thinking of her ex, who'd kept his affairs at work well hidden from her. It still irked her. She must've been the only one who didn't know Xander cheated on her with heaven knew how many women and for how many years. Surely Trevor wasn't like that, was he?

"Would it help if I asked you questions to sort out the entire issue?" Louise said when Zoe's nervous fingers shredded more banana bread. Did she reduce all her food to fragments? Louise wondered. Skinny as she was, the young woman must eat like a bird.

Her gaze at the restless hands didn't go unnoticed. Zoe wiped her sticky fingers on a napkin and sat demurely, hands folded in her lap.

"Okay, so let me sum up my impression. Carol, who was Trevor's great-aunt, used to own the house you're now living in. I assume she found it too big for herself and moved into this place, renting out the one next door."

Zoe nodded again and said, "Yes, she already owned this cottage and rented it out before. I don't know when she switched over. Must've been ages ago when Trevor's uncle died. Well, great-uncle."

"Dennis mentioned last night Trevor's dad was the black sheep of the family. Do you know what he meant by that? Of course, he shouldn't have told a stranger like me, anyway." Louise felt uncomfortable bringing it up.

"What a jerk Dennis is. Trevor's dad was just unlucky." Zoe seemed to relish the opportunity to defend her late father-in-law. "He invested in some scam and got his aunt—I mean Auntie Carol—to invest, too. Or lend him the money or something. They didn't talk for years. But Trevor says she came to his dad's funeral, and Trev and Auntie grew close."

'Oh, dear.' Louise suppressed a sigh. One might sympathize with the glib Dennis if irresponsible borrowing ran in Trevor's family. A learned, rather than an inherited, trait.

"Trev's cousin is just jealous. He's lucky Auntie didn't disinherit him."

"Who is?" Louise asked, losing track of the convoluted family relations. Nephews and cousins who were great-nephews and cousins once or twice removed. Who was the real thing? Nor was she sure it mattered. Unless in a legal dispute where kinship played a role. Or in a police investigation.

"Dennis is." Zoe's glance implied a certain doubt at Louise's brightness. She explained in a patient tone, "Dennis always sponged on his dad. Aunt Carol's husband. And then he wasted it on mad start-up schemes. After his father died, he took his inheritance and emigrated to Australia without a goodbye to Auntie. His mother, I mean. They lost contact for years."

"What a sad story. Poor Carol," Louise commented softly, not to interrupt the flow.

"Auntie didn't care. It's awful, but I think she didn't like her son."

"I guess one can love one's children without liking them," Louise said and hesitated before adding, "The same could be said about parents."

"Oh, that's so true," Zoe said as if Louise's comment had been profound and echoed her feelings.

"Do your parents live in this area? Can you turn to them for support?"

"No. Trevor and me grew up in Saskatoon. My parents live on a farm. I couldn't wait to get away. They don't talk. Maybe it's the air up there," Zoe said, her small mouth twitching into a lopsided smile. "Anyway, I should get going. I feel all better for talking with you."

"Ah, don't go yet. Tell me quickly. How did the meeting with the police go? Did they tell you why they're investigating?"

The young woman sank back onto the chair, shoulders sagging. A haunted look darkened her eyes.

"Funny," she said with no amusement, "that's what I came to talk about. From what we can make out, they think Auntie died of poisoning."

Chapter Thirteen

Zoe's announcement left Louise speechless. Her mind told her she should have expected something of the kind. Maybe it was not malicious. Then Kendra's words bubbled up like from a bog. What had she said? 'If there was poisoning, the old gnome did it.' No, garden gnome was her own mental imagery. Either way, it referred to her neighbor, Mr. Simpson.

Aloud, as if to ward off the sinister possibility, she said, "Do they suspect food poisoning? Like from unsanitary food handling?" The police wouldn't investigate general food poisoning, or would they?

"I don't think so. They questioned us about Auntie's birthday. Who was there? Did we bring any food or drink? What did Aunt Carol eat while we were there? You know, it was an open house kind of thing. Friends and people dropped in."

Zoe's hands tightened the already tight ponytail. It pulled the corners of her eyes toward the temples, which looked painful to Louise.

As Zoe swung her legs sideways in preparation to rise, Shadow scrabbled into a sit.

"Was that all they wanted to know?" Louise said without emphasis.

Her visitor gazed at Shadow and reached for his ears. Her fingers kneaded them like dough. "They asked about financial stuff. I told you what Dennis is saying. Police questioned Trevor about it. And me, too."

"Goodness, how stressful for you. Trevor looked a little frazzled when he came for Daniel. I wondered how it went." Louise rose as her guest got up. "I am sure they are only doing their job. But what on earth triggered the sudden interest after weeks?"

"An anonymous tip, they told us. Someone gave them the name of a lab and claimed they should check for test results or something like that. The sergeant actually started by saying the lab's name and asked if we'd heard of it. How could we? We've only lived here for a short time. I can't even remember it now."

"How very odd," Louise said as she walked Zoe to the door. In passing, she noticed Magic's tiny head peeking around the upper bend in the staircase, irises startlingly yellow against the black face. A slow blink as if the kitty agreed with her assessment. Louise had an uncanny feeling Magic followed every word of the conversation. 'Don't be fanciful,' she chided herself.

After Zoe had left with renewed thanks, Louise cleared the table and put the untouched loaf slices into a tin. It felt wasteful to toss Zoe's crumbled piece into the compost bin. At least, it would one day fertilize some plants. She sighed. The circle of life was so reassuring.

While she unearthed the cat crate from the storage closet and made it more comfortable with a soft towel and some enticing cat treats, her mind puzzled over what she'd heard.

Food poisoning remained a possible explanation. But malicious intent appeared more likely to trigger a police investigation. Someone must have sent a sample of something from the birthday party—or maybe from anything consumed the day Carol died—to a lab for analysis. Not officially done, or else they would have postponed the funeral and done an autopsy. Not an efficient lab if it took so long for results. Else, the police investigation would have started much sooner after Carol's death.

But who had access to what was consumed that day at Rosewood Manor? Anyone who worked there, Louise's mind instantly answered. And the residents. Don't forget all the well-wishers at the birthday open house and anyone who dropped in during the day or evening.

It very much looked like someone among them didn't wish Carol Benson well at all.

Crating the opinionated feline proved a struggle. Magic seemed to suspect imminent eviction and went into hiding. With patience, treats, and soothing whispers, Louise lured the cat out from under the bed and maneuvered her, bum first, into the crate. What kitty didn't see coming, kitty didn't fear. Or was it blind trust in her foster parent?

When Louise backed the car out of the garage into the lane, she realized with satisfaction it had been almost a week since she'd used it last. Village life must be a health boon with all the walking she did.

Magic mewed non-stop on the short drive.

Located in the annex to a modest Victorian red brick home, the waiting room of the vet's office was small and exuded the usual antiseptic odor. Louise had already supplied her contact info over the phone. Within minutes, a teenage receptionist led her to an examination room overlooking a treed backyard.

"Dr. Wexford will be with you in a moment," the girl said and closed the door softly.

Louise placed the crate onto the stainless-steel surface of the table. Except for a cabinet unit, sink, a monitor and keyboard on the counter, the room contained only a visitor chair. Posters of all kinds of cat and dog ailments plastered the lime-green walls. They advertised anti-parasite protection. Huge images of pests, like fleas, ticks, and heartworm, served as unpleasant reminders of what was in store for one's beloved pets.

Why did doctors, for animals and humans alike, create such gloom and doom vibes? Louise wondered. Everyone knew how important positive thinking was for mental and physical health. Why these constant reminders of medical horrors?

Annoyed, she bent to be face-to-face with Magic, who meowed in protest of being held captive and eyed Louise through the crate's grid.

"We'll be out of here in no time. I promise," Louise whispered. With one finger, she reached between the bars and stroked Magic's head. The kitty's tongue curled and licked her finger.

"Hello there."

The cheery voice startled Louise. She hadn't heard the inner door open.

A woman, at most in her early 30s, wearing a white lab coat, entered briskly. She was as tall as Louise and wore her wiry black hair closely cropped. The topaz blue eyes sparkled. Despite the broad welcoming smile, Louise felt under intelligent assessment.

"Emily Wexford. Pleased to meet you, Ms. Penfold, isn't it?"

"Call me Louise. Glad to meet you, doctor."

"Just Emily is fine. I see you're bringing in Magic. Did you adopt her? Were you a friend of Carol's? So sorry about her passing." The young doctor stepped around the table and, like Louise had done, reached through the grid to let the cat sniff her finger.

"Oh, no. Not yet," Louise heard herself say. Confused, she amended, "I offered to foster the kitty until a forever home can be found."

Dr. Wexford gave a shrewd glance and grinned. "I understand. This little pussy is magical, isn't she? What a beauty. May I take her out?"

"Sorry. Of course. And, no, I never met Carol. Did you know her well?" Louise said. "I'm a dog person. Cats are a mystery to me and make me feel out of my depth."

As soon as the doctor opened the crate, Magic strutted out, sinuous back curved high. With a meow that sounded like 'about time!' she leaned against her foster person and rubbed a toothy cheek against Louise's arm.

The young woman laughed. "Seems to me Magic has adopted you. She's always been rather particular about likes and dislikes."

"I am honored. How old is she now?" Louise felt her cheeks burn. Her hand glided along the kitty's back.

"She's a few months over two. We'll print out her ID card later. Was there anything in particular that brought you in today?" The doctor's fingers flew over the keyboard until a colorful spreadsheet appeared on the monitor. "Magic's last checkup was in December. So, she isn't due for quite a while."

"Well, a rather odd encounter triggered this visit, Emily," Louise said while the vet's experienced hands gently prodded Magic's body. "Do you happen to know Carol's, or I should say, my neighbor, Mr. Simpson?"

"Ah. Yes, I do." Emily looked up, but her gaze gave nothing away. Nor did she expand.

"When I met him out in the backyard the other day, he claimed Carol's cat attacked his Pekingese." Magic's eyes blinked at Louise. "Since I found this kitty on my roof, she hasn't aggressed against me or my Shadow. He's a sweetie—a setter-lab cross. Same age as her. They might not be furrific friends yet, but Magic and Shadow get along just fine."

The vet chuckled and rolled startling blue irises up just a fraction, then grew serious.

"You understand, Louise, I can't comment on a client's pet. But I can tell you, this little beauty has a mind of her own." She tickled the kitty under the chin. "Her records show no sign of her being a bully. Magic was brought in once, last June to be precise, with a bite wound just above her tail. You can still see the scar."

With gentle fingers, Emily parted the hair on the cat's rump and revealed puckered marks of sutures.

After a quick scroll through the chart displayed, eyes still on the screen, the doctor said, "We were told the cat had been attacked by a neighbor's dog, and we advised keeping the cat indoors to prevent further harm to her."

"Oh, I see. When you say 'we,' does that mean 'you'?"

Emily grinned at her. "Nothing slips by you, does it? No, I meant 'we' literally. My dad and me. My father owns this office. While at vet school, I was his assistant and took over from him a few months ago when his health forced him to take a break."

"I'm sorry to hear of your father's health issues. He is lucky to have you to lean on," Louise said and meant it. The young doctor appeared very competent and confident.

Emily's deep, warm laugh was soothing. "My parents are touring Europe as we speak. It seems a life of leisure suits them so much, Dad finally might listen to my mom and retire."

"What a coincidence. My parents are touring, too. In a beaten-up VW camper on the hippie trail through India, of all things," Louise added ruefully.

"Wow, that sounds amazing," Emily said. "What fun. I'm afraid my parents are conventional by comparison."

"So am I." Louise grinned. "As a kid, I believed I was a changeling. Mixed up at birth and sent home to the wrong family. Sometimes, I think my parents must've wondered, too."

Again, Emily chuckled. She stroked Magic's head with her forefinger. "Do you want to have her blood work done? I don't think it's necessary unless you have specific concerns. We tested after the attack and again at the last checkup to be on the safe side."

"No, not really. What you told me alleviates my concerns on that score." Louise hesitated. She bent over the kitty who lay stretched out on the table as if ready for a nap.

"But there's something more, isn't there?" The astute doctor's gaze sought hers.

"I realize you can't release any information, Emily. Still, I need to get it off my chest. My neighbor implied his dog was poisoned. He seemed to link it to the alleged attack on his dog by this poor kitty."

Emily's eyes narrowed while Louise spoke, and a tiny, probably involuntary, headshake gave Louise a partial answer.

Slowly, Emily opened the door of the crate. Louise scooped up the docile kitty and placed her bum first into it.

"I see she taught you already how to crate her." The wide grin faded, and Emily grew serious. "As a general point, if a client were to inform us their pet died from poison, we would advise to run tests and send samples to our lab. Alternatively, we would suggest an autopsy. If the client refuses our recommendations, we can only note it in our records." Louise felt Emily's insistent gaze.

"Let me add," the doctor continued, "Even when pets pass away at a venerable age, it's not uncommon for grieving pet owners to lash out against others and insist their pet died before its allotted time."

"I can see this happening very easily," said Louise. "No matter how old our pets grow, their passing devastates us."

"It certainly does. Let's not think about that now. Your pets are still kids. I hope your visit settled some of your concerns. Magic is a healthy kitty and seems remarkably happy despite her recent loss. You are doing a wonderful job, Louise."

"Thanks so much, Emily. Since I know nothing about cats, it helps to have my intuition about the kitty confirmed." A loud meow from inside the crate hastened her to add, "I do trust her. How could I not when she snuggles up in bed and looks at me with those big amber eyes?"

"Ah, I knew it. Kitty has wrapped you around her little paw already." With an amused chortle, Emily walked Louise and Magic to the door. "We'll meet again, I'm sure. Welcome to Cascade."

When Louise asked for the bill, the girl behind the reception desk checked the computer screen and said, "There's no charge for today. Dr. Wexford marked it as a follow-up. Here's the cat's ID card for you."

"That's amazingly kind. Please thank Dr. Wexford from Magic and me." Louise dug out her purse and inserted a bill into the local Humane Society's collection box.

Outside in the parking bay, she stored Magic's crate on the car's passenger seat rather than in the back and secured it with the seatbelt.

Once in the driver's seat, she turned to the kitty, who watched her through the grid.

"Now listen, Magic. Don't get any ideas. I might have said 'yet,' but that doesn't mean we are on the road to 'forever.'"

The kitty sneezed.

Chapter Fourteen

Left with two hours before heading over to Rosewood for her first reading session with Mrs. Norton, Louise yielded to a sense of duty and returned to proofreading. Yet her mind wandered, revisiting what she'd heard from Zoe and the vet. Shadow sensed her restlessness and sat up to scratch his ear. Head leaning into his paw, he regarded her.

"Leave your ear alone," Louise said, getting up. "You'll be sorry if your nails hurt it. Come, let's go outside for a few minutes."

The pooch pounced ahead to the door. Louise slipped on her wellingtons and a raincoat. Though the rain had petered out during the last hour, the trees continued to drip, and the mist persisted.

Shadow looked at her, tongue lolling sideways, eager for any games she might suggest.

"Go ahead. Have a good sniff. You'll get your walk this evening," Louise said.

Lots of scents for him to follow in this damp weather. Even her infinitely weaker sense of smell picked up earthy whiffs tinged with a fungi flavor.

As she paced the flat part of the yard that divided her house from Zoe and Trevor's, a momentary tightening inside her chest caused her to pause.

The tall evergreens dribbling moisture seemed so much darker today. Why this sudden pang of desolation?

Yesterday, life looked so bright when she and the little fellow played fetch with Shadow and dug in their make-believe sandbox.

That was just it. The change in the weather brought with it a transformation of the peaceful village atmosphere. Better face it. Something deadly festered under the picturesque surface.

She needed to know exactly what it was. Rosewood Manor might well hold the answer.

With renewed determination, Louise called Shadow. He abandoned whatever trail he was on among the wet weeds and followed her inside.

On the stroke of three, Louise entered the reception area at Rosewood. Rain threatening again, she'd used the car to avoid arriving like a soaked sponge cake. The same staff smiled vaguely from behind the glass enclosure and wished her a good afternoon.

"Hello again. I'm here to visit Mrs. Norton. We've arranged a reading session. Louise Penfold is my name."

"Oh, yes. Matron mentioned it. Hang on while I buzz someone to take you up." The receptionist spoke into the phone and then ignored her. Amused, Louise reckoned her volunteer status demoted her from prospective client to 'that reader for Nora.'

A few minutes elapsed until the door behind the desk opened. The girl, Uma, approached.

When Louise greeted her by name, the young nurse's brows contracted. Then her forehead relaxed. "You came to see Matron. I remember now. Sorry, I didn't catch your name."

"Louise Penfold. We only met in passing, and you were busy."

The girl's brown skin seemed to turn a shade darker, and the frown returned. "Would you come this way, please? I'll take you upstairs."

They mounted a solid oak staircase. Its banister gleamed, but a non-skid material hid the wooden treads.

Louise said conversationally, "My, what a beautiful house. The parlor downstairs looks so inviting. I'm surprised to see it empty. Don't the residents like to use it?"

Uma glanced at her with a vacant expression. It cleared in a moment. "I get it. You mean the events room? It's for special stuff. Like receptions at Christmas or for open house."

"Hm, where do the residents gather on ordinary days, then?"

"There's a TV lounge in the back with tables for playing cards or board games. Plus, we have a den with a few computers and video games. Keeps them busy."

"Ah, I see. I take it Carol Benson celebrated her birthday in the events room?"

The glance Uma shot her struck Louise as none too friendly. Nor did the girl answer.

Instead, the nurse pointed down the carpeted corridor as they reached the top of the stairs. Cream-colored bead paneling covered the lower half of the walls. Framed watercolor paintings of pastoral scenes in soothing pastel tones created a serene ambience.

They only had a few steps to go until Uma knocked on one of the solid wood doors. She opened it and announced, "Your reader's here. Can she come in?"

"Uma, Uma. Will you ever learn?" a cultured female voice fluted. Without even seeing the occupant, Louise expected a dainty, elegantly dressed lady, so strong was the image the voice conveyed.

The reality did not disappoint. What Mrs. Norton lacked in height, she made up in vivaciousness and poise. The tasteful, burgundy wool dress accentuated a petite, slim figure. Silver-white hair, cut and styled becomingly in gentle waves, framed a surprisingly smooth complexion.

Like her own mother, Louise figured, Nora Norton might be a mere 70.

"Dear Ms. Penfold. Come in, come in. I'm so pleased to see you." In an endearing gesture, silver bracelets tinkling, the beringed hands reached out.

Louise clasped them gently with her own. "A pleasure to meet you, Mrs. Norton." Attracted by the lovely room, Louise's glance traveled over the smaller woman's head.

Of generous proportion, the room featured a sitting area in front of a bay window. Floral chintz-covered armchairs faced each other across a low table. An upright mirror next to a handsome mahogany armoire reflected the ambient light from floor and table lamps.

The three-fold mirror of a marble-topped vanity perpetuated lights and images in 3D fashion. Framed photos and knickknacks adorned occasional tables. Several oil paintings looked like originals.

At first, Louise thought it was solely a private sitting room. But then she noticed the paneled casing of what must be a fold-up bed on one side of the room, next to another door, which presumably led to an en suite bathroom.

Mrs. Norton stood, hands folded under her chin, watching Louise eagerly.

Embarrassed at being caught in visual snooping, Louise said, "Goodness, how rude of me. I apologize for staring. But it's such a cozy room."

"Do you like it?" Nora Norton asked diffidently, like a young girl. "I furnished it with some pieces from home when my husband and I came to Rosewood. Come sit with me, and we'll have a chat."

A graceful hand gesture invited Louise to the window nook. The deep pile of an expensive blue and gray rug cradled her moccasins as she walked across.

Displayed on the table, a library book's lurid cover caught Louise's eye and made her heart sink. Romance, no matter how famous the author, hadn't been her go-to reading since her teens when she devoured Georgette Heyer's regency romps.

The trilling laugh of her hostess showed her dismay was all too obvious.

Mrs. Norton leaned over and whispered, "Camouflage. I've got sterner stuff for us to read."

This sounded so sweetly out of sync with the genteel personality Louise grinned conspiratorially.

Her hostess wriggled in the armchair, far too large for the tiny figure, and reached for a purse behind the cushion. "I'll always keep it with me," she confided and chortled. "Like our dear late queen."

Though a Canadian, Louise had never thought of the queen in terms of 'our' but recalled images showing the monarch carrying a purse even at home.

"Whatever you like us to read is fine with me, Mrs. Norton."

"Call me Nora, please. May I say Louise?"

"Of course." Louise reached over to relieve Mrs. Norton of the proffered paperback. The black cover showed a blonde in a red cocktail dress. In red ink, the title and author's name stood out. Raymond Chandler, *The Lady in the Lake.*

Louise grinned. "Ah, you prefer noir thrillers to romance."

"Do you mind? Is it too dark for you?"

"Not at all. In fact, I edit for a true crime writer. Her books and the research we do can get pretty grim."

"How exciting!" Nora all but clapped her hands. "We have to try one someday." Again, diffidence snuck in. "If you enjoy reading with me."

"I'm sure I'll love it." Louise smiled reassuringly. "Would you like me to start?"

As though she hadn't heard, Nora whispered, "We have a true crime right here at the Manor." She glanced toward the door as if worried someone might overhear.

"Oh?" Louise said, hoping for more.

"A friend of mine was offed."

If she hadn't known how real the death was, Louise would have grinned at the lurid phrase coming from such mild, discreetly lip-sticked lips.

To avoid later awkwardness, she said, "I'm so sorry. I should tell you, Nora, I know who you are referring to. I bought Carol Benson's house on Charlotte's Lane. The day I met with Matron Juniper, the police showed up. This must be so upsetting for you." Though Nora seemed excited rather than perturbed to her. "Was Carol a close friend of yours?"

Her hostess sat very straight on the edge of the armchair, silky legs sideways and small feet in low-heeled pumps crossed at the ankles. The silver bracelets tinkled when the fragile hands fluttered to touch the string of pearls. Only the knobby finger joints and knuckles spoke of advanced years.

Nora's eyes were misty when she responded after a thoughtful pause. "Don't think me callous. Death no longer frightens me. Of course, it's sad, but I've made my peace with life's reality."

With a tiny laugh, she added, "Now I've shocked you. You see, we had to move here because my husband needs full care. I visit him every day in the nursing wing. Most days, he doesn't know who I am." The gray-blue eyes lost their focus, and the features sagged.

"I'm sorry," murmured Louise.

Animation returned to Nora's face. "That's how I met Carol again. I've known her for years when we were both on the village committee. While she was here in the nursing wing, I made a point of dropping by for a chat once she felt up to it."

"I heard she was well enough to celebrate her birthday. Did you see her that day?" Louise was now very curious, indeed. "It was an open house kind of affair, wasn't it?"

Mrs. Norton leaned forward, keen eyes regarding Louise. "You are just as interested in Carol's death as I am. Aren't you? Why is that, I wonder?"

Asked so directly, Louise shifted uncomfortably in her seat. The spine of *The Lady in the Lake* cut into the flesh of her palms. She hadn't realized she was still clutching the book. Carefully, she placed it on the low table.

'You've got to give if you want to get,' she reminded herself.

"I'll come clean," she said lightly. "Cascade and the lovely cottage on Charlotte's Lane beckoned as a peaceful refuge from the harsh reality of city life. My marriage didn't end well, and I'm starting afresh."

Nora eyed her, puzzled where this was going, Louise realized. So, she switched from flowery to prosaic. "Then, a neighbor insinuated Carol poisoned his dog. I found out the police are investigating Carol's death. My idyll is shattered. For my own peace of mind, I need to know what really happened."

Like a dainty bird's, Nora's head nodded in little spurts. "You and I." The blue-veined hand reached across the table, not quite touching Louise's that still rested on the paperback. "Let's team up and find out. With your true crime experience and my insider knowledge, we'll beat my godchild any day," Nora said, eyes sparkling.

Confused, Louise asked, "Beat your godchild? What do you mean?" How far Mrs. Norton's insider knowledge went was another question, she thought.

"Raymond. He's with the RCMP. They investigate Carol's death." Nora's forefinger tapped the tabletop. "He doesn't take me seriously. I told him I'll help. Be his eyes and ears here. You know what he did? He laughed at me! Keep your nose out of police business, he said."

Louise almost smiled at the righteous outrage showing on Nora's face. "Is Raymond the one who came here with the female sergeant the other day? Uma called him inspector. Is he in charge?" The female officer had looked about ten years older, but equity was not what characterized policing.

"No, his staff sergeant is in charge. That's why I tell him he must prove himself to get promoted. He just laughs and says, 'Godmother, stay out of it.' I feel like Al Capone's wife when he calls me that." The rueful smile told Louise that Nora didn't mind the association.

There could be no question of involving this spritely lady in any amateur sleuthing venture. But it wouldn't hurt to find out what Mrs. Norton knew about the events on Carol's last birthday.

Conscious of skirting her volunteer duties, Louise pointed to Chandler's book. "We got a little off-topic, didn't we? Should I—"

A knock on the door interrupted. Instead of answering, Nora pushed the romance toward Louise and half rose to grab the thriller, stuffing it behind her seat cushion. "Quickly, read to me. No, just open it in the middle," she muttered when Louise turned to the beginning.

Mrs. Norton sat back, adopting a genial expression when she twittered over Louise's reading voice. "Come in, dear. It's open."

The outer door swung in soundlessly. Framed by the entrance stood Alfred, a tea tray in hand.

Chapter Fifteen

Louise closed the book, her forefinger still marking the passage she'd read. Across from her, Mrs. Norton beamed at the head nurse.

"Ah, our tea. So kind of you, Alfred," she said as he walked in. "Leave it here, please. Louise will pour."

He bent to deposit the tray on the table. Louise saw a gleam in his eyes as they strayed to the romance she was holding.

"No need to pretend," he said. "I know what Nora got you up to."

'Oh, no!' Louise's mind raced. Had Nora already involved the nurse in her Nancy Drew act? Not a good idea at all.

"Louise and I were just—"

With an unladylike coughing fit into her sleeve, Louise interrupted Nora's twitter.

Her hostess and Alfred regarded her with concern. Mouth still covered by her raised upper arm, Louise apologized.

"Can I get you some water?" Alfred asked politely. "Or tea?" He raised the porcelain pot.

"Yes, Alfred. Please do," Nora said.

As he poured, Louise tried to catch Mrs. Norton's eye. Understanding dawned, or so it seemed to Louise, as the gray-blue eyes sparkled, and Nora's chin gave a tiny nod.

"Thank you, Alfred." Accepting the fragile rose-patterned cup and saucer, Mrs. Norton's hand reached under the cushion and withdrew the Chandler. With a mischievous smile, she said, "Alfred knows all my vices, Louise. We can't hide anything from him."

Louise looked at the nurse, who had straightened up. She couldn't read his expression when their glances met.

"Oh, dear," Nora said. "How remiss of me. Have you met before?"

"We have," said Alfred. "Louise saved me from getting squashed." He grinned at Louise.

"Goodness gracious. Whatever happened?" asked Mrs. Norton, wide-eyed.

"Nothing heroic, I am afraid," Louise said, taking a sip from her cup. "I merely lifted the motorbike when it toppled while Alfred was working on it. We both live on Charlotte's Lane, and I happened to pass his place with my dog this morning."

"Well, I'll let you get on with your tea and crime fix," Alfred said, which earned him a delighted titter from Nora.

Louise watched his departure thoughtfully. After the door closed with a soft click, she turned to her hostess.

"I'm not sure it's wise being too trusting after what happened to Carol. The last thing I'd want is to alarm you. But until the police find out what happened, it's better to err on the side of caution."

Mrs. Norton regarded her over the teacup's rim, pinky tucked in. "I see what you mean. But Alfred is such a caring nurse. My husband responds to him better than to anyone else. It makes me so grateful."

Louise recalled the off-duty Alfred and reserved judgment. "Still," she said. "Please, do be careful. Just for the moment."

"I have police protection, don't I?" Nora giggled. "Everyone here knows Raymond is my godchild."

If someone thought the sweet lady knew more than was good for her, didn't it make Mrs. Norton more vulnerable? Her work with the true crime writer client taught Louise sharing knowledge might reduce the risk if the recipient was trustworthy. Since Nora intended to play sleuth, it would be best to plumb her for information.

"Can we return to our earlier conversation, Nora? You said your godchild wasn't willing to listen. I certainly would. Did you notice anything out of the ordinary on Carol's birthday? Were you at the open house celebration?"

Her hostess, who had nodded eagerly while she spoke, pushed a small plate of plain cookies across the table. "Have one. French Sable. They look boring but are quite good."

When Louise tested a cookie and pronounced it tasty, Nora said, "Raymond took my statement but only wanted to hear who dropped in, what food or drink they brought, and how long they stayed. He wouldn't listen to my theories."

Mrs. Norton emphasized the last word. "I was there the entire time, you see. We rarely use the beautiful parlor. Quite silly if you ask me. Much nicer than the TV 'lounge.'"

Even without Nora's fingers tapping scare quotes in the air, Louise would have heard them in the refined voice.

"An ideal observer. Can you remember everyone who came?" Louise asked.

"I can do better." Mrs. Norton broke into her trilling laugh. "In my younger days, I wanted to be an actress and, for years, was in amateur theatrics. I'll show you. Enjoy your tea and watch. Pretend you are Carol in her chair down in the parlor."

The idea made Louise a little queasy. Playing someone soon to die was not a comforting thought. Yet, she agreed.

Nimbler than her age led Louise to expect, Nora sprang up and dashed to the door. When she turned, miming an entry, Louise was astonished at the convincing transformation of the mobile features.

"Auntie! How lovely to see you." Nora came rushing toward her. Louise could've sworn a vision of Zoe materialized, so convincing was the mimicry. When two hands reached for hers, and an overly eager, smiling grimace leaned close as if to kiss her cheek, Louise recoiled as far as the armchair allowed.

"Perfect! That's just how Carol reacted." Nora said in her normal treble voice and clapped her hands. "Now, you don't know your lines as Carol. So, I'll speak for you."

Again, the amazing lady's voice and features changed completely. Her jaw dropped. Her cheeks drooped and eyes contracted, aging Nora by 25 years. She suddenly looked closer to 95.

In a raspy, weak voice, yet full of authority, she said, "Don't be a fool, girl. I look like death warmed over, and you know it. Did you bring my cat, as I asked? And where is that child of yours?"

"But Auntie, you know they won't let us bring in a cat. Daniel is at a friend's house." The speed with which Nora switched roles had Louise gaping. Mesmerized, she watched the features adapt as if they were made of putty.

"Stuff and nonsense," countered the Carol imitation in a gruff rasp. "How can you know if you never bother to try?"

Seconds later, Nora was back in her chair, smiling her sweet, joyful smile, while Louise sat still spellbound, blinking as if to dispel a mirage.

"You are quite the actress, alright. I could virtually feel Zoe in the room with us."

Nora laughed. "I won't role-play a whole script. Maybe just one or two of them are too good to pass up," she said. Red roses bloomed on her pale cheeks. "The rest, I'll just tell you."

"Too bad," said Louise. "I can see it would take a while to enact."

"Exactly. So, then Trevor came forward. You know them, I assume?"

"Yes, I do. Yesterday, I babysat little Daniel. Such a lovable child."

"Carol found him ill-behaved. Terrible twos—or threes—I told her. Anyway, Trevor brought a gift bag and a box from the local bakery. Carol told him to place it on the folding table the staff had set up for beverages and snacks. Nicely done with a white tablecloth and streamers."

Louise motioned to the teapot and, without waiting for a response, refilled both cups. Nora sipped slowly before continuing.

"Some of the seniors dropped by," she said. "Owen arrived with more cake boxes. He showed Carol the special birthday cake Jeremy from the patisserie created. Carol's favorite petit four as a tiny birthday cake for one.

We all crowded around to see. It looked lovely with Carol's name in tiny white script on the bright green icing and a twirly, white-green candle in the center."

"Jessie at the shop mentioned it to me," Louise said. "Did Carol like it?"

"I think she did. She certainly ate half of it later. It was a little odd. Everyone brought her petit fours. As if someone in her condition could eat so many sweets."

"They meant well, I guess," said Louise. "It seems to have been an open secret that Carol adored Jeremy's little pastries. Who else dropped in?"

"The woman from the local antique store must have come in at some point. You see, I was sitting in a chair off to the side, knitting a jumper for Raymond's baby girl." Nora pointed to a lidded wicker basket next to her chair. Two long needles poked out.

"Were you able to see Carol the entire time?" Louise asked but realized it was unlikely.

Mrs. Norton's knobby hand rose to her temple. Her eyelids closed, perhaps looking back into the past. "No," she said. "People moved about. Carol told them to help themselves to the treats on the table."

"So, Carol ate from the special birthday cake," Louise repeated when her hostess's shrewd glance returned to her. "Did you see her eat or drink anything else, Nora?"

No immediate answer came. Instead, the sprightly lady jumped up again and scurried to the door. Louise watched as the trim body sagged and contorted.

In slow motion, she turned and had Louise exclaim at the horrible transformation. The spine curved to rival the hunchback of Notre Dame. Head jutting and jerking forward, the figure scuttled toward Louise. A venomous grimace writhed the genteel mien beyond recognition.

The hand appeared gnarled in clutching a phantom offering to a torso, hollowed by the hunched, boney shoulders.

Though the slower approach prepared Louise, she tried not to recoil but couldn't suppress a moue of distaste. An *ugh* escaped her when the apparition's head bobbed close.

"Surprise!" It sputtered and cackled. One claw reached as if withdrawing something from a bag.

Louise's hands shot up to ward off the imaginary gift.

The wheezing cackle dissolved into a titter, and the impersonation metamorphosed into the sweet and dainty lady who clearly cherished the artistic effect she'd wrought.

Speechless, Louise gazed at her hostess, seated again, complacently brushing the hem of the burgundy wool dress into place below the knees.

Nora pushed back the silver bracelets and almost coyly asked, "Didn't you recognize who that was supposed to be?"

"You left me dumbstruck. What a performance. Mr. Simpson to a T. Frightening. Nora, the world lost a remarkable actress when you left the stage."

"Goodness," said Mrs. Norton. "The third-class amateur theatrics I left behind hardly qualify as 'the stage.' True, maybe I should have studied acting instead of letting myself be swept off my feet by the love of my life."

For a moment, the mobile face looked wistful. "Water under the bridge. I've had a good life."

"What was Mr. Simpson's gift? And how did his former lover react?" Louise asked as much trying to divert Nora from melancholy life reflections as to gather details on what happened.

"I couldn't say because just then Dennis Benson made his entry. He is Carol's son. Did you know?"

"Yes. I've met him." Louise wasn't ready to share her strange encounter but wanted Mrs. Norton's view of him. "How did that go?"

"Dramatic," her hostess said. "He knows how to take center stage. I won't act it out for you, but it was quite effective."

"Oh? How so?"

"Well, my poor imitation of Carol's old beau—that's what she used to call the poor misshapen fellow—was nothing compared to the real-life impression he made on the birthday guests. Our eyes were on the old beau when this outraged shout came from the door. One word, 'You!' But, oh, what lovely passion."

Nora beamed at the recollection.

"Of course, he had our full attention. There in the doorway stood Dennis, right arm stretched out, finger-pointing at the little man. 'How dare you?'" It seemed the actress could not resist imitating Dennis's growl.

In her own voice, she explained, "I was just getting up to grab him by the sleeve of his designer suit and tell him it was no way to act—though I enjoyed it as a performance—upsetting Carol with his dramatics when Alfred came up from behind."

"Oh, my. That all must've been so distressing for Carol in her state of health," Louise said.

"Carol was not above creating a scene. But, yes, she was still fragile from the bout of illness she had suffered. Whatever it was Alfred said to Dennis, it deflated him. Owen somehow coaxed the little man away from Carol, and Dennis went to sit with her."

"Did they get along well?" Louise asked, aware Zoe implied quite the opposite. Yet, animosity might affect the great-niece's judgment.

"From what Carol let slip, my impression is she had no illusions about her son," Nora said. "In for the money. For years, she had not a word from him. I understood her lawyer contacted Dennis in Australia when Carol was hospitalized after her recent attack."

"Maybe it shook him up, and he regretted having neglected his mother," Louise suggested, though she doubted a benign motivation for such regret.

"Maybe."

As Nora's glance met hers, Louise felt sure they thought the same thing.

"Did the party disperse after Dennis's performance?" she asked.

"Not immediately. Someone proposed toasting the birthday girl. There was a bottle of bubblies. I believe Alfred brought it in. But Carol hated champagne and wanted a glass of her favorite liquor. She was crazy about absinthe. That was in the green icing and cream filling of the birthday cake."

"Yes, Jessie at the patisserie told me," Louise said.

"Somehow, a bottle of the foul-smelling stuff—sorry, I can't stand the smell of anise—stood on the side table next to Carol's chair. I hadn't noticed

94

it before. Only Carol wanted it. We all had champagne in plastic flutes. Carol got a small glass of the green—"

Nora broke off. Her face turned even paler than her natural complexion. It took on a greenish tinge.

Alarmed, Louise half rose. "Nora? Are you alright?" This long talk must've exhausted the dear lady, she thought. "I'm so sorry. I should have—"

"No. Not you. But don't you see? The absinth was poisoned!"

With a thud, Louise sank down onto the chair again and stared at Nora. Slowly, she said, "That might be it."

Mrs. Norton's cheeks regained color. Animation returned. "It must be. We all had champagne, except for Carol."

"Let's slow down," Louise said. "We don't know if whatever she ingested during the birthday party killed her. If this was in the afternoon, she might have consumed plenty of other things during the evening. Also, didn't you say she ate half of the special birthday cake? Did anyone finish it?"

"Huh? No one would. It would be like eating someone's leftovers. People don't do that," Nora said with conviction.

'Our kind of people,' Louise thought, remained unstated. Yet, she agreed. One didn't polish off someone else's cake slice unless it was among close friends or loved ones.

"Who was present to toast Carol's health? What a sad irony," Louise added quietly.

"Let me see. I think everyone I mentioned. Trevor and Zoe. Dennis. Mr. Simpson. I believe about three or four of the residents. Oh, the bakers had just come in. The woman who keeps the antique store—what's her name, now?"

When Nora frowned to recall, Louise put in, "Kendra."

"Anyway," Mrs. Norton waved it aside. "Matron Juniper joined us with Uma. Like I said, Alfred was there already and poured the champagne." Nora gazed at her hands, eyes narrowing in concentration. "That's it, I think."

"Had Owen left?"

"You are right. No, he was still on a stool by my side, talking to me. Such a nice man."

Despite the effort of appearing lively, Mrs. Norton's face looked drained. Worried about taxing the older lady's resources, Louise glanced at the gilded Ormolu clock on an occasional table. Though she couldn't make out the time, she exclaimed, "My, it's getting late. I'm sorry, but I must dash."

When her hostess's features slackened in sadness or disappointment, Louise regretted the suddenness of her announcement.

Gracefully, Nora rallied. "You'll visit again soon, won't you? I haven't felt so alive in ages." With the mischievous smile, so unexpected in such a gentle lady, she added, "And we haven't done our reading yet." She pointed to *The Lady in the Lake,* lying abandoned on the table.

"I'll be back soon, I promise," Louise said. "Would you like my phone number?"

"Yes, please." Nora rummaged in her purse and handed Louise a late-model iPhone. "Here, punch in yours, and I'll drop you a line. I love texting." The amazing lady giggled in delighted anticipation.

"Before I go," Louise said, adopting a sober tone despite her amusement at Nora's enthusiasm for SMS contact. "Will you promise me to be very careful? If anything worries you, please promise to call your Raymond. Or me."

"Fiddlesticks. Nothing will happen to me." Mrs. Norton fluttered her hands, bracelets tinkling.

Louise wished she could feel the same certainty.

Chapter Sixteen

When Louise passed the Witch's Brew on her drive home, she stopped, though she still had more pastries from the patisserie at home than she could eat.

Two customers were leaving as she entered. One told her, "They are closing."

A girl in a long black apron upended chairs onto the tables while another cleaned the espresso machine, releasing hissing bursts of steam.

'Oh, well,' thought Louise, 'tomorrow is good enough,' and made to leave.

"Louise!" called Owen's voice. "Don't go."

Not waiting for a reply, he entered from the kitchen and made his way around the serving counter.

An empty tray tucked under his arm, he grinned at her. "Just in time for a quiet bite. Perfect timing. Staff's ready to go home, and I was about to have soup and salad. Won't you join me?"

"So kind of you to ask, Owen. If I'm not intruding," Louise said, pleased at an opportunity to talk to him away from customers. Of course, she would insist on paying for her meal. "Do you always close at five?"

"Just one day a week. A man needs a night off." He chuckled, catching her raised brow. "And so does a woman. Girls, too," he added when the chair-swinging employee rolled eyes at him.

"Leave the table over there," he told the staff. "Louise and I want to sit by the window. Don't we?" His questioning gaze had Louise nod. "What would you like to drink? "Afraid cappuccino's not an option. Machine's put to sleep."

"I'd love a glass of water. I've had too much tea at Rosewood."

"What brought you to the Manor? Do you have loved ones living there?" Owen grabbed a glass from a rack behind the counter and held up a jug of water, rattling the floating ice cubes. "Cold? Or bottled? Maybe you prefer it fizzy?"

"Cold, please. No, I volunteer as a reader at Rosewood and had my first session today."

"How did it go?" Jug and glasses in hand, the café proprietor walked her to the table. "Your voice sounds perfect for audiobooks. Do you do it professionally, too?"

"Thanks. No, I never considered it. My work as an editor occasionally involves testing the oral flow of a piece. Today was more of a meet and greet. Mrs. Norton and I had a pleasant chat."

"Nora Norton? She's a dear."

Louise glanced at Owen, who lingered, hands resting on the vacant chair opposite. "She mentioned you."

His eyebrows shot up. "You talked about me? I am flattered."

"Nothing much." Embarrassed, Louise floundered. She didn't want to appear a town gossip in the making yet relished the chance to hear his impression of Carol's party.

"Nah, you won't get away that easily. I'll grab our din-din and be right back. Chicken soup, okay?"

Louise thanked him and leaned back to mull over her intense visit with Mrs. Norton.

The café's staff shot her curious glances and called 'good night' upon leaving.

Minutes later, Owen returned with steaming bowls of soup and plates of spring baby leaf salad, garnished with cucumber wedges and red, yellow, and speckled heirloom tomatoes. He placed a basket of baguette slices and a dish of butter crowns on the table.

"This looks lovely," Louise said as she inhaled the soup's delicious aroma. She hadn't realized how hungry she was. Sable biscuits weren't filling, and her frugal lunch was a distant memory.

"Dig in." Owen watched her with a pleased grin.

For a few minutes, the food kept them busy.

Her host refilled their water glasses and sat back. "Now tell me. What made Nora mention me? Did she give you a rundown on the village population? She's lived in the area her whole life and knows just about everyone."

Louise hesitated. Without being specific, she would have no chance of getting his views. Yet, she felt reluctant to confide. After all, Owen had delivered Carol's birthday cake. Still, Louise couldn't imagine what on earth might motivate the café proprietor to poison an elderly woman. Nor was there a shred of evidence for the cake as the modus operandi. Though Jeremy or Jessie had the best opportunity to mess with it.

Aware of Owen's scrutiny, Louise pretended to chew and gulped down water as if to clean her palate before speaking. Did he even know of the police investigation?

Her mind groped for an innocuous phrasing that wouldn't seem devious if he knew yet enabled her to question him if he was unaware.

"We spoke of Carol because I mentioned my move to Charlotte's Lane. Nora told me about Carol's birthday party and the people who dropped in. Your name came up. I sensed she rather likes you."

"Ah." Owen played with his soup spoon.

Louise speared some salad and chewed it thoughtfully, leaving the conversational ball in his court. It worked.

"So, you've heard about the police nosing about," he said. She nodded and waited. "And dear Nora, being a crime buff and a bit of an actress, can't wait to play Ms. Marple, can she? Par for the course, with that godchild of hers."

Louise almost sputtered salad. Then played for time. "Whatever do you mean?"

"C'mon. You don't want to tell me you ladies chewed over Carol's final birthday, with her dying the same night, and the cops deep-diving into her so-called suspicious death, and our Nora showed no interest?"

"Well, of course, she's interested, like everyone else. You seem to know her quite well. How come, Owen? Is she a good customer?"

"Sure. She's a regular, like most of the mobile seniors at Rosewood. They often meet here to get away for a while. Nora comes from an old Cascade family who's owned land in the area for generations. Served on the town committee, just like Carol."

"So she said," Louise murmured when he stopped to drink some water.

He topped up the glasses. "Did she now? Told you about my run-in with the committee about the patio, I bet."

Louise looked noncommittal, hoping for more. She scooped up the last bit of her soup.

"They sure didn't succeed." He rocked back on his chair, mouth widening in a complaisant smirk.

Intent on fishing for details without showing her complete ignorance of the issue, Louise said vaguely, "How could they, anyway?"

"The busybodies on the committee hoped for a majority vote to take the complaint to the municipal council. Ridiculous. As if my patio caused the traffic jams. Folks come in droves for the scenic beauty of our area. So what if the bikers and cyclists park their machines all over the place? We've got cops to see to traffic violations, don't we?"

The café owner seemed to work up a steam and notice it. He wiped his mouth with the back of his hand. "Sorry, Louise. Didn't mean to go on a rant. But that committee and its pet peeve got my goat."

"I'm keen to learn about the village dynamics," Louise said mildly. "A newcomer can really put her foot in if she's ignorant of people's opinions."

"They'll tell you their opinions, all right." His laugh sounded cynical.

"Your friends on the village committee supported you, though." It was a safe bet, she figured, since he'd said they didn't succeed. A glance from the window revealed the evidence. Fresh annuals studded the planter box enclosures around the patio. Rain drenched now, dry warm weather would bring back the crowds.

Owen's complaisant grin spoke for itself. "Most shop owners are on my side. They'd lose customers if the village was a no-parking zone on weekends. Hey, my place attracts tons of people. They stop for a bite and hang out in the village." He pushed out his chest and puffed it up in mocking self-congratulation.

The sight made Louise chuckle. "I see you are the town benefactor. The village people were against you? I can hardly credit that."

"Nora was on the side of reason. My side." He grinned disarmingly. "As was old Simpson. Just to spite Carol. She'd still be chairing the committee if her health hadn't failed. And launching another attack, too." With a rueful grin, Owen shook his head. "Undefeatable."

For a moment, neither of them spoke. Then, he added, "Poor Carol. I almost wish she had another go at it. What a trooper she was. Dominated the committee for years. I've seen members cringe at her tongue-lashing."

"Yet, she was outvoted in the end, wasn't she?" Louise said, keeping her voice even.

"Secret ballot."

"Are you on the committee, too, Owen?"

"Me? Not on your life. Me and some others sit in as spectators to the village antics. Need to keep abreast of their shenanigans. Plus, keep them on your good side." A wide grin split his face. "I donate the beverages and Jeremy the treats. Kendra would lavish her junk on them if she'd find any takers."

Louise could well imagine the antique lady trying it. "Isn't Kendra on the committee?"

"She'd hoped to succeed Carol as the chair. But no luck."

His neutral expression didn't tell her if that was a good thing.

"My, you have all the fun in this town, don't you?" His earlier comment offered a gambit for turning the conversation back to Carol's last day. "Is Mr. Simpson still on the village committee? I heard he was upstaged by Dennis's dramatic entry at the birthday do. Carol's son is quite the guy."

The café proprietor shot her a curious glance. "You've met Dennis?"

"*Uhu.*" She nodded as if it was of no consequence and buttered the last piece of bread. One can't be expected to speak with one's mouth full.

"Simpson resigned when Carol's health forced her to give up committee work. The old rascal thrived on their spats. I bet he found the meetings too dull with our respectable new chairperson."

"I've heard he and Carol used to be an, er... in a relationship." She had almost said 'an item' like Zoe had put it.

Owen must have noticed her involuntary smile but misinterpreted it. "Yeah, I know. Go figure. They tell me Carol used to be quite a looker. Beauty and the Beast, eh? I feel sorry for the poor geezer. Can't have had an easy time of it."

"So do I," Louise said. "Yet, no reason to be venomous. I only met him briefly, and he insinuated Carol poisoned his Pekingese."

"What? That's ridiculous. Carol loved animals. She'd never harm one. Besides, the pup was a hundred if he was a day. Old man Simpson used to bring him here. Don't get me wrong. I am a dog lover, but that little brute was vicious. Snapped at your fingers after you'd given him a biscuit."

Louise could imagine Peek-a-boo and his person sharing such a characteristic, even if the human stuck to verbal snapping. A glance at the empty dishes on the table reminded her that time for questions was running out. Nothing for it but jump right in.

"If Mr. Simpson convinced himself Carol killed his dog, do you think him capable of retaliating?"

Owen's head jerked back as if the idea came unexpectedly. "You mean poison Carol?" His tone conveyed incredulity. "Melodramatic, wouldn't you say?"

"Agreed. But someone did."

"There's that. Did Nora put the absurd notion about Simpson into your head?" As if planning a getaway, he stacked their bowls and plates.

"Let's be realistic, Owen. Carol died the night after her birthday party. The police are investigating her death as suspicious. It stands to reason to wonder who killed her."

She grabbed her purse and dug out her wallet to have it handy.

"I meant to ask you," she said in a more casual tone. "Did you happen to notice what Mr. Simpson's gift was?"

On his feet now, the proprietor regarded her closely. "Can't say I did. A bottle of wine, maybe?" He seemed to consider, screwing up his nose and eyes in thought. "Yeah, could be. Two or three sat on the table in gift bags. You know, the ones you get at the liquor store. Why?"

"Oh, just wondering what people would bring to someone of Carol's age and state of health." Aware of how thin it sounded after mentioning her neighbor as a potential poisoner, she rose and reached for the water jug to help carry things to the counter.

Nor was Owen fooled for a moment. "Carol didn't drink any wine at the open house. At least, not while I was there," he said with conviction.

"There's no knowing what she might have consumed during her last evening," Louise countered. "And while you all toasted her good health with champagne, she, unlike everybody, drank absinthe."

Into Owen's gasp, she added, "And she ate half of the birthday cake Jessie sent along with you."

The last bit stopped Owen in his tracks. Dishes rattled when he spun around to face her.

"Boy, you do know how to hit hard, don't you? But let me tell you, if there was anything fishy about that cake, it wasn't me who messed with it. I'm not a killer."

Chapter Seventeen

As she drove up the rain-soaked lane to her house, Louise cringed at the memory of her departure from the Witch's Brew. Her attempt to mitigate Owen's impression of being cast in the role of poisoner had failed. He remained aloof. To her embarrassment, she couldn't pay for her meal because the café's computer system was shut down already. She'd have to pop by tomorrow to straighten her account.

At this rate, she'd lose all goodwill in the village before ever gaining it. 'Comes from sticking your nose into business of no concern to you,' Louise told herself. The café proprietor had an influence in the village. She felt sure his venue wouldn't flourish if he weren't respected in the community. If word got around that she was a doo-doo disturber, the villagers would ostracize her.

Downcast, Louise pulled into the garage at the top of her driveway. The metal door's rattle echoed unnaturally loud in the damp evening stillness when she lowered it.

A cough and throat clearing close behind her made Louise pivot and stumble on the loose gravel.

"Sorry, ma'am. Didn't mean to startle you." The young man in a dark three-quarter raincoat with an upturned collar looked familiar.

"Oh, it's you," Louise said. The inspector—no, sergeant—she'd seen at Rosewood. Without thinking, she said, "You are Raymond, aren't you? Nora's godchild."

His cheeks pulled down in surprise. "You know my godmother?" Alert eyes scrutinized her. "Is that whom you visited at Rosewood Manor the other day?"

"Not quite," Louise said. So, he'd recognized her, too. "Can we move under my portico if you want to talk to me? It's starting to spit again." She felt heavy drops on her face.

The sergeant followed her as she hastened toward the front door. Torn between curiosity about Nora's uncommunicative godchild and guilt for making Shadow wait for his promised walk, she stopped under the portico roof.

"Do you mind if I let my pooch out? He's been cooped up for most of the day." She rummaged in her purse for the keys.

"Go right ahead." Raymond, as Louise couldn't help but think of the sergeant, smiled. Rain dripped on his bare head from the tall maples as much as from the sky. The front stoop was too confining for two people without invading the other's personal space.

Louise unlocked the door and gently eased it open in case Shadow stood too close. A black snout pushed into the gap, impatient for a bois-terous greeting. Vigorous tail wagging swayed his entire rear end as he nuzzled her legs.

"Dear me!" Louise's mouth broadened at such welcome.

Shadow switched his attention to the sergeant and stopped mid-wag.

The young man went into a half-squat, tapping both palms on his trouser legs in a doggy invitation to play. A dog person. Louise grinned. No need to interfere.

Shadow pounced, front legs pawing the ground, rear end aloft, clearly ready for a game.

Raymond raised one arm, reached far back as if readying to throw a ball, and let it shoot forward.

In a comical pantomime, Shadow's head spun, snout pointing into the air. His eyes followed the trajectory of the invisible missile. With a giant leap, he launched himself into hot pursuit.

Louise laughed. "He falls for it every time. Otherwise, he is a smart dog."

"Better to pursue the odd curveball in vain than miss out on a home run."

"Is that the baseball player speaking or the detective?"

"Both." The sergeant's answering grin transformed his face, just as she'd noticed at Rosewood. Not handsome, Raymond's square features were memorable.

Shadow abandoned the unavailing search and came back at a gallop.

"Go do your business," Louise called. "There's a good dog."

"A well-trained dog," Raymond commented when the pooch slowed and sauntered up to a tree to lift a leg.

"Won't you come in, er? Should I call you 'sergeant' or will 'Raymond' do?"

"It's not an official visit, Ms. Penfold. So, first name is fine," he said as they went in and removed the damp coats.

"Please call me Louise. Don't worry about your shoes," she said as she slipped off her own. "I know police must keep them on." Her mouth twitched, imagining cops who aimed at looking tough and authoritative, unlacing their regulation boots before arresting a suspect at home.

Shadow bounded in. "Stop. Paws first." Her reminder brought him to an abrupt sit. Obligingly, he lifted a front paw to get towel dried.

When Shadow turned his rear end toward her upon being told, "Hind legs," Raymond chuckled. "What a guy."

As they entered the living room, Louise noticed the sergeant's unobtrusive scrutiny of her home. Not wanting to sit too close, she pointed to the club chair rather than her favorite spot by the window.

"Make yourself comfortable. Can I offer you anything? Tea?"

"Thanks. I'm fine. I won't keep you." His eyes swept the bookcases. "An avid reader," he said with a smile. "No marks for a brilliant deduction, I know."

Shadow sprawled halfway between her armchair and the visitor.

Louise's glance wandered to the stairs in search of Magic. When her gaze returned, she noticed the sergeant's scrutiny relax into bland amiability. Was he wondering if someone else lurked upstairs?

"This place looks fantastic," he said, nodding admiringly in all directions as he leaned forward in his chair. "Freshly renovated, isn't it? Or did you buy it like this?"

Unsure if this was merely small talk, Louise said, "My contractor did a thorough job. It was in a dismal state when I bought it. Were you hoping to get a feel for how the deceased lived?"

Her bluntness, she noticed, took him aback. "I didn't," he said but interrupted himself. "All right. I did wonder. Sometimes, it helps to get a sense of the personality."

"Are you investigating Carol's death as a homicide?" She wanted to hear him confirm it.

"We are treating Carol Benson's demise as a suspicious death. You will appreciate I cannot share information about an ongoing investigation." Raymond's face was expressionless, but she sensed alertness.

"Nora told me you weren't forthcoming with details. But, yes, I understand."

"Have you known her long? I don't recall Godmother ever mentioning your name. You moved here a few days ago, didn't you?"

She felt uncomfortable under his searching gaze. To divert his interest from her, she remarked, "Nora said when you call her godmother, she feels like Al Capone's wife."

Into his laughter, Louise added, "She's a wonderful lady with unique interests and talents."

"Absolutely." The sergeant's eyes softened for an instant. "I owe her and Uncle Hank a lot."

"Oh?"

"Didn't she ever tell you? They took me in during my final years at high school when my parents passed away. If you are a friend of my godmother, I'm surprised she didn't mention it." Though his eyes narrowed, his face kept its amiable expression.

Louise sighed and smiled ruefully. "Okay. I'd better come clean. I met

Mrs. Norton this afternoon for the first time. The other day, I volunteered as a reader at Rosewood, and the matron assigned me to Nora. We hit it off immediately, you might say."

"I'd say." A hint of exasperation swung in his tone. Then he chuckled. "She made you read a thriller, did she? Her taste, I know, veers toward hard-boiled."

"Well." Louise hesitated. Maybe forthrightness paid. "We never got to the reading part today but talked about Carol's birthday party instead. You know, the open house just hours before she died."

Now, he really seemed exasperated. Chin raised, his eyes rolled up to regard the ceiling. "I should have known. She can't resist playing sleuth. I just hope you didn't encourage her. It's a dangerous thing to do. Interfering with a police investigation is also against the law," he said with a stern glance at her.

"Doesn't the police appreciate the public's help? I'm sure Nora is worth listening to." His didactic demeanor irked her. After all, he must be a good twenty years her junior.

"Did my godmother share something with you we ought to know about?"

"Why don't you ask her?" Hardly spoken, she regretted the sharpness. "If you are interested in how Carol's place looked when I first viewed it, I can let you see the photos I took. Of course, things might have already been changed by the time the house came on the market."

"Were her personal effects still in place?"

"I believe so. It certainly was not empty. Presumably, the content belonged to Carol." Louise got up to grab her iPad from the shelf. She scrolled through its photo library until she came to what she was looking for.

"Here, have a look for yourself while I feed this poor boy. Come, Shadow, let's get your dinner."

Raymond took her tablet and thanked her.

When she returned from the kitchen a few minutes later, she found the sergeant in front of the crime section that took up a major stretch of the shelving. Still holding her iPad in one hand, his other hand browsed along a row of her client's true crime books.

"Found anything interesting among the photos?" Louise asked. She had taken them for decision-making purposes, not trusting her memory when viewing multiple properties while house hunting. She couldn't recall having looked at them closely.

"Thanks. It helps to get a feel for the person." He smiled at her. "Mostly, they are a testimony to the incredible renovation job you've done."

"The contractor deserves the kudos," Louise said, though she appreciated the praise.

"I see you are a crime devotee." Raymond's finger tapped one of her client's books. "Odette Vérité's true crime novels have the merit of being very well researched," he said.

"Oh? You have read Odette's books? She's a client of mine. Yes, she's a meticulous researcher," Louise said with pride. "I edit her manuscripts and run fact checks for her."

Raymond's forefinger tilted the volume forward. "May I?"

"Of course." Her client's meticulous work ought to tell him how much an editor and research assistant learned about crime. Perhaps he'd think twice about dismissing her so-called interference, she thought, watching him scanning the first pages, where her client named her as the editor and praised her contributions to the research and to solving the cold case.

"Great job editing," Raymond said. "I noticed the quality of workmanship when I read her books but never considered the editor's efforts."

He pushed the volume back into its place and handed her the tablet. "Thanks so much for inviting me in. I'd better let you get on with things."

As they turned to leave the living room, Louise spotted Magic at eye level with them on the stairs.

The sergeant noticed, too. "Shadow has a buddy. What a beautiful cat. May I say hi to her? Or is it a Tom?"

"That's Magic. She was Carol's cat. Strange. Usually, she hides while anyone visits." Amazed, Louise heard the kitty purr when Raymond slowly reached and tickled the white patch under Magic's chin.

"This gorgeous creature came with the house? Lucky you."

Louise wasn't sure if the last bit referred to her or to the kitty. "I'm only fostering her until a permanent home is found."

When Magic meowed assertively just then, she and the sergeant looked at each other and laughed.

"Seems your kitty has decided to stay." He grinned and gave Magic a last stroke down the sleek back.

Shadow, who'd wolfed down his kibbles, pranced up to them, mouthing a tennis ball.

"Sorry, pal, can't play catch inside," Raymond said when the pooch offered the toy with a hopeful gaze.

"Just toss it for him in the yard," Louise said and opened the front door to let the sergeant pass. Out on the front stoop, she added, "You still owe him for the blind."

"Right you are. C'mon, bud." Raymond took a step back and let the ball fly. Shadow yipped in eager pursuit.

'Nora's godchild's a good sport,' thought Louise. Good shot, too, she acknowledged, watching the missile slice through the air.

The sergeant crouched, saying, "I'm sorry, I must have kicked over your plant." He straightened a small pot wrapped in clear cellophane.

"Uh? Where did that come from?" Louise stepped closer, examining his find. Pale pink blossoms hung like limp trumpets from two straight stalks encircled by leaves lower down.

"There's a gift tag with it," Raymond said and stiffened.

Shadow pushed between them and dropped the ball. His snout inspected the man's hand as it moved swiftly to guard the plant.

"Don't touch." The sergeant's tone seemed unnecessarily sharp to Louise. Her dog wasn't prone to damage things.

"Sorry, fellow. Not good for you." Pinching the top of the cellophane bag with pointed fingers, he lifted the pot and showed it to Louise. "You didn't buy this?"

When she shook her head, he asked, "Mind if I check the card for you?"

"What's wrong? It's just a plant. Maybe my neighbor dropped it off. I babysat their little son yesterday." Almost accusingly, she added, "While you questioned them down at the station."

"This is foxglove," he said. "It's toxic. You don't want Shadow nosing it. I'm wondering why someone would give you a toxic gift."

"Oh, my." Louise felt her jaw drop. Even if she didn't recognize the pretty flowers of the immature plant, she'd come across the properties of foxglove in past research.

"Digitalis," she said aloud. "Fatal for the heart in the wrong dosage. Or for anyone with certain heart conditions." She grabbed Shadow's collar and told him to sit on the front stoop. "Go ahead, Sergeant. Please check the card." Her mind raced. If only the plant wasn't Zoe's token of thanks.

Raymond set down the pot and pulled latex gloves from his pocket. Thus equipped, he extracted a tiny card. With a frown, he read aloud, "'Sorry about your crawlspace.'"

"Well, of all the nerve," Louise burst out.

"I take it you know the sender?"

Again, Louise hesitated. The sergeant wasn't forthcoming at all. So why should she be? Dennis's visit wasn't relevant to the police investigation. As the thought surfaced, another chased it. The son was the most likely suspect.

To gain time, she asked, "How come you recognized the plant so quickly?"

His raised brow told her he realized she was stalling. "Cops get some toxicology training," he said wryly. "Foxglove is far easier to spot when it's fully grown rather than a mere eight inches like this one. My wife is an avid gardener and bans toxic plants from our yard."

"A good idea with the little one. Nora mentioned knitting for your baby girl."

"We also have a pup who loves playing outside."

"What kind?" Louise couldn't resist the lure of dogs.

"A golden doodle." He regarded her with a half-smile and pointed to the plant. "You still owe me an answer. Who's the sender?"

"Well, all right. It's an odd story." She gave him an abbreviated account of her encounter with Dennis but skipped any comments the man had made about Carol's family affairs. "Dennis probably grabbed the first plant in sight at a garden center and dropped it off to make amends for his intrusion," she ended.

The sergeant looked skeptical.

Not sure why she would want to defend the odious Dennis, Louise said, "In fairness, I wouldn't have recognized it if you hadn't told me. Without a label, I'd have just stuck it into the flower bed." She cringed at the thought. "Carol's son didn't strike me as a gardener type. Not that one can tell by appearances unless you'd find someone knee-deep in potting soil."

"There is a label," the sergeant said mildly.

"Well, it certainly won't find houseroom in my yard. Not with my neighbor's tyke visiting and Shadow roaming free." Louise's glance swept the area around the house. "I'll need a book on plants to figure out what's what and uproot anything toxic."

"You can download a nature app. My wife uses it wherever she goes. Take a photo, and it tells you what you've found." With a glance at the foxglove, he asked, "If you like, I'll dispose of this."

"Be my guest." She felt sure he'd do no such thing. The latex glove treatment spoke for itself.

Raymond stripped off the glove on his right hand and bent to fondle Shadow's ear. "A pleasure meeting." He grinned up at Louise and finished, "All three of you."

"Likewise," said Louise.

His face grew solemn. "As a police officer, I must remind you to let us do our job. Interference of civilians is dangerous for everyone concerned."

"I'm sure I'm not interfering with anyone's job," Louise said primly.

"Please, don't encourage my godmother to play sleuth." His eyes softened when he added, "I don't want her to get hurt."

Louise sighed. "Encouragement is the last thing Nora needs. She's got a mind of her own. All I could do was to caution her not to trust anyone and to call you if anything disturbs her, Sergeant."

His skeptical gaze reminded her she didn't have his contact info.

"Would you leave me your card, just in case?" Like deciding to tell him about Mr. Simpson's accusations against Carol, she thought.

The young man reached into his pocket and, with a lopsided grin, handed her his card. "Don't laugh, and note the 'el,'" he said. "The joke wears thin."

"Pardon?" Her mouth twitched as she scanned the card.

RCMP - GRC

Raymond Marpel

Sergeant

Despite his injunction, Louise laughed.

"Well, Sergeant. You certainly don't look a bit like the sleuth from St. Mary's Mead."

As Louise watched Sgt. Marpel's long strides toward the lane, her expression sobered. Digitalis might easily kill someone of Carol's age. But no killer would be stupid enough to draw attention to it. Or would he?

Chapter Eighteen

The next day, Louise got up bright and early to work several hours before the mid-morning dog walk.

Too tired last night for nitty-gritty proofreading of the true crime writer's manuscript, she'd skimmed a few chapters of another author's epic fantasy but found herself distractedly musing the day's events. Curled up in bed with Magic by her side, she'd vowed to discover the truth about Carol's death despite—or was it, to spite? —Raymond and his injunctions.

Now, Louise glanced at the display on her laptop. Just past 10 a.m. Perfect time to catch her lawyer during a morning coffee break.

It took Louise a minute to convince the lawyer's senior secretary to put her through. The woman could be a fierce dragon when protecting the boss.

"Louise." The lawyer's soprano vibrated through the digital ether. "How's life in the cultural desert?" Peals of laughter followed.

"Don't be a snob, Estelle," Louise said, imagining her family's friend and legal adviser leaning back in the luxurious leather desk chair, power-dressed and spa-pampered. High up in First Canadian Place, Toronto's tallest office tower, the Lake Ontario view would be stunning even on an overcast day like this.

"Yeah, no. I'm a country gal at heart," drawled Estelle, dropping the clipped downtown lawyer talk. "Any news from your parents? How are they making out?"

"A one-liner from Mom. If there's more, I'll text you. Or you me if you hear from them first. Let's get down to business. Your right-hand says you're expecting a high-profile client. Meaning I'm low profile and shouldn't keep you."

With another trilling laugh, Estelle said, "The dragon is partially correct. We all stand in awe of the man who's to swoon down on us in— exactly eleven minutes. Spit it out. What do you need me for?"

"It's about buying this place."

"Why?" the lawyer cut in. "I thought you love it."

"Wait. Tell me whose power of attorney it was sold under. Did the lawyer act for the previous owner or her heirs? You told me back then you only dealt with the lawyer."

"Standard practice. In real estate transactions, we don't meet our counterpart's clients. Hang on, I'll pull up the file and check the POA."

Louise heard Estelle hum to herself.

"Here we are. The lawyer, a Mr. Fox, holds power of attorney and is also Carol Benson's executor. As principal, she arranged it years ago. Why do you ask?" Estelle sounded wary. "Something wrong?"

"Well, not where the house is concerned. Carol's death is a bit of a problem. Turns out to be murder."

"What?" The high-pitched shriek reverberated in Louise's ear. "You're kidding me, right?"

"Of course not." Offended, Louise added. "It's far too serious for jokes. What I'm asking, did this Mr. Fox say anything about his client or heirs?"

"No occasion for discussing his client. Hardly professional to do so. You know that, Louise. From our end, we checked the POA and the usual things. Like the title search, liens, etc. Everything above board. Or else I wouldn't have let you go ahead with the purchase."

Over Estelle's speakerphone, Louise could hear the creaking chair and tapping fingernails before the lawyer asked, "Where do the heirs come in now?"

"Exactly what I'd like to know. Can one get access to the will?"

"In Ontario, anyone can request access. As executor, Fox will have filed probate. The public can apply to the relevant court in person." Estelle's tone changed to urgent concern. "Louise, you're not mistaking a real-life death for one of your clients' novels, are you? Murder is not a game."

"My client writes about real-life deaths," Louise countered, barely suppressing a rising impatience. "I need to figure out what happened here. How can I enjoy the serene village life I yearned for when I don't know who killed my predecessor and why? Just text me the info on how to access the will."

Louise almost wished she hadn't called her family's lawyer. Worried now, she added, "And don't tell Mom and Dad."

"If you must see the will for your peace of mind, I'll have my assistant search the database. Quickest way. Sorry, got to run now. The dragon is breathing down my neck. Red light's flashing. Talk soon. Promise to loop me in."

"Thanks, Estelle. I will, and I owe you."

"You bet." Her legal adviser's words ended in a hoot.

While Louise donned wool slacks and sweater for her walk, she mulled over what to do next. Four of the people who attended Carol's birthday were obvious suspects. If Dennis inherited his mother's estate, he'd have a sizable financial motive, increased by his hope of getting Carol's investments via disputing his second cousins as beneficiaries.

What if Dennis Benson assumed he was the sole heir, just as he'd assumed to inherit the house next door? Since Carol took back a second mortgage, he might still gain from the transaction now unless the will stipulated differently.

Aware she was avoiding what worried her most, Louise tied her walking shoes and slipped on a rain jacket in case the governmental weather frogs were wrong in their forecast.

"Let's get some fresh air, Shadow," she said and clipped the leash to the patiently waiting pooch's collar. "I can think better while we walk."

A leaden sky greeted them. The trees were still damp but no longer dripped. As they reached the end of the driveway, Louise heard voices behind the tall evergreens dividing her property from the one next door. She was about to detour to the neighbors to say hello when a faintly familiar male voice rose to a threatening growl.

"You've got until Monday. Pay up, or else—"

Louise stopped dead in her tracks. Either he left the rest open or spoke too low for her to catch. Shadow sank to his haunches. Decency demanded a retreat to her own door. But her sleuthing instinct overrode any scruples.

She snuck a little closer and heard the man hiss, "Want me to put the screws on that little wife of yours?"

Then, Trevor's shout, "You touch my wife, and I'll beat the—"

The man's laugh drowned the rest. A car door banged.

Louise stepped sideways behind the shelter of her garage wall, pulling Shadow along. Heart beating too fast, she waited.

A moment later, an engine roared, and a black sedan shot down the lane. She glimpsed a dark-haired driver wearing mirrored sunglasses.

Troubles grew serious next door. A sickening feeling suffused Louise, thinking of the danger Trevor put his family in. Had he succumbed to temptation and—

'Don't jump to hasty conclusions,' she cautioned herself. 'Wait and see what the will says.'

Stifling a deep sigh, she counted another two minutes before venturing into the lane. Only when she had gone a few yards down did she realize, with the revving motor, she hadn't heard Trevor's door close.

As they approached Mr. Simpson's driveway, Shadow's ears pricked. Thus forewarned, the hunched figure lurking with clippers in hand didn't surprise Louise. Was that his standard outdoor equipment?

This time, he wore a wide-brimmed straw hat adorned with a pink ribbon. It lent a jaunty air to the sagging pants and frayed tweed jacket. Yew hedge clippings stuck to him like tinsel.

He spotted her and stepped into the lane, clippers dangling open from one hand. They seemed disproportionately large for the man's small stature.

"Maniac!" He sputtered, swinging the tool.

Taken aback at such a greeting, Louise veered sideways. Shadow growled. The man couldn't possibly mean her, could he?

Yet, a soothing tone was her best bet. "Good morning, Mr. Simpson. A perfect day for yard work, isn't it?"

"Drivel," he muttered, only to startle her with a squeak. "Did you see that maniac? Tore down the street like the devil was chasing him." His cackle made her wonder who was crazy here.

"Yes, indeed," she responded in measured tones. "The person drove much too fast for a narrow lane."

"Lucky, he didn't kill your hound."

Louise assumed his giggle was a habit rather than a sign of mirth. Still, when he moved forward with a birdlike neck jerk, she involuntarily drew back.

"That no-good-for-nothing son of Carol's been sneaking around," he spluttered. His free hand tilted the hat toward his neck. Rheumy, almost colorless, eyes glared at her as if Dennis's presence was her fault.

"I know. He came to—to visit," she amended.

Her neighbor pounced on her hesitation. "Snooped. Didn't he?" The last sounded like a challenge. Dare to contradict, it said.

Why not see if he could shed light on Dennis's true intentions? As Carol's former beau, Mr. Simpson might be well-informed about the mother-son relations. Not to mention Simpson's own post-affair relations to the victim, she thought.

Aloud, she said, "Come to think of it, there might be some truth to what you said." Just like the night before, she recounted her crawlspace adventure, much to Mr. Simpson's glee. He reminded her of plovers she'd watched picking at wet sand on a beach, their heads incessantly bobbing up and down.

"Well," she ended her tale, "he came back yesterday evening to apologize. At least, I assume so from the little gift and note to say how sorry he was."

"Don't believe it for a moment." The elderly gent straightened as far as possible for him. "Carol's son never was sorry for anything he's done. He's a loser. Always has been, always will be."

Just when his serious tone convinced her, the volatile man grabbed the clippers with both hands and snapped at the air, issuing staccato bursts of cackle.

"Do you mind?" she said, stepping out of accidental reach.

"Carol fixed his little wagon," he cried. "Burned through what his imbecile dad left him and came crawling back to Mom for more. Not a penny he got from her." Tears of mirth coursed down the shriveled cheeks.

"You mean Dennis inherits nothing from Carol?" Hard to believe, she thought while speaking.

Her question appeared to sober the venomous fellow. Startled, he confessed, "That, I don't know."

His abrupt pivot left her standing speechless, watching him scurry along the driveway to his bolt hole.

When she arrived at the Witch's Brew, a group of cyclists clustered the patio. Some lounged against their bikes, munching from paper bags. Two older cyclists with jumbo-sized takeout mugs chatted on a bench.

"What a good-looking pup," a young guy in a colorful biker tunic said.

Louise thanked him for the compliment but was glad he made no move to pet Shadow. She didn't want the group crowding around her dog while she was inside.

Pooch securely fastened within reach of the water bowl, Louise entered the café. With some trepidation about Owen's reception, she made straight for the counter to settle her bill but saw no sign of him.

From the corner of her eye, she noticed several customers at tables. Two cyclists on barstools at the window ledge hunched low over their beverages as if still fighting a headwind.

A man sat alone in front of the bookshelves. On second glance, she realized it was Dennis Benson. The discovery changed her mind about 'pay and run.'

She grabbed a cold latte from the cooler and settled last night's bill. Just when Louise pocketed her wallet, Owen emerged from the kitchen not in his usual work-a-day clothes but in cycling gear.

Half turning, he said something to whoever worked there and then saluted the girl behind the cash with, "See ya later, alligator."

His laugh broke off abruptly when his glance fell on Louise.

Glad she had spotted him before, Louise greeted him. "Hi, Owen. Out for a cycle?" She cursed the inane remark as soon as she spoke.

His eyes seemed to agree with her thought, but his mouth mustered a weak smile. "Hello again. Sorry, gotta run."

With that, he was out the door. She could hear the cheers of his buddies, who made for their machines as if they'd only waited for the café owner to join the pack.

Louise strolled over to Dennis's table. Bent low over his phone's display, he took no notice. When she greeted him, his head flew up as if caught in some illicit act.

"Mind if I join you?" Aware he could hardly say no without blatant impoliteness nor rush off since his ceramic mug was still half-full, she hoped for a few minutes' conversation.

With interest, she watched his features rearrange themselves into a semblance of delight.

"Ms. Penfold. What a pleasure," he gushed and jumped to pull out a chair for her.

"Thanks. Likewise. So unexpected to run into you here," she said. "Are you staying in the area?"

"Not exactly." He looked as vague as he sounded. "I prefer the city when I come to visit."

"Toronto's entertainment certainly offers more than this village. Quite a drive, though, if you need to come out frequently."

"Duty demands my presence." He sighed like someone resigned to a huge sacrifice.

Louise nodded, commiserating, and unscrewed her drink and poured a bit into the mug she'd received from the server. "I'm glad for this opportunity to thank you in person for the gift you dropped off last night. So thoughtful."

Dennis shifted in his seat, stumbled into a deprecating, "No, no...least I could," and didn't finish.

"Are you a gardener?" No subtle approach occurred to her, and blunt means might work, she thought.

"Eh?"

"Just wondered at your choice of foxglove."

"My choice?" His bewildered frown seemed genuine. Then his brows relaxed. "You caught me out. I plead guilty."

Into her gasp of surprise at the admission, he smiled ruefully. "The girl at the supermarket picked it. Don't you like it? Looked pretty to me."

"No, it's fine. Just an interest of mine, matching flowers to the personalities of the givers." As no reaction came, she switched topics. "How long are you staying in Canada this time? Are you on leave from your job in Australia?"

His glance shifted from his mug and roamed the café. "Depends," he said, still avoiding her gaze. "No telling how long it'll take to sort my mother's affairs. Probate, you know. Lawyers' stuff." Exaggerated eye-rolling underlined the last point.

Quite misplaced, thought Louise, considering it was Dennis who disputed Trevor and Zoe's claim to Carol's investments.

"Does it require in-person presence?" she asked. "Lucky you. Not every boss extends a vacation." Though he'd be entitled to a leave of absence on compassionate grounds. Then it hit her. Police might require him to stay. 'Don't leave town' kind of thing.

"I'm my own boss," Dennis said, raising his chin and looking down his nose.

"Oh? Are you in business? What do you do for a living? I found switching to freelancing was a game changer for me. Master of your own destiny and whatnot. Don't you think?"

The gambit worked to draw him out.

"What kind of freelancing do you do?" Keen now on sharing, he didn't wait for a response. "I'm an entrepreneur. Start-ups. I get them up and running and sell at huge profit." He pushed back the sleeve of his designer jacket to reveal a clunky gold watch.

Before he could use the time as an excuse to leave, Louise asked for the name of his current venture. It didn't mean a thing to her when he named it.

"Well, it was good talking to you," she said when he gulped down his coffee. "I'd better get going. My dog's waiting."

"Here's my card." Dennis withdrew a gold pen from his shirt pocket and scribbled on the back before proffering it. "My Canadian phone number. If you venture downtown Toronto, give me a buzz, and we'll have a drink."

'Fat chance,' thought Louise, as she thanked him. Still, she might have reason to get in touch. One thing for sure, their conversation had not bumped Dennis from the top of her suspect list.

Chapter Nineteen

After working through lunchtime and early afternoon, Louise ventured out on her own.

Armed with a good excuse, she hoped to tap into the antique lady's store of information on Carol's relationship with family and community. A businesswoman much involved with local affairs and a friend of the victim —as Louise now thought of Carol—Kendra was ideal. If the prickly lady chose to cooperate.

The overcast sky didn't improve the appearance of the antique shop's grime-streaked windows, making the display seem dustier than on her first visit. Nor did the beckoning totem pole attract customers. For no one browsed the interior when Louise entered. No sign of Kendra, either.

While she waited for the proprietress to appear, Louise meandered around various obstructions designed to ensure a visitor's circuitous route. As far as she could tell, the same items awaited customers. Pieces like the ornamental Upper Canada jam cupboard, artfully stripped of its paint to leave some tell-tale residue, wouldn't sell within a few days. Nor would the massive pine armoire and drop-leaf tables. She peeked at the tools in the rummage box below the copperware shelf with its eye-catching vessels and found it still loaded with miscellaneous stuff. Even if the market for farm equipment proved tepid, reminding Kendra of the junk pile at the back of her property served as a reason for dropping by.

Oddly, this time, the antique lady didn't give a sign of life. Then Louise realized no tinkling bell had announced a customer. A quick glance confirmed the brass bell was raised out of reach of the shop door.

Louise cleared her throat with a gentle cough before navigating the armoire hiding Kendra's desk. The empty chair faced a chaos of paper, catalog piles, and an array of other items.

Maybe the proprietress stepped out for a moment or went to the washroom. On Louise's first visit, Kendra appeared unconcerned about pilfering. Now, Louise noticed a vintage wide-angle street mirror mounted strategically high on the wall. Grime-free, it yielded a perfect view of the shop behind her.

Louise smiled. So much for lack of concern. Nor would one suspect a shrewd businesswoman of blind trust. Yet, where was a vigilant Kendra to monitor things?

Half-hidden by bulky furniture pieces, Louise noticed the mouth of a corridor leading to the back of the premises. Time to draw attention to her presence. She didn't feel comfortable left unattended in this shop.

Both walls of the hallway displayed artwork. As an aficionado, Louise couldn't resist the lure and slowed her step. Price tags on some items proved this gallery to be part of the showroom. Unless overpriced, she might consider a purchase for her collection. Several pastoral landscapes, older oils in ornate gilded frames, and light aquarelles of the type she preferred lacked tags and might be costly.

A high-pitched grinding startled her. It came from the rear of the building. On a closer look, she noticed a sharp bend at the corridor's dimly lit end. The screech that followed sounded like a revving saw.

Louise strode toward it, calling, "Anyone home?"

No answer. Rather than startle someone handling a saw, she waited for the noise to abate.

When it stopped, she hollered, "Yoo-hoo. Kendra. It's me. Louise."

As Louise peered into the hallway extension, a masked and goggled head poked around a door jamb a few steps ahead.

There stood the antique lady, sleeves of a checkered blouse rolled up, a tan-colored woodworking apron bulging over her midriff, its pockets studded with tools of the trade. In one hand, she held a vicious-looking saw, finger on its trigger. Her eyes seemed huge behind the curved safety goggles. Nor did she appear happy at the interruption.

"Hi, Kendra. I'm sorry to butt in." Conscious of being out of bounds of the area open to the public, Louise half regretted her foray.

The shop owner pulled down the breathing mask. "How did you get in? We're closed this afternoon."

The greetingless abruptness struck Louise as rude. "I didn't see a 'closed' sign, and the door opened. Your bell isn't working, though."

"The scatterbrain of a helper left without flipping the sign and locking up, I guess." Kendra's tone softened, and a gleam entered her eye. "Did you come back to buy something you saw?"

"Er, no. Yes," Louise stuttered, then plunged for her earlier inspiration. "One of the landscapes. And I dropped by to arrange a convenient time for you to inspect the vintage items at the back of my property." Better stop calling it a junk pile, or the woman would devalue it unseen.

The bait for selling a painting worked.

"Give me a few minutes to finish what I'm doing, and my time is yours," Kendra said with a wave of the saw that triggered the blade. "Oops! Sorry."

Louise jumped back in reflex. Curiosity aroused, she ventured closer when Kendra got on with the job. Back turned to Louise, the woman appeared to mend an antique dresser perched on the workbench, its drawers removed and stacked on the floor.

The workroom contained countless pieces of partially dismantled furniture and other items. Perhaps chaos was not merely the shop owner's strategy but her way of life. A potent smell of paint thinner and other solvents accosted Louise despite the powerful fan Kendra now engaged. Next to the workbench sat a pot with sawdust and shavings. At least, the worker tidied her place to that extent. Or was it collected as a wood filler for the antique enhancement?

The whirring of the saw blade ground to a halt. Kendra pulled the mask down to her chin and raised the goggles. As she turned, she slid them back over the strawberry blond hair, lifting it off her forehead. The goggle strap tightened the skin at the temples. Under the bright, fluorescent work light, her eyes appeared vacant and naked.

Caught spying the tricks of the trade, Louise blushed. Her discomfort increased when Kendra pointed to the sign on the workshop door. 'NO ENTRY UNLESS AUTHORIZED.'

"Well, I didn't really come in," Louise said mildly. "Woodworking's so fascinating. One can't resist a peek."

As the woman's bulky figure ambled forward, Louise caught sight of a watercolor in a far too ornate frame leaning against the wall. "Oh, how lovely," she cried. "I'm a fan of the painter. Wish I could afford her work."

Kendra pivoted as if surprised at what was in her own workshop. Then she snorted dismissively. "A cheap mass-market print. I'm framing it for a friend as a favor."

She grabbed the offending piece and stored it in a large crate that held a whole load of other frames as Louise could glimpse before the lid came down with a thud.

Caught loitering, a gruff "You still here?" made Louise inch back into the hallway, mumbling, "Sorry. See you by the paintings."

A few moments later, the shop owner joined her. Sleeves rolled down and apron discarded, the wavy hair and the dark skirt still showed traces of wood dust. A seller's smile snapped into place when Louise idly glanced at an oil canvas, at least three by two feet, in a bombastic frame high on the wall.

"Isn't it lovely? Such character. The old boys still knew how to paint," the dealer proclaimed.

Louise didn't care for somber, poorly executed hunting scenes and hastened to say, "Er, I guess so. My taste tends toward airier, pleasant vistas, like this watercolor here." She pointed to a delightful aquarelle in a modest white frame that peeked out shyly from among its hefty neighbors.

"A pretty picture." The shrewd seller sounded bored. "If it takes your fancy, I can let you have it for two-fifty. Basically, at cost."

'Yeah? Really?' Louise felt like saying but engaged in the haggling dance. "Ah, not quite what I'm prepared to spend. Too bad. It's quite a nice little picture." With a shrug, she took a step toward the front room.

From the corner of her eye, she saw Kendra's nose twitch as if picking up the scent of prey.

"At a special new customer discount, let's say two-twenty cash," the dealer bargained.

"Make that two hundred on credit card, and you can wrap it up for me," Louise tossed back in an uninterested tone.

She'd barely reached the desk by the armoire when Kendra came, frame in hand.

Louise suppressed a grin. Since she already owned a painting by the artist, she knew the lower price was reasonable. Not a steal but an investment in future value. More importantly, gazing at it would give her years of pleasure.

While the dealer selected packaging, Louise engaged her in small talk about gardening and the late advent of spring. Then she slipped in, "An odd thing happened the other night."

"Oh? What was it?" Kendra rummaged for tape and didn't look up.

"I found Carol's son, Dennis, in my crawlspace."

This time, startled icy-blue eyes met hers. The antique lady's small mouth pinched tightly, creasing the surrounding skin like a prune, only to relax when she said, "Sounds intriguing. What was he looking for?"

Aha, Louise's mind commented, an interesting immediate assumption if, indeed, it expressed Kendra's initial reaction.

Casually, she replied, "Nothing but a few rusty gardening tools down there. Anyway, I mentioned the encounter to the police sergeant when we spoke last night."

She watched Kendra's hands stop what they were doing. "How come? Did you report it as a break-in?" The woman's piercing glance didn't match the off-hand tone.

"Of course not. The sergeant happened to come by, and it cropped up."

Aware of how thin this sounded, Louise switched tack. "Do you know Dennis Benson? Did Carol talk about him? I can't quite make him out, and the whole episode was a little disturbing."

She decided not to mention the foxglove yet. From Dennis's reaction at the café, he might be clueless about what he'd gifted.

A penetrating glance assessed her. The professional mask slipped, and the voice was far from friendly when Kendra asked, "What is it to you?"

Perhaps she regretted the bluntness. The calculating gaze vanished, and an affable smile puffed out the fleshy cheeks. "You know how it is, Louise. When one of us comes to harm, the community draws together. Personally, I still think the police are barking up the wrong tree. People don't get murdered in this village. We're peaceful folks. But we protect our own."

With unnecessary force, the dealer tightened the bow of the wrapping string. "There you go. Two hundred, and it's yours."

"Thanks," muttered Louise and fished in her purse for a wallet. "So, your point is, the community doesn't welcome outsiders or newcomers sticking their nose in?"

"Only in your best interest, Louise. I want you to be careful about asking too many questions." Kendra reached over to touch Louise's sleeve. "We wouldn't want you to get hurt. It's too nice having you come to live here."

"I appreciate it, Kendra." Louise passed a credit card. "Still, you must realize, living in a house whose previous owner was murdered, one gets drawn into things. If you'd assure me Carol's son and, of course, her great-nephew and niece wouldn't possibly harm an elderly lady, I'd sleep much sounder." Any such assurance would be meaningless unless Kendra knew the killer. Yet, it might provoke some reaction.

"You don't feel in danger, do you?" The woman eyed her curiously.

Louise lifted her shoulders a fraction and tilted her hand in a show of uncertainty.

Silence paid, for the other went on, "If you want my off-the-cuff impression, I wouldn't lend money to any of Carol's family. She was naïve that way. Or maybe played some dangerous game, snubbing her son and favoring that great-nephew. Ask yourself, would youngsters like that come back from Europe to care for an old aunt? They were out to get her house and get it cheap. What? She about paid them to move next door."

The fluffy strawberry waves wobbled in unison with the jowls when the antique lady shook her head at such folly. "The son is no better, mind you," she added soberly. "Not a word from him for years until he thought his mother was at death's door. Then he swoops down like a vulture."

Maybe feeling she'd said too much, Kendra pushed herself up from the desk chair she'd perched on while finishing the transaction. She handed over a credit card receipt.

With a glance at it, Louise said, "I hate to trouble you, Kendra. Would you mind filling out a sale slip specifying which picture I've purchased and the name of the painter?" When the dealer frowned as though it was an unreasonable request, she explained, "Just for my own records, and in case I'd ever consider parting with the lovely aquarelle."

With a shrug, the woman sank back into her chair, which squeaked under her weight. After a few minutes of rooting in desk drawers, she unearthed a yellowed receipt pad.

It didn't speak well for integer business practices if such an item needed searching for, Louise figured. Then she remembered her other errant. "Before I forget, Kendra. Would it suit you to come out sometime this week to check the vintage items on my property? I'd love to get them sorted."

"Eh? Sure. If you leave me your number, I'll give you a buzz when I can spare the time." She handed Louise a receipt with an outdated postal address of Precious Treasures rubber-stamped at the top. Nor did it show a phone number. The price entered was almost illegible.

'How sloppy can you get?' thought Louise but didn't feel like complaining. Instead, she dug in her purse for a business card. "Please text me before dropping by."

All affability, the proprietress walked her to the door.

"One last thing before I go," Louise said. "Remember, we spoke of my neighbor, Mr. Simpson? You seemed to believe him capable of poisoning an animal. Do you think he'd harm his former—I guess, lover?"

A cold blue stare bored into hers. The eyes narrowed as a frown contracted the sparse eyebrows into a sharp crease over the bulbous nose. The woman's finger squeezed Louise's lower arm as if confiding a secret.

"I wouldn't put it past him."

Chapter Twenty

When Louise knocked at the neighbor's door a few minutes after 6 p.m., she still questioned the wisdom of accepting a dinner invitation with a poisoner at large. Her inability to picture either Trevor or Zoe as murderers didn't convince her for a moment. Yet, here she was, telling herself no one was stupid enough to mess with a guest on their home turf while already on the police's radar.

'You read too many crime stories,' she chided herself as she gave the wrought iron door knocker a polite whack.

The door opened within seconds, and a tousled redhead pushed through the widening gap, chanting, "Ant loose, ant loose," or so it sounded to Louise. A compact little body propelled itself into her extended arms.

"My, what a greeting," Louise mumbled, hampered by a damp cheek pressing against hers, the child's locks tickling her nose. "Hello, sweetie. Lovely to see you."

"Daniel, you'll get Auntie Louise all dirty," said Zoe, opening the door wide. "Great you could make it, Louise. And sorry again for the short notice."

"Not to worry. Hi, Zoe. It's so nice of you to ask me over. Would you grab the bottle before I knock it over?" Louise shifted the toddler's weight to nod at the gift bag she'd deposited on the step to save it from the careening child.

"Oh, you shouldn't have." Zoe stroked back the flowing, calf-length dress, this one in earth tones, and knelt to retrieve the bottle. "Come on in. Trevor's checking on the lasagna he's made. I hope you like vegetarian."

"Love it," Louise said as they entered the tiled mud room, lined with practical shelving above a bench on one side and coat hooks on the other. Not having bothered with a jacket for the short distance, she kicked off her shoes.

Daniel wriggled in her arms, and she lowered him to his feet. Still, he didn't let go but pulled her along, shrieking, "Takto, takto."

"He means tractor." Trevor advanced from the stove in the open-concept kitchen, a striped apron with the legend 'Chef' covering his jeans. He waved his hand, clad in an oven mitten. "Good to see you, Louise." His other hand pointed to a green miniature John Deere tractor with yellow hub caps.

Louise's greeting was drowned as Daniel picked up the toy and thrust it at her, switching from shrieks to an engine roar.

The dad stepped in. "Easy does it. Go play in the living room until dinner's ready."

The tyke obeyed after Louise admired the vehicle, ruffling the little fellow's red curls. When he zoomed to the room next door, Louise withdrew a Kinder chocolate bar from her cardigan's deep pocket and asked, "Can he have that for later?"

"Thanks, he'll love it," Zoe said and placed the gifts on the wide kitchen island.

"What a beautiful room," Louise said. "Did you renovate the house?"

"Aunt Carol did a couple of years ago," Trevor replied. "We lucked out. It was in great shape when we bought it."

"Goodness, yes. Knocking two rooms into one must have been a major job." Louise admired the cream-colored cabinetry and eyed the beams and massive side supports. They marked where a wall once separated the dining area from the kitchen proper. "The wall removal was an earlier reno, wasn't it?"

"Right. They opened it up back in the 90s when my great-uncle was still alive," Trevor said. "Would you like a glass of wine before dinner? Beer? An apéritif?" He pointed to a liquor collection on a top shelf.

Curious to see what was on offer, Louise checked it out. Campari, vodka, brandy, sherry, vermouth. But no absinthe.

From behind her came Zoe's anxious voice. "It's just for visitors. We don't drink all that stuff. Trevor's business friends like it."

Her spouse laughed. "C'mon, Zoe. You adore apéritifs." He turned to Louise. "Special occasions merit special drinks. What can I get you?"

"A dry sherry, if that's all right?" She pointed to an unopened bottle. While Trevor took a knife to peel off the seal and pour, she continued, "Dennis mentioned he grew up in this house. He seemed fond of it."

As he grabbed a couple of tumblers and mixed vodka and vermouth over ice, Trevor said without looking up, "I bet he'd be fond of getting his grubby hands on it. My cousin threw a fit when he found out Aunt Carol sold it to us."

"Oh?" Her mild interjection didn't prompt Trevor to expand.

"We weren't there," Zoe remarked. She'd been standing by the entrance to the living room, presumably keeping an eye on Daniel, whose engine roars dissolved into a moist putter. Now, she slid on a barstool next to Louise at the island counter.

Trevor pushed a tumbler toward his wife and raised his own. "To the new lady of Charlotte." He clinked glasses with them both. "What Owen calls you," he added, grinning at Louise.

"Not sure Owen's appellation is a good omen," Louise joked wryly.

"We're so glad you've come to live next door," Zoe said.

"Thanks. To great neighbors." Louise raised her glass again, then turned to Zoe. "What did you mean? There, for what?"

When his wife's brows contracted into a frown, Trevor explained, "At Rosewood, when my precious cousin accused his mother of cheating him out of his birthright."

"And Auntie so ill!" Zoe's dark eyes flashed. "The creep shows up after years, and first thing he does, he upsets Auntie. She told us when we got here."

"Zoe." Trevor's tone sounded like a caution. He pushed an appetizer plate to their side. "Have some olives," he said to Louise.

Not fond of olives, Louise speared a cocktail pickle with a toothpick from a tiny barrel Trevor passed them. From what she'd seen of Dennis, she could image him lashing out. But at an elderly and weakened parent in nursing care? That sounded brutal to her.

Aloud, she said, "How did the sale come about? Was it a long-standing plan for you to move here?"

"Auntie asked us when she took ill last December," Zoe said, and sipped her apéritif.

"Oh, I didn't realize your aunt was ill for months." Puzzled about the sequence of things, Louise twirled the empty toothpick between her fingers.

"She called us after she'd a gastrointestinal attack. I said I'd fly out. Carol didn't want me to," said Trevor. "But she asked if we were interested in buying this place. Her tenants told her they'd leave in spring."

"I was so homesick for Canada. We've moved around so much." Even now, Louise could hear yearning in Zoe's voice.

"That must have been tough with a baby. What luck it worked out with your jobs," Louise said.

"My company made no fuss," Trevor said, "and Zoe works remotely, anyway. Makes no difference where she is."

"Ah, yes. I find it's such a bonus of freelancing. What kind of field are you in, Zoe?" Louise asked.

"Marketing for online sales. Not very exciting."

Trevor chuckled. "Pays the bills. Isn't that what life's all about at the end of the day?" He tossed the salad he'd been preparing on the other side of the island. "Grab some plates, honey."

"Can I help?" Louise asked.

"Sure. Care to get the monster from the lion's den?" He raised a comical eyebrow.

"Love to." Louise slid off the barstool, surprised she hadn't noticed the putt-putting sounds for a while. Neither parent seemed aware. Worried now what mischief her new friend might be up to, Louise hastened through the doorway.

The green tractor lay abandoned on the rug in front of a squishy sofa in off-white canvas fabric. A cozy family feeling immediately registered in Louise's consciousness. The large happy family portrait, Zoe holding a younger sweetly smiling Daniel in her arms with the proud dad next to them, underscored the impression. Something about the photo rang a bell.

Louise's gaze traveled over the room. Child-size pieces, like a miniature rocker, an easel with flip-chart paper showcasing Daniel's wildly colorful artistic imagination, and overflowing toy boxes on wheels, dominated the room.

No sign of the toddler. Where could he have gone? A child-proof safety bar secured the patio door against escapees.

Then she spotted the tyke. Curled up under a blanket in a play tent at the far side of the room, Daniel was fast asleep.

Louise tiptoed back to the kitchen to pass on the tidings, unsure if they were good or bad.

"Let him sleep." The father took the news with equanimity. "He's had a healthy snack at five and probably won't eat his dinner, anyway. We'll enjoy ours and put him to bed after."

The lasagna smelled heavenly. Louise inhaled the aroma as she sank into a chair at the dining table and watched Trevor prepare three pieces on plates.

"Take your pick," he said, offering her first choice.

With a grin, he grabbed a fork and announced, "Wait. Taste testing. Just to make sure it's well done before you dig into yours."

Eyelids lowered, he made a show of savoring the flavor like a Michelin gourmand, ready to pronounce judgment. He swallowed and said, "Not bad. Fit for general consumption."

Zoe giggled and toyed with her fork.

"Dig in, honey." Trevor looked at his wife with mock sternness. "Set a good example, or Louise will think my cooking sucks."

"Oh, no!" cried Zoe, and scooped up a sizable chunk of pasta. "Trevor's an awesome cook. I could never make something like this." She munched as if to prove her point.

"Bon appétit," said Louise, aware her host intended the tasting ritual to reassure her. A moment later, she agreed with Zoe. "This lasagna is outstanding. Kudos to the chef."

As if by mutual consent, the dinner talk revolved around innocuous topics. The young couple related episodes from their European experience. Among other places, they'd lived for briefer periods in Munich and Zurich. Pricey places for a young couple, Louise thought.

After dinner, she helped clear the table and load the dishwasher while Zoe saw to Daniel, whom the dad had carried upstairs.

"We'll have dessert when Zoe's back," Trevor said. "Decaf or the real thing?" He shook two coffee tins for her to choose from.

"No caffeine for me, please. Or I won't sleep a wink."

Bent over the coffeemaker, Trevor said softly, "I saw you leave with Shadow this morning when my loud-mouthed visitor took off, tires squealing. Did you hear him?"

Since the car noise would have awakened the dead, Louise assumed he was referring to the man's parting shot about the money. Cautiously, she admitted, "A word or two. Hard not to hear."

"Not to worry. I realize that. It's just— All right. Zoe has no clue I borrowed." The plea not to tell his wife came through loud and clear despite the low volume.

"Wouldn't it be better to tell her? The man threatens harm. You need to protect your family and let police know." Without meaning to, her own voice also dropped to a whisper.

"Jeez, the last thing I want. Police's already breathing down my neck. I'm not serving them a motive on a platter. Dennis is doing that for me."

"But loan shark collectors are dangerous. Er, I'm assuming that's what the man is. Think of Daniel." Her mind conjured horror scenarios of child snatching.

"I do," said Trevor. "Once the investment firm pays up, I'll discharge the loan. Just let me do it my way, and don't tell Zoe."

"Don't tell Zoe what?" The spouse's voice came from the doorway. An angry face with flaming cheeks followed. "What are you two talking about?"

Chapter Twenty-One

'Yikes.' Audibly, Louise sucked in air between her teeth. She felt awful. Though an innocent bystander, she'd no wish to conspire or get involved in a financial family drama. For a second, she closed her eyes to ward off the sight of an outraged hostess.

She heard Trevor sigh and mumble an oath. Resigned, it seemed, he said, "Let's have coffee." He handed her three mugs and grabbed the glass pot from the coffeemaker.

Zoe still stood, hands on hips, then joined them when they sat at the table. Not touching her coffee, she crossed her arms over her chest and glared at Trevor.

He stirred sugar and cream in his mug and spoke without glancing up. "I didn't want to worry you, hon. So, here goes. Moving back here was way more expensive than we figured. Plus, we spent a fortune on furnishing this place from scratch."

"But it's only cheap Ikea stuff." The pitch of Zoe's voice rose to a wail. One finger twirled and tugged at the end of her ponytail.

"Adds up. Anyway, I borrowed. A lot." Trevor sat back, took a gulp from his mug, and waited.

If they started with nothing and furnished an entire house, the cost was staggering, Louise thought. Yet she noticed Zoe visibly relax.

After drinking some coffee, the young woman said nonchalantly, "Everyone gets loans. What else are banks for?" She turned to Louise. "It's so hard for our generation to start a family and buy a house. Not like it was for the boomers."

"Well, I'm sure previous generations found it just as tough. But I agree, a fresh start is terribly expensive," Louise said and thought of how her ex had taken her for a costly financial ride.

Covertly, she glanced at Trevor. Would he leave Zoe under this misconception about a bank loan? As if reading her thoughts, he gave a tiny head-shake and gulped down his coffee.

He spread out his hands an inch above the tabletop. "Sorry, hon," he said in a toneless voice. "It's not just what we owe the bank. When they refused to lend us more, I got sucked in by one of those ads. You know, 'pay off your debts' money lenders kind of thing. Turns out the interest is over the top, and they're putting on the thumbscrews."

Zoe stared at Trevor, apparently at a loss for grasping the meaning. 'Doesn't she get it?' Louise wondered. Then, she saw the lips pout and the color ebb from the pointed features. Louise wanted to reach out to comfort her but realized it wasn't the time to interfere.

Almost petulantly, Zoe turned on Trevor. "You said we'd be okay when we get Auntie's money."

'Oh, no.' Louise wanted to cry out, 'Don't say such things. Don't even think it.' She bit her tongue and remained a silent and unwilling onlooker. Yet, she felt she might learn important facts about the couple.

"I still say it. The point is *when*." He emphasized the last word by spreading his hands. To Louise, he said, "My aunt made us the sole beneficiaries of her investments to avoid it going into the estate."

"I assume it's in segregated funds, then?" Louise said. From her financial adviser, she knew it avoided probate delays and complications. "The payout probably only takes a few weeks."

Zoe burst out, "The creep, Dennis, got his lawyers to stop the payout."

To calm things down, Louise explained, "It would be difficult to dispute the allocation of a beneficiary. Your cousin would need to prove the principal, I mean Carol, wasn't of sound mind when she stipulated beneficiaries. Or similar—"

"Auntie wasn't crazy or demented!" Crimson-cheeked, her hostess glared at Louise, who wished she hadn't interfered.

"Calm down, Zoe." Trevor sounded embarrassed at his wife's temper. "Louise is talking about mental incompetence, which can be temporary when someone's ill. Didn't you?" His glance seemed to plead with Louise.

"Yes, I wondered if your cousin might use her illness. When did your aunt name you as beneficiaries? Was it a recent change?"

"No, years ago," Zoe said, visibly relieved. "After I had Daniel. I'm so sorry, Louise, I was rude. I know you only want to help."

"Not to worry." Louise reached across the table and patted the young woman's tense hand that clutched the empty coffee mug.

"We got married a couple of months before Daniel was born. My aunt was very supportive," Trevor said.

Louise nodded. "She sounds like a nice lady. Were you and Carol always close?"

"Nah, not until my dad's funeral," Trevor said. "I was surprised she came because they hadn't talked in years. After that, we kept in touch."

"Tell Louise what your jerk of a cousin did to your dad." Zoe's dark eyes flared, and red patches rose to her cheeks again.

"What's the point of raking up old stories? It's got nothing to do with anything."

"Yes, it does. Once a creep, always a creep," his wife hissed. "If you don't, I will."

"Cool it, hon."

To judge by his clenched jaw, the husband needed to chill, too, Louise thought. She shifted in her seat, increasingly uncomfortable about witnessing the spousal dissent.

Quietly, she said, "Maybe we talk more another time. It's getting late." Yet, she was keen to hear about Dennis's past actions.

"It's so unfair. People thinking Trev's dad did something wrong when it was Dennis all along." Close to tears, Zoe's voice quivered. "I hate injustice!"

"Don't upset yourself," Louise murmured and glanced at Trevor, hoping he'd reach out and console his wife.

Misinterpreting her look as a request for an explanation, Trevor said, "What Zoe means is a bad investment tip my dad passed on to Carol. She was his aunt, really. Anyway, they both lost tons of money. My dad had invested far more and went broke. Carol never spoke to him again. The point is, Dad got the tip from Dennis."

"Oh, my," said Louise, thinking, 'Who'd act on a tip from a guy like Dennis?' Maybe he hadn't the flashy salesman vibe back then.

"Well, yeah. Cousin Dennis, of course, claimed it wasn't his fault. Dad only blamed his own stupidity for sinking all his money into a scam. My dad felt awful about Carol and thought he deserved to be cut out of her heart and will, as he put it."

"What a sad story." Louise shook her head in empathy. "I'm so glad she reconnected with you. Family estrangements hurt everyone."

Her mind pictured a widow getting on in years and the son cutting ties when moving to Australia. Alienated from her other relatives, Trevor's dad and his kin, plus separated from her lover—no matter how unlovely—what a lonely life for Carol. At least, the close-knit community in Cascade sustained her.

Curious now, she asked, "Did you ever tell Carol her son was behind the fateful investment tip?"

"Of course not," said Trevor. He shrugged. "My dad didn't want to rat on him."

"I did." Zoe sounded defiant yet proud.

"You did—what?" Outrage made Trevor sputter. "You had no right to."

"I had so. You didn't say a word when the creep told Auntie we were out for her money. So unfair when it was him who ruined your dad. The creep only came to visit because he thought she'd cut him out of her will. And she would have."

"What are you talking about?" Trevor's angry voice rose. The couple seemed to forget they weren't alone. "When did you tell my aunt?"

"The day after she told us Dennis threw a tantrum about the house here. Remember? She'd asked me to buy some toiletries at the drugstore. When I dropped it off, she had one of her good days, and I figured I tell her before the creep bad-mouthed us even more."

Though she tried not to glance at him openly, Louise saw Trevor stare at his wife as if feeling utterly betrayed. To her mind, there was a kind of justice in telling Carol. Still, Trevor's dad acted on dubious advice and chose to pass on the investment tip back in the day. But Carol was a woman capable of decision-making. Both were responsible for their own actions.

To find out at such a late stage her own son was implicated made things worse, no doubt. "Was Carol terribly upset about learning the truth?" Louise asked.

Zoe gazed at her as if she hadn't considered Carol's emotions before. Slowly, she said, "I don't think so. She said something like, 'Good thing the lawyer is coming next week.' That's why I thought she'd change her mind about her will and cut Dennis out."

"Ah," said Louise. Next to her, Trevor heaved an exasperated sigh. Louise persevered. "And did the lawyer come? Do you know?"

When Zoe started to speak, Trevor coughed. His wife ignored the caution.

"Auntie died that week."

Chapter Twenty-Two

Back in her own place, Louise soon retired to the loft, not yet to sleep but to do some thinking and googling at the desk by the window.

Magic, who'd led the way up the stairs, perhaps in hope of an early cuddle, sat nonplussed in the middle of the bedroom.

"Go ahead. Have a nap," Louise told her. "I've got work to do."

After the awkward finale to the dinner next door, none of them had felt like the promised dessert. Home with the pets, Louise felt wound up and in need of sorting the impressions she'd gained over the past few days. Some answers might emerge. Like what Dennis was up to. She typed the name of his start-up into the search bar.

From behind her came the unmistakable sound of scratching. Louise glanced over her shoulder.

"Not again. Magic, please. Go use your scratch post downstairs." She'd forgotten all about her promise to get a scratch mat for the loft.

When the kitty paid her no heed and continued to sharpen her claws on the drywall, Louise rose and scooped up the cat. Armed with a pillow from the bed, she deposited the cat on the desk in the soft nest. "There. Now watch me work or have a snooze."

The amber eyes examined her critically, one paw raised to lick its spongy pad.

"Have it your way." Louise adjusted her reading glasses and scanned the search results to no avail.

After entering various search strings and browsing results, she struck lucky. A bankruptcy notification of an Australian start-up by that name appeared but dated back to the year before. This didn't bode well for Dennis's avowed business success. Carol's son might need cash as urgently as her great-nephew and niece.

Why had the man even mentioned a dead company to her?

"Wait here, kitty. Be right back." Sure she'd emptied her pockets when changing pants after the morning walk, she got up and rifled her nightstand for Dennis's card.

At the time, she'd thought how little information it gave. Nothing but his name with the addition of a middle initial, Dennis P. Benson. Instead of a company name, it stated Consultant. The address, Christurn, Australia, and a phone number didn't tell her much either.

Back at her laptop, she searched for the name and found lots of people, even consultants, by his last name. None matched his full name and personal appearance. A reverse number lookup informed her the number was not in service.

Puzzled, Louise sat back and misused the eraser end of a pencil to scratch her head. Too worn out for more in-depth research on the elusive Dennis, she grabbed a notepad to jot down a suspect list. Somehow, paper felt safer than committing her thoughts to the digital no-man's-land.

Distracted, she watched Magic's paw spin a pen on the slippery desktop. Louise's pencil wrote the first header of its own accord.

Dennis P. Benson

- Son of victim (60-65 yrs.) lives in Christurn, Australia.
- Self-proclaimed successful entrepreneur (contrary evidence: latest start-up filed bankruptcy).

- Motive: money

- Means: ?
- Opportunity: present at birthday party

Grounds for suspicion [sources might be unreliable]:

- Might urgently need money.
- Only reconnected with mother when she was gravely ill. [Genuine concern?]
- Set his lawyers to dispute beneficiaries of Carol's investments.
- Expected to inherit house(s) on Charlotte's Lane and perhaps to be sole heir.
- Acts oddly (entered crawlspace without permission; gifted toxic plant; lies about his success).
- Sketchy history (appealed to mother for money after spending inheritance from father; gave fateful investment tip to Trevor's dad but denied responsibility).

When Louise reread her notes, she told Magic, "None of this means much. Lots of people pretend to success they don't have. Our sources may give their own spin on things. Or lie."

The kitty blinked. Louise took that for agreement. "We'll keep an open mind."

She scribbled the next header.

Trevor [last name?]

- Great-nephew of victim (early 30s), 55 Charlotte's Lane, Cascade, Ontario.
- Employed by a Canadian company for work assignments in the EU and recently returned with Zoe and Daniel to live next door to Great-aunt Carol.

- Motive: Money
- Means: ?
- Opportunity: present at birthday party

Connections to victim, affecting motive:

- Carol benefited the young couple in many ways, e.g. sold them the house, lent the down payment, and took back a 2nd mortgage.
- After Daniel's birth 3 years ago, she made them beneficiaries of her investments to bypass probate and informed them at some point of this legacy. (When did she tell them?)
- (Are they also among the heirs in her will?)

Grounds for suspicion:

- Trevor (and Zoe) urgently need money.
- They spent well beyond their means to finance a new start and furnish the house.
- After exhausting bank loans, Trevor secretly borrowed from dubious money lenders but can't meet payments. He's under severe pressure to repay.
- He (and Zoe) counted on Carol's investments to solve their financial troubles.

Zoe (ditto)

Only noteworthy additional points:

- Zoe didn't know about the loan sharks and the increased urgency for cash.
- She told Carol that the fateful investment tip originated with Dennis and might have hoped Auntie would disinherit Dennis.

Louise stared at the page and sighed deeply, waking the cat-napper in front of her. Magic yawned and stretched.

"Kitty, I'm afraid things look dark for our new friends next door." A vision of the adorable redhead flashed across her mind. Too horrible to contemplate the parents having a hand in Carol's demise.

The cat's paw toyed with the window curtain, parting it far enough for the desk light's reflection to sparkle on the dark pane. Absentmindedly, Louise reached and stroked the kitty's sleek black back.

The penny dropped, and Louise perked up.

"Ah, I get it. We've got another neighbor to consider, don't we? Thanks, Magic." Her pencil already flew over the next page.

Mr. Simpson

- Victim's former beau [boyfriend or lover] (85+) 47 Charlotte's Lane, Cascade, Ontario

- Motive: Revenge, scorned love, hatred?
- Means: ?
- Opportunity: present at birthday party

Connections to victim, affecting motive:

- Relationship dissolved approx. 10 yrs. ago.
- Subsequently on acrimonious terms with the victim.
- Claims Carol's cat attacked his Pekingese and that Carol poisoned the dog. [Vet appears to doubt this.]

Grounds for suspicion:

- Appears to be a spiteful person.
- Shows some signs of mental and psychological instability.
- Seems to lie about Magic attacking his dog [sources claim the dog was aggressive].
- Antique shop owner, Kendra, believes him capable of poisoning his own dog and Carol (but gives no reason for this belief).

"Well, kitty. The man might be your all-time favorite for the role of evil poisoner, but unless he has stronger grounds for bearing a murderous grudge, it looks thin compared to the motives of the son and great-nephew."

In answer, Magic contorted her body to lick her rear end.

"Yikes! Must you do this right in front of me?" Louise rose. "I'll get tea while you're at it. Can I bring you anything?"

Not waiting for a reply, she descended to the kitchen.

When she returned with a mug and biscuits for herself and a few cat treats for her companion, the cat snoozed. Louise settled in the desk chair and read over the notes.

Might as well add the maybes, she thought and jotted down the next name.

Owen (last name?)

- Proprietor of Witch's Brew café (50+)
- Calls himself a friend of Carol.

- Motive: eliminate opponent (very weak)
- Means: possibly the mini birthday cake he delivered.
- Opportunity: present at birthday party with access to means

Grounds for suspicion:

- On opposing sides over patio and parking issues. (Carol spearheaded move to file complaint with the municipal council.)
- Carol might have revived the issue in the future. [Unlikely since she resigned from chairing the village committee.]
- Owen delivered the birthday cake, which possibly contained the poison. He had access before bringing it to Rosewood Manor.

While her hand wrote the last sentence, her mind considered Jeremy and Jessie. They had the best opportunity to mess with the cake. What motive, though? Would parking restrictions affect them? If so, then all she'd written about Owen would apply to them and to anyone else operating a business in Cascade. A conspiracy to eliminate Carol?

'Get real,' Louise told herself.

She massaged her aching fingers and glanced at the time on the laptop. Half past ten already. As she planned an early start on her real work, as her mind ruefully called it, she ought to quit. Maybe just jot down some questions to prevent them from churning in her brain and robbing her of sleep.

Questions:

- Which poison was used?
- What contained the poison?

Working hypothesis:

The birthday cake or the absinthe was poisoned, since no one else consumed either of these.

[If poisoned after the party, the field is wide open.]

Louise scratched her head with the eraser again. Everyone might have known Carol's passion for absinthe. Thoughtfully, she wrote the next question.

- Who brought the bottle of absinthe?
- Or was it Carol's, and she brought it to the parlor herself?

Frustrated, she tossed the pencil onto the pad. The sound woke Magic, who opened a quizzical eye.

"Sorry, kitty. How on earth am I to find answers? The police won't tell me anything."

Other questions crowded in.

The cat got up and stretched her sinuous back into a dome shape. Then she stalked over and rubbed her cheek on Louise's hand.

"Right, Magic. I'll scribble a few more, and then we'll go to bed. With all your snoozing, you must be exhausted, too. Poor Darling. Your brother is snoring away, I'm sure."

When Magic licked her pinkie, Louise laughed. "That tickles." She pulled her hand out of reach to continue her list.

- Who sent the samples to the lab?
- Who tipped off the police about the lab?
- What are the conditions of Carol's will?

The pencil hit the paper so hard its tip broke off when she jabbed the dot of the question mark.

"Let's take that as a sign to call it quits for tonight."

By a quarter to eleven, Louise snuggled under the duvet with the kitty in the crock of her arm. Amazed at how used she was growing to a furry bedroom companion, she smiled in the darkness and closed her eyes.

Sleep, however, refused to be courted. Stray bits of thought circled and swirled. Not wanting to disturb the dozing cat, Louise willed her body to remain immobile. Time to resort to her proven remedy for bouts of insomnia so frequent during the harrowing months of divorce proceedings. In slow, deliberate steps, her mind counted down from ninety-nine, mentally enunciating each syllable of the numbers to keep monkey thoughts at bay.

By the time she crossed the threshold to the fifties, her consciousness gradually dipped into oblivion...

Chimes like church bells wove into a dreamy daze. With a start, Louise resurfaced to awareness and a wriggling sensation in her arms.

Through the mental haze, the mobile chimed and vibrated on the nightstand. Magic struggled free from the covers and burst into an annoyed meow.

Raised onto one elbow, Louise groped for the phone she'd forgotten to switch to night shift. Estelle's name appeared on the display. Its sight shook Louise wide awake.

Her lawyer friend's chirpy voice bombarded her before she could say a word.

"Did I wake you? You took ages to answer. I know it's late, but it's the first chance I got. Tomorrow will be worse, and you were in a hurry—"

"Okay, okay, Estelle. I'm glad you're calling." Louise did her best to chase away remnants of sleep.

"The dragon stuffed a paper copy into snail mail, but I figured you'd want to get the gist of it right away. Don't you?"

Louise switched to speakerphone and propped up the pillows, mumbling, "Sorry," to the kitty, who retreated to the foot of the bed.

"Don't be. No trouble at all," Estelle's high voice fluted into the room, setting Magic's ears twitching.

Not bothering to correct the lawyer's misconception, Louise said, "Thanks, Estelle. I appreciate it. What does it say?"

"A lot. I won't go into details. You can read the testatrix's, shall we say, explanatory remarks at leisure. Seems she wasn't happy with her son. Did you know?"

Estelle paused long enough for Louise to say, "I gathered relations were strained."

"To put it mildly. In short, barring a minor bequest or two, the estate is to be divided in equal portions among the son, a Dennis Parker Benson, and the great-great nephew, Daniel Parker, son of Trevor Parker. The child's portion will be held in trust by the executor or successor—Lawyer Fox, remember?—until Daniel turns twenty-five."

When Estelle ceased to speak, Louise murmured, "Oh, my. Doesn't look good for Trevor."

"Eh? Should've thought he'd jump with joy at the boy's windfall. Young parents usually do. Wait 'till you hear the codicil, added in January of this year."

"There's more?" Louise scrabbled at her scalp with her fingernails.

"Yep. Apparently, the testatrix sold a house to the great-nephew and his wife. If the deal closed last month—"

"It did," Louise interjected.

"Well, then they don't need to repay the second mortgage nor the down payment she lent them. She must've liked them a lot," Estelle commented. "That's it in a nutshell."

Louise sighed. "I see," she said, feeling dispirited. If the police saw the will, which was a certainty, Trevor must be their number one suspect. "Thanks so much, Estelle."

"You're most welcome. The details of the will, however, are not. Are they?"

"Isn't it obvious? It gives Trevor and Zoe a whopping motive for poisoning Carol Benson. They stand to gain far more than Carol's son."

"True," Estelle said, far too chirpy for the late hour and occasion. "Cheer up. They'd need to have known the terms of the will beforehand. Did they?"

The thought made Louise perk up. "Hard to say. They seem to count only on the payout of the investments." Which looks bad enough, her mind supplied. "Carol made them the beneficiaries."

"Smart woman. By-passes probate. Speaking of which, there's a memorandum referred to in the will, which specifically instructs the executor to forego a reading of the will until probate is completed."

"Goodness. That sounds spiteful. Why would she make them wait?"

"Your guess is as good as mine. Spite the son? Pointless since the heirs could apply to the relevant court for access during the probate period. Few people realize this. Maybe she banked on that."

"The young couple doesn't strike me as legally savvy enough to be aware of the option. Nor was I until you told me," Louise said. "Well, you've given me—"

"Wait. I almost forgot."

Over the speakerphone, Louise could hear the clicking of a computer mouse.

"Here we are. There're a couple of things worth mentioning. First, a smaller, oddly worded bequest says, 'To my former Beau, Gilbert Simpson, should he have the audacity to survive me, I will CAD 10,000.'"

"Did she really? How strange, I'm amazed," said Louise. "The last person I'd expected her to leave even a penny."

"Here's a stranger one still. It reads, 'My treasure I will to the happy finder. May they use it wisely.'" Estelle's high-pitched laughter filled the loft and made the kitty jump.

Louise shook her head in disbelief. Something floated to the surface of consciousness, only to sink again. Annoyed that it escaped her grasp, she muttered, "I can't make her out. What a puzzling person Carol must have been."

"Compared to some odd wills, this one is quite straightforward," Estelle said. "You'll see when the print copy arrives. Might take a few days to snail its way to the boonies. Meanwhile, have a good night. And Louise? Do be careful. Promise?"

"I will. Thanks so much. Sleep tight, Estelle. Whenever you call it a night, that is."

Another volley of laughter ended the call at the other end.

Lost deep in thought, Louise's consciousness took moments to locate an unpleasant sound. Preoccupied, she chided, "Magic! That's enough! Stop scratching the wall." She swung her legs out from under the duvet and slipped into the felt clogs. "You go back to bed, kitty, while I fetch a sleepy-time tea."

She very much doubted slumber would descend any time soon.

Chapter Twenty-Three

Ten o'clock the next morning found Louise completing a final scroll-through of her true crime client's manuscript. Another half-hour, and she could hit 'send.'

Pleased with her early bird efforts, she turned to Shadow, who lay stretched out on his side in a pool of sunlight filtering through the window.

"Once I'm done, we'll go for a proper walk."

His tail thumped in agreement onto the laminate floor. Magic was too busy to spare them a glance, monitoring a woodpecker whose ra-ta-ta-tap drilling filtered through the open window. The kitty, Louise thought with a smile, loved perching on the table with a view of the sun-dappled ravine just as much as the foster mother enjoyed working by the living room window.

A sudden vibration of the phone rattled the wooden tabletop and startled them both. Magic hissed and jumped to a stand, her back curving high.

"Got it. Relax." The soft tone soothed the feline temper. "Just a text."

A glance at the snippet ruffled her own calm. She thumbed the app's icon.

NORA

> Important! Hi Louise, it's Nora. Could you come over asap, please? Disturbing news about our case!

"Goodness! What's she up to?" Louise muttered. Or was the actress dramatizing again? A dangerous game. With a sigh, Louise offered to come by around 11.

NORA

> Thank heavens! Do come!

LOUISE

> Stay calm and safe.

Ten after eleven, an unfamiliar Rosewood staff member escorted Louise to Mrs. Norton's room. A couple of spritely seniors in golfing outfits passed them on the stately staircase. They beamed at her.

"Can't ask for more gorgeous weather, eh?" said one of them.

"Too nice to stay inside," added the other.

Mindful of missing her morning walk, Louise wholeheartedly agreed.

Any thoughts of the weather faded once her attendant knocked on Mrs. Norton's door. It burst open without delay, and a flushed Nora ushered Louise inside.

Before closing the door, Nora yanked a 'Do not disturb' sign from a hook and looped it over the outer doorknob.

"There. That will give us some privacy. We can make our own tea. I keep an electric kettle in the bathroom." Somewhat breathlessly, Mrs. Norton led Louise by the elbow to the now familiar sitting area in the window nook.

Though Louise had uttered a greeting while entering, barely suppressed excitement made her hostess dispense with social niceties.

155

Sure Nora needed a heart-to-heart more than tea, Louise said, "Unless you'd like some, let's forget about tea for now."

"I've been on tenterhooks all morning, dear." Mrs. Norton patted Louise's arm and pointed to a chintz-covered chair. "So kind of you to fit in a visit on a workday."

Dressed today in a becoming, natural linen pantsuit over a black top, she appeared groomed and stylish. A blue-pattered silk scarf softened the contours of an unmistakably aging neckline.

Perched on the edge of the seat, Nora leaned close as Louise sat down across from her.

"My pleasure." Louise smiled reassurance. "I got an early start and needed a break. The perks of freelancing." No need to mention her missed walk. "So, what's on your mind, Nora? I take it something happened?"

"Yes! Important developments." As though nervous about eavesdroppers, Mrs. Norton twisted to glance at the door. "Pull your chair closer, Louise. One never knows who might be about."

Eager to soothe her hostess's evident agitation, Louise rose and moved the low table out of the way to make room for her chair next to Nora's.

"Good like this?" she asked and tilted her torso in an attentive posture.

"Thank you, dear, for humoring an old lady." The rueful smile had Louise demure. "I've done a little sleuthing," Nora confided. One hand lightly covered her mouth as if surprised at some naughtiness.

'Please, no,' Louise wanted to say. 'Here we go. Trouble ahead.' Instead, she murmured a tried and proved, "Oh?"

"Last night, I couldn't sleep," Nora said. "Too many unanswered questions."

"Same here," Louise admitted.

"Really?" Her hostess regarded her with keen interest. "After our last talk, I've puzzled over who sent samples to the laboratory. Who ratted to the police? Might it be the same person? Was that on your mind too, Louise?"

"Hm, yes. If we knew who contacted the lab, we'd be a huge step forward."

"We do know now." The petite lady in her elegant outfit sat back and smirked a wee bit smugly.

For a few seconds, Louise remained speechless. Did Nora succeed effortlessly when she didn't even see the way to an answer?

"You amaze me, Nora. I doff my cap to you." Louise lifted an imaginary hat and sketched a bow. "Who is it? Spill," she added lightly, though growing anxiety about Mrs. Norton's safety gnawed at her.

"Promise to be patient? Let me have my moment of glory. There's lots of time to worry after." Nora wriggled a forefinger at her. "Yes, your face is an open book, Louise."

For the first time since Louise arrived, Nora's tittering laugh relieved the tense mood.

Glad of a respite, Louise chuckled. "Got me in one. I'll stay mum. Just don't keep me in suspense for too long."

"Don't spoil my fun. It gets serious soon enough." A sigh escaped before the irrepressible actress smoothed the creased fabric of the linen jacket and recomposed her features for animated storytelling.

Bent close to Louise, she continued her tale. "As I was saying, I mulled over the questions and dozed off only in the wee hours. Next thing, bright daylight woke me. Or perhaps the sound of Uma. There she stood by the bed, ready with the needle."

As Nora's fingers mimicked the action, thumb pushing a plunger, Louise gasped and shot bolt upright at the imaginary Uma wielding a syringe. Unaware of Mrs. Norton's medical condition, she hadn't considered the possibility of messing with an injection.

The tiny lady's dismissive hand waving hardly reassured. "It's just insulin. I'm diabetic. Don't worry. It's under control." A mischievous smile stole over the fragile features. "You never suspected the cookies I served were sugarless, did you? Jeremy makes them for me, low carb and monk fruit sweetened."

Reluctant to alarm her hostess with dangers of another kind, Louise murmured, "Glad to hear it."

"You see, it was something in the girl's glance when she bent close to insert the needle. I knew it right that moment."

Hair rose on Louise's shivering arms, visualizing the needle coming closer. "Knew what?" she whispered.

"She's the snitch, I said to myself. And I was right." A self-satisfied grin creased the pale skin and brought a rosy hue to her cheeks.

"How can you be sure?" The nurse's glance was not much to go by, Louise thought.

"She admitted it. You might call it a blunt approach. But it's effective. 'You informed the police and set off the investigation into Carol's death, Uma,' I said. Everyone at Rosewood knows Raymond is my godchild. She assumes he confides in me."

"My goodness! Nora. How reckless of you. What if the girl killed Carol?"

"Of course, she didn't. I'm surprised at you, Louise. Uma wouldn't tip off the police if she murdered someone, would she?"

"Not the first killer to do so," Louise pointed out. "Never mind. Tell me what she said. Did she send in the samples, too?"

"No. Alfred did."

For a few seconds, Louise closed her eyes. Did those two collude? To what aim? Aloud, she said, "I see. Or more, honestly, I don't. Were they in it together?"

"Sort of. Let me explain. The girl hadn't been herself for a while. Fidgety and jumpy. Uma and Alfred got along fine in the past. Not anymore."

When Nora again peered at the door as if waiting for someone to burst in, Louise remarked, "Yes, I noticed Alfred's rather sharp with the nurse, and she seemed petulant in response. Strained working relations, for sure. Not in the best interest of patients, is it?"

The tiny headshake didn't move a hair in Mrs. Norton's perfect coiffure. Still, her hand reached to pat it lightly. "At first, she wouldn't answer me, though I could sense she needed a friendly ear. Once started, there was no stopping her."

Louise shifted in her seat, wishing Nora would come to the point.

Her perceptive hostess smiled knowingly. "I won't spin out my yarn any further. Blame my fondness for theatrics." The trilling laugh carried a tone of disappointment.

A pang of guilt prompted Louise's, "Take your time." With so few opportunities to indulge her acting skills, it seemed mean to hasten Mrs. Norton.

"No. I shouldn't keep you in suspense. Here's what happened. Both Uma and Alfred attended to Carol after Uma found her dead in the early morning hours. Alfred had just come on day shift. He paged Matron and requested sending for the doctor."

"Is that standard procedure?" Louise asked.

"I assume so. Uma mentioned it matter of fact. She doesn't have much experience, and her mind was on what happened after." Nora dabbed a lacy handkerchief to her lips.

"Sorry, dear," she continued. "This is unpleasant. You see, they found Carol in quite a mess. Soiled herself and had chucked up."

Louise empathized when Nora's hanky went up to cover her mouth in an unconscious movement. "Only to be expected," she murmured.

"Yes. Quite right. Anyway, before the cleaning staff arrived, Alfred secured samples and requested Uma to sign a note stating she'd been present throughout the entire time and observed the collection of specimens."

"Was Matron with them? Did she—"

"No! That's just it. Alfred said it was in Uma's best interest not to tell and kept her with him until he had packaged and addressed it to the lab. She had to sign off for that process, too."

"And she didn't find that irregular? Why not go to Matron? Hard to believe the nurse didn't speak up and then confided in you instead." Afraid that sounded odd, Louise added, "I can understand she chose you, though, as a kind listener."

"Nice of you to say so, but choice is the wrong word. The girl was scared. She believes Alfred suspects her of wrongdoing or neglect during the night shift when Carol died. People misjudge him because he can be a little abrupt and gruff." Nora's lips twitched in a rueful smile. "Never with his patients. He's an angel. So gentle and caring."

"Still—"

In an imperious gesture, the older woman's hand rose. "Remember, the girl is so very young. They pretend to be tough when underneath they're anxious and insecure."

"If she contacted the police, she obviously had second thoughts and regained her nerve," Louise said.

"Not at all. Her father made her. Just like me, he noticed something wasn't right. She'd grown skittish and nervy. When she told him she was quitting her job, he sat her down and talked until she owned up."

"The father made her give an anonymous tip to the police? How very strange."

"Consider their background. They left their homeland to get away from corruption and injustice. From what Uma let on, they don't trust authorities to be unbiased. But the father is also a religious man and believes in doing the right thing. In the end, they compromised."

"Hm. I can understand their point of view. Not a smart move in the long run. Police are bound to find out. An awkward position for both father and daughter."

"Exactly what I told Uma this morning. After a good cry, she promised to call Raymond. I assured her my godchild is a decent person and passed on his work phone number."

"Did she call?"

"Yes. That's just it. Raymond and another officer came right away. What's so awful, they took Alfred to the station." The voice petered to a halt.

Before Louise's eyes, Mrs. Norton seemed to shrink and age. The earlier animation completely evaporated.

Puzzled, Louise said, "They need to question him. The lab samples triggered the investigation and are the key evidence. Why ever didn't Alfred call in the police at the very start? Something about Carol's death made him suspicious. Why the secrecy? I don't get what he planned to do with the lab results if his suspicions were confirmed."

Aware she'd spoken vehemently and distressed her hostess further, Louise added softly, "I'm so sorry, Nora. It's not your fault—"

"But it is! If I hadn't persuaded Uma." The older woman's mouth quivered. "Alfred wouldn't be held for questioning."

"Don't blame yourself, Nora. I think you've done right. The police probably suspected the staff here or Matron Juniper. They're the ones with access to...whatever was sampled." Louise touched Nora's knobby hand, which cramped on the armrest of the chair. "Alfred must have realized that all along. As head nurse, he ought to have acted responsibly."

"You don't know him as I do," said Nora. After a brief hesitation, she stretched out her hand. "Will you promise to tell no one?"

Unsure what she was agreeing to, Louise temporized. "I guess so unless it protects a criminal."

"Alfred got into trouble with police before." Palm raised to forestall a comment, the head nurse's champion went on, "No. Not what you think. Nothing to do with his job here. A few years ago, he was charged for possession. He was an addict back then."

"Goodness." Louise's eyebrows shot up. "I'm surprised he kept his job. Scary stuff. The risk to patients, one can just imagine what might happen."

"Well, he didn't. The place he worked fired him. Give him credit, Louise. He admitted himself to a treatment clinic and overcame his addiction. Matron Juniper hired him and never regretted it."

'Until now,' Louise meant to say but kept quiet. The fervent tone of Mrs. Norton's defense might show an unquestioning belief in Alfred's integrity or a desire to persuade herself.

Her face must have mirrored her doubts. For her hostess insisted, "Trust me. I know Alfred."

"Well, substance use and abuse presumably is an issue in the medical profession," Louise said. "What with easy access to prescription drugs and high levels of stress, it's all too tempting."

"So true," Nora agreed eagerly. "Just think what the pandemic has done to nurses, paramedics, and doctors. Legalizing cannabis makes it worse."

Privately, Louise figured the head nurse's judgment might be seriously impaired. His conduct implied it.

"The investigators will hold his past against him," said Nora. "'A prior,' they call it." The bony fingers snapped scare quotes in the air. "As if a subsequent was inevitable."

Did Nora's confidence in Raymond's integrity only extend to Uma? Louise thought. Or did the sergeant's godmother realize Alfred's actions gave far more cause for suspicion? Mildly, she pointed out, "If only Alfred had called in the police instead—"

"Don't you see?"

Whatever it meant remained unclear to Louise because a loud rap on the door startled them.

She caught a glimmer of fear on the pale features. "Would you go see who it is?" her hostess whispered.

"For sure." Louise rose, grateful for the interruption of their tense exchange. A brief break would calm ruffled feathers.

As she opened the door, a now familiar voice said, "May I come in? I must speak to Mrs. Norton in my official capacity."

"When he talks like this, I'm in for a sermon." Nora's gentle titter didn't convince Louise.

"Well, I'd better make myself scarce, then," Louise said. "Please, come in, Sergeant Marpel."

Chapter Twenty-Four

"Dear Raymond. Yes, come in and make yourself comfortable." Mrs. Norton's hand fluttered, beckoning the sergeant to her side.

Louise detected a nervous tremor in the gesture.

Without hesitation, Sgt. Marpel grabbed the frilly stool from the mirrored vanity table and placed it squarely across from his godmother's armchair.

When Louise gathered her purse and buttoned her cardigan, ready to depart, Nora urged her, "No, please stay." To her godchild, she added, "I want Louise with me when you grill me, Raymond."

Despite the sergeant's disapproving glance, Louise resumed her seat. Though she empathized with the awkwardness of the situation for Nora and Raymond, her curiosity won out.

Sgt. Marpel unzipped his sports jacket, crossed his legs, and made a show of flipping through his notepad, then sat at ease, pen in hand.

Next to her, Louise sensed Nora fidgeting. Nervous fingers straightened the sleeves of the linen jacket. Time to break the artificially induced tension, she decided, and said, "Should I make us a cup of tea, Nora? You must be parched after our chat."

The sergeant frowned at her. Then his lips twitched.

Mrs. Norton's veined hand restrained her. "Later, dear. Let's get the official stuff over with." Still, the interruption buoyed her. Poised, she regarded her godchild sternly. "Get on with it, Raymond. No need to resort to interrogation tactics. You want to hear about my interview with Nurse Uma this morning, I presume?"

"Er, yes, if you don't mind, ma'am." This time, his grin proved irrepressible but fleeting. "Tell me in your own words how you came to discuss the matter with the nurse and repeat to me what was said."

Nora wagged a finger at him. "Now, you're pulling my leg, Raymond. Playing the ponderous bobby of a penny novel, really, dear."

"Right," the sergeant said. The smile transfigured his square feature. "Okay, let's have it then. Tell me what happened, and I'll throw in questions."

"Much more sensible," Mrs. Norton agreed and launched into a repeat of her earlier performance.

Soon, Louise realized it was a much-abridged rendition, purged of any reference to Uma's father. The sergeant asked only about the time the conversation took place but didn't query any other statements.

From facts, Nora glided into suppositions of Alfred's innocence. Or was it wishful thinking? Louise wondered, catching the anxious flicker in the gray-blue eyes when the older woman's tentative hand reached out to the sergeant but withdrew with a sigh.

To Louise, it seemed almost a studied gesture of suppliance. So did the tone when Mrs. Norton said, "Of course, Alfred should have left well enough alone. I'm convinced he meant well. You can't blame him for not trusting the police after what he's been through."

Sgt. Marpel pocketed his notepad and made to rise. Rather pompously as it seemed to Louise, he pontificated. "I can't say it often enough. Interfering with police matters is a serious offense. We can't take it lightly when someone covers up a crime."

"But don't you see?" Mrs. Norton cried, rising to the occasion. "If Alfred hadn't sent samples to the laboratory, you wouldn't be now on the trail of a merciless killer."

For a moment, Louise worried if Nora the actress would take the stage. The sergeant wasn't moved but pointed out the flaw in the reasoning.

"If your Alfred had done his duty and called us in immediately, forensics could have collected evidence instead of it being destroyed. It took an anonymous informant to get the ball rolling."

When he rose, his expression was grave and unyielding. "Let us do our job. Don't meddle."

Despite seeing his point, the peremptory tone caused Louise's hackles to rise. A quick glance showed her hostess felt irked, too. Neither of them commented.

Raymond's voice softened. "We'll talk again, Godmama. Say hi to Uncle Hank for me. I'll pop in to see him first chance I get." His gaze shifted to Louise. "You have my card. Please stay safe. Both of you."

Mrs. Norton rose unsteadily as if all her energy had evaporated. Raymond sprang forward to assist her.

"Thank you, my dear boy. So good of you to come by instead of sending your constable." The voice sounded tired and frail. With one hand resting heavily on her godchild's arm, she walked with him to the door.

He leaned down for a peck on the elderly lady's pale cheek before wishing them both a good day.

Concerned, Louise moved closer, ready to guide Mrs. Norton to the armchair.

As soon as the door closed on the sergeant, Nora sprung around, spritely as ever. Her eyes sparkled with mischief.

"Now, it's time for tea and strategic planning. Don't look so disapproving, Louise. You didn't think I'd have a fit of the vapors like some Victorian damsel? No need for smelling salts."

Louise shook her head in exasperation mixed with a touch of admiration.

With a light step and a girlish titter, Nora led the way to the inner door. "Come help me get tea. If dear Raymond wants to believe I need mollycoddling, I play the helpless little old lady for him. But you, at least, know I'm made of sterner stuff. We'll crack this case."

It didn't take long to brew tea in the tiny alcove tucked in a recess by the bathroom entrance. Equipped with a mini-fridge, microwave, and storage cabinet, it provided a modicum of independence for the resident.

Soon, they sat again, comfortably ensconced in their armchairs, sipping tea.

"Now, Louise. You see how it stands. As much as I love my godchild, we cannot rely on him solving this case."

When Louise made to remonstrate, Nora's hand rose in a quick gesture.

"No. Let me finish. I know my Raymond. He's a good and smart boy but awfully stubborn. Once he makes up his mind, he sticks to his guns."

At this image of the sergeant, Louise couldn't suppress a chuckle. "I'm sure he'd hate to hear you talk of him like this."

"Oh, he would," Nora agreed earnestly. "You see, I've known him from when he was in diapers. He's the son of my dearest friend. She and her husband died tragically. Never mind. A different story." The elderly hands rummaged for the purse behind the seat cushion and extracted a lacy white handkerchief. Mrs. Norton dabbed her lips and, surreptitiously, the corner of her eyes.

Touched by such emotion at the memory of a long-lost friend, Louise's heart went out to Nora. A nagging little doubt remained. How much was real and how much playacting? Louise took a sip from her cup to drown the uncharitable thought.

The sergeant's admonition didn't diminish her own desire to unravel the mystery of Carol's death. She felt certain her predecessor would haunt her dreams, if not the house if she left the cruel death unpunished. Though she didn't share Nora's conviction of the head nurse's innocence, the man's actions hardly fit a killer's.

Why would he draw attention to foul play by collecting samples for testing when everyone assumed natural causes? Only a convoluted idea of preempting later suspicions by an atypical action might account for a killer collecting such evidence of his own crime.

"...don't you think?" Mrs. Norton's words penetrated Louise's cogitations.

"So sorry, Nora. My mind was wandering. What were you saying?"

"Wouldn't it be nice to arrange a memorial gathering to commemorate Carol's life and death?" Nora eyed her with a sweet yet watchful expression.

The suggestion caught Louise off guard. "Er. Perhaps. Wasn't there a memorial service at the funeral?"

"Oh, I meant a get-together of Carol's friends. Right here at Rosewood. We'll use the parlor. They call it the *events room*. Such an ugly name, isn't it?"

"Hm. But wouldn't that reawaken unpleasant memories?" Louise floundered, not wanting to veto the idea outright. "After all, Carol died in the wake of the last gathering of her friends."

Mrs. Norton gave a gentle cough, covered by the lacy handkerchief. "Don't you see how fitting it will be?"

The prospect of rounding up the birthday guests in the elegant parlor sent a shiver down Louise's spine.

"Nora, let's not play with fire. Someone at the birthday open house poisoned Carol. Isn't that what we assume?"

Her hostess nodded eagerly. "Exactly. All we need is an admission. The great detectives gather the suspects in one room and eliminate them one by one."

Laughter bubbled up in Louise's throat at such naivety. Helpless to suppress it, her palm covered her mouth. The hurt expression on the older woman's face sobered her.

"My apologies, Nora. No cause for merriment. I just pictured myself in the role of Poirot, browbeating the killer into a confession."

"If anyone is the right person for that role, it would be me," said Nora. With a mischievous smile at Louise's involuntary pout, she added, "The egg-head detective is pint-size, just like me. You're the right height for Hastings."

Put thus in her place, Louise said, "Right size maybe, but we're not in a play featuring the famous Belgian. Please, give up the idea. A memorial gathering should wait until the killer is safely behind bars. At this stage, it's far too dangerous. Your Raymond would have a fit. We don't want the killer to have a go at you."

"Don't you worry, Louise," said her hostess with a sweet smile. "Of course, you and I won't touch any of the food or drink we'll serve."

Louise closed her eyes and groaned.

Chapter Twenty-Five

It was a rather shamefaced Louise who drove back to Charlotte's Lane several hours after leaving Mrs. Norton and Rosewood.

Though the trip to the pet store in the nearest market town was necessary for dog food and the promised scratch mat, lingering for lunch and the impromptu purchase of a patio table set were pure indulgence.

No way for a responsible freelancer to act, she told herself. Yet, she'd felt too wound up to go straight to work. Worried about Nora's mad scheme, she needed a distraction. How could she trust the actress not to go ahead with the memorial gathering? The ardent hand-to-heart promise to let Louise know might have been just so much playacting.

There was nothing for it but to find the killer before Nora got into trouble. With a sigh, Louise pulled into her driveway on Charlotte's.

She saw him immediately. Crouched low, a grimy baseball cap hiding the eyes, there was Alfred. Spade in hand, he appeared to watch her.

Louise cut the ignition and got out of the car. "So, they've let you go." The thought verbalized without preamble.

"Why shouldn't they?" he retorted and used the spade to hoist himself up.

No need to mention who 'they' were.

"Nora worried about you," Louise said.

He swiped at his dirt-streaked face with the sleeve of his flannel shirt. The knees of his jeans were darkened from the damp soil.

She pointed to the spade. "What are you digging for?"

"Soil needs turning," he said. "Always put things to rights before May's long weekend. I got a late start this year."

"I see," Louise said, though she didn't.

Her face must mirror her feelings, she thought, for Alfred said, "Hey, no obligation to take me on. Owen told me you need help around the yard."

"I do," she admitted. "Kind of you to step in the breach."

His dirt-stained hand waved off such a notion. "Can't afford to lose my usual gardening gigs. Just give it a try. See if you like what I'm doing. If not, tell me to get lost."

"Fair enough," she said, hoping she wasn't employing a killer.

When she opened the trunk and wrestled with the dog food, Alfred came to her aid.

"Here. Let me carry the stuff."

"Leave it at the door, and I'll take it from there, thanks."

"Where does the table go? Out front?" His arm swiped in the direction of the narrow patio next to the portico.

"It's for the deck on the backside," she said. "If you don't mind."

As soon as she unlocked the door, a bundle of fur hurdled at them.

"My goodness, Shadow. Slow down." Such an energetic greeting warmed her heart. "He heard you and wants to know what's happening out here," she told Alfred when the pooch went from nuzzling her legs to the much more interesting earthy scents of the gardener's knees.

Her helper rested the kibble bag against the doorjamb and crouched for a proper canine greeting.

"So much for my guard dog," Louise said, seeing Shadow lick the man's cheeks.

"He barked alright when I got here. Told him it was just me, and he settled down." With a last pat on the dog's rump, Alfred rose. "I'll shift the rest."

Head shaking, Louise watched the dog pounce along at the man's side. This pooch definitely wasn't cut out for guard duty.

When she stepped out onto the deck through the living room's patio door, Alfred had set up the folding table and chairs close to the house wall.

"Good place?" he asked. "Carol liked hers here. Not too much sun in the summer when the maples are in full leave."

"Perfect," Louise agreed. Her sense of hospitality inclined her to offer him some refreshment, but prudence recommended avoiding a too friendly footing. Yet she wanted a chance to talk to him.

"Did Carol employ you on a specific schedule, or how did you work it?" she asked.

"Depends on what needs doing. Plus, on my shifts at Rosewood. I do for a few people. Snow removal and stacking firewood, too."

"Ah. Good to know," she said. 'Unless he gets arrested,' her mind supplied.

As if reading her stray thought, Alfred's mouth twitched. His eyes, she noticed now, were an inscrutable pewter, the whites shot through with broken veins.

"If Matron has to let me go over this whole mess, I'll have lots of time on my hands."

Driven by curiosity, Louise asked bluntly, "Whatever made you do such a thing? If Carol's death looked suspicious, why not raise the alarm and call the police?"

No answer came. The shield of the cap hid his eyes when he lowered his chin. Yet Louise saw the jaw muscles tighten. His fingers clawed the upper rung of the slatted backrest as he pushed a chair closer to the table.

"Cops swarming the place?" The words rolled like a growl, making Shadow snap to attention. "Last thing I wanted. A whiff of homicide, and they pounce on dudes like me."

His chin came up, and she felt a shrewd glance examine her face. "Anyone tell you? Had some run-ins with the law." Acknowledging her slight nod, he added, "Matron's been good to me. I didn't want trouble coming her way."

"But Alfred." Louise felt frustration mount. "Didn't you realize how much worse it'll be for everyone once the police find out? How could you let the cleaning staff destroy evidence?"

"Yeah, well. Don't I know it? Now. Wasn't thinking straight, was I?" He slapped the chair's backrest and winced. Shadow yipped as if sensing the pain.

'Bodes ill,' Louise thought, 'if the head nurse can't think straight in an emergency.'

To Alfred, she said, "Then why take samples at all? Why not let it go when the doctor assumed natural causes?"

"With a killer at loose among my patients? I had to know. Besides," he added, wiping his nose on the sleeve of his shirt, "I owe Carol."

"What did you plan on doing if the results were positive?" Louise watched him closely for a reaction, but he eyed the maple canopy as if nature held the answer.

Then he shrugged. A helpless gaze grazed her before shifting to the pooch. "Track down who'd done for her? Tip off police? Didn't think that far. My mind was on couriering the vials to the lab as quick as I could."

He yanked the baseball cap off. Fingers spread wide, he combed back sweat-darkened hair. "Listen. I know I've made a bloody mess of things. Don't need no one to tell me. I'll quit before Matron's got to fire me."

His stare challenged her to contradict him. "Hell, if you want me off your property, just say so."

Before Louise could decide, a phlegmy cackle announced they weren't alone. With a growl, Shadow lurched forward. Snout wedged between the bars of the porch railing, he barked at the intruder below.

Appalled, Louise followed the pooch. Half-hidden by the evergreen boughs, her neighbor peered up at her. He must have snuck along the fence unseen while they were too distracted to notice. Maybe the wind blowing in the opposite direction prevented her canine's nose from sensing the alien presence.

Louise shushed the yipping dog and called down, "Good day to you,

Mr. Simpson. What brings you to *my* side of the fence?" emphasizing 'my' to deter future sneaking.

"Want me to leave?" Alfred muttered.

Unsure if he meant get off her property or leave her alone with the prowling neighbor, she said, "Please stay."

Yet, her mind questioned the wisdom of a tête-à-tête with two suspects as she grabbed hold of the dog's collar and led the way down the porch stairs.

Her neighbor remained sheltered among the trees, the prickly branches camouflaging his presence. The motley tweed jacket and baggy brown trousers blended in well. So did the Tyrolean hat adorned by a tattered Gamsbart brush.

Relieved, Louise noticed the little man came unarmed today. No danger of shear snapping.

Verbal sniping sufficed in a pinch, she thought wryly when he rasped, "So you're playing sleuth, I hear. Dangerous game for a lady." His hee–hee–ing made her take a step backward, knocking into her would-be gardener.

"Sorry," she mumbled in reflex. Then, straightened to address the intruder. "What on earth gives you that impression?"

When Simpson cackled in response, Louise caught Alfred's eye-rolling.

"Nothing escapes the village watch," her neighbor spat and shook a grimy finger at her. "Curiosity killed the cat. Never forget."

Over the renewed cackling fit rose Alfred's voice in the commanding tones Louise had noticed him using with Uma at Rosewood. "Cut it out, Gilbert. Louise isn't a fool. She sees right through your mad hatter's act."

To Louise, who felt by no means foolproof, he said mildly, "Don't mind Gilbert. He likes to play mind games with people's prejudice. Deep down inside, he's quite sane and not a bad guy."

This drew a shrieking hoot. Spasms shook the hunched figure.

Under Louise's restraining hand, Shadow went still, ears flattened back, and lip curled. Concerned about the dog's reaction, Louise aimed to de-escalate through soothing tones. "Let's go out front, and you can tell me about the garden plans, Alfred. Why don't you come along, Mr. Simpson, and give us your advice?"

Under no circumstances did she want to appear intimidated by the odd little fellow's antics. Nor did she wish this erratic neighbor roaming the far side of her house unobserved. Without overt confrontation, she must discourage trespassing. Did he stalk Carol while still living here?

For the next ten minutes, Louise listened to an almost comical interlude of Alfred's landscaping ideas, punctuated by Gilbert Simpson's caustic remarks and derisive snipes that pearled off the gardener like useless sweat.

The botanical lore washed over Louise and became a blur. It mellowed Shadow into slumber by her feet.

"Why don't we leave Alfred to get on with his work?" she eventually said to her neighbor. "I want to ask your advice on a different matter, Mr. Simpson."

Her new gardener shot her a grateful look and said with a grin, "I'll drop off a list of what we might plant so you can decide in peace."

Raymond's warning occurred to her. "What about pulling poisonous plants?"

Her neighbor's shrill laugh forestalled Alfred's reply. "Lady, you might as well pave over the whole lot," Simpson rasped. "Nature's store of poisons is infinite. See the pretty lilies of the valley? Toxic. Azalea? Kills your mutt if he's stupid enough to munch them. The list goes on."

For Simpson, she thought, a remarkably sensible speech.

"He's right, you know," Alfred put in. "You're best-off teaching Shadow not to touch things. A smart dog like him learns quickly. Won't you, handsome?" His long fingers caressed the dog's ears and received a lick in response.

"What about little Daniel?" Louise asked, though she realized the truth of the men's words.

"Kids learn, too," Alfred said.

"Wouldn't know about that. Never had brats to fret me." With that, Mr.

Simpson turned to go, not down the lane they stood closer to, but again cutting across her yard.

Louise hastened after him, Shadow at heel.

"Gilbert?" she called. "A word."

Abreast with the entrance portico. Ready to pick his way around the side of her house, he stopped and peered from under his jaunty hat.

At a loss of how to broach the subject foremost on her mind, Louise said somewhat aimlessly, "Gilbert. Mr. Simpson, I mean," she corrected hastily when he swiveled briskly as if to walk off. "Please, stay a moment."

No choice but to address his back, the extreme curvature noticeable despite the XL-size tweeds, Louise said, "You've known Carol the longest of people here. Your close relationship must give you insights into her—"

With a cry of pain, he wheeled around. "Close rela–relation—" Trembling lips broke off the sputtering.

"Oh, I'm so sorry. Didn't mean to—to offend. I'm sure—" The emotional violence of his reaction had her stammer. After a steadying breath, she tried again. "I heard you and Carol were...er." Her mind groped for an innocuous term. "In a partnership."

Some tremor set his loose clothes shaking. Hands pressed over his mouth, he uttered muffled whooping sounds.

Was he laughing or crying? Louise couldn't tell. "I'm so sorry," she repeated, conscious of Shadow's low growl.

Whatever emotion had gripped the fellow, it ceased quite as abruptly. When his forefinger tipped back the ridiculous hat, the rheumy eyes' sudden sharpness surprised her.

"Too curious for her own good," he muttered. His fingers pinched the trembling lips as if to still them. His voice shook, saying, "You think Carol would stoop to the likes of me?"

His crowing sounded forced to Louise. Nor did he expect an answer. "More fool me to think she'd marry me when old man Benson went the way of all flesh." He peered at Louise with a sneer. "Know what she did?"

Louise shook her head, though the question was rhetorical.

"Laughed me right in the ugly mug. 'Marry you? Might as well wed the bellringer of Notre Dame.'"

"Oh, my God," whispered Louise, appalled at the cruelty.

"Only spoke what everyone's saying behind my back," he said, quite sober now. "We were good friends for so many years, I'd forgotten what I looked like to her."

A wave of compassion made Louise reach out. She dropped her hand when their glances connected. Pity was the ultimate insult, she realized.

Matter of fact, she said, "Sorry it didn't work out for you. After a nasty divorce, my opinion of marriage has hit rock bottom."

Furrowed skin around his thin lips deformed in what might pass for a smile.

It encouraged her to change topics. "What I meant to ask you, back when you were still friends with Carol, did she ever mention her nephew, young Trevor's dad, giving her a disastrous investment tip?"

"Lost her a packet. That fool of a man went broke. Gullible fellow he was, and she plain greedy." Though he answered readily enough, the questioning tone and flicker in his eyes signaled he expected an explanation in return.

She didn't yield but pushed her luck. "They never spoke again after the incident, did they? Carol held on to her grudges, it seems."

Fingers like talons clawed at his mouth as though to stifle a response. Louise saw how gnarled the hand was. Thick veins protruded dark blue.

Still attempting to figure out Carol's personality without revealing what she'd learned thus far, Louise continued vaguely, "But generous to a fault if she liked someone. Isn't that so?"

At this, the little man threw back his head as far as his hunched posture allowed and reverted to his habitual shrieking mad act.

"Blood-sucking viper! Gets her fangs into you and never lets go."

With that vampire image of the late Carol Benson, the dear departed's former beau scurried off.

Chapter Twenty-Six

After stowing away the dog food and providing both pets with new toys, a wind-up furry mouse for Magic, and for Shadow, an equally furry squeaky vaguely resembling a fox, Louise retired upstairs to fix the scratch mat. That done, she settled at the desk up there to focus on her much-neglected editorial duties.

It didn't take long for the kitty to sneak into the loft, the synthetic rodent firmly lodged between her fangs. Louise wound it up for her twice and watched the cat crouch and then pounce in a giant leap. The hapless play mouse got a few whacks from a hooked paw that sent it scooting under the bed. Magic eyed Louise expectantly.

"Don't think I'd crawl on my knees to retrieve your toy. It's your job."

After a disdainful glance at both the bed and Louise, the kitty opted for a thorough grooming session.

With a roll of her eyes, Louise returned to the laptop screen to devote her full attention to a client's manuscript she'd received that day. For the next hour, the urban fantasy world engrossed her.

Once, Louise thought fleetingly of Alfred out in the yard and wondered if she should check on him. Reluctant to break her concentration, she resisted the impulse. Only her long training prevented her mind from revisiting all she'd learned today. Reflection must wait.

Despite her absorption, a familiar sound teased the fringes of awareness. With a jolt, the synapses of her brain fired. Louise spun around in her chair so violently her back muscles screamed in protest.

"Kitty!" The involuntary shout startled Louise more than the cat, who stood upright, sharpening her front claws in the same groove as before, scratch mat pushed aside.

"What's wrong with the new mat? Looks just like the tattered one downstairs." Maybe this one smelled too new, though she'd rubbed catnip over the carpeted surface and filled the pouch on its back, just like the shop clerk recommended.

As if tuning into her thoughts, Magic set the mat swinging with a few well-aimed paw swipes. An idea of how to trick the fussy cat crossed Louise's mind. No time but the present to test it out.

Scratch mat unhooked, Louise went to exchange it downstairs for its worn and balding cousin. A few minutes later, she viewed her handiwork critically. Still might need a screw at the bottom to keep it in place, but it should do for now.

"There, kitty. You like it?" Louise asked the cat, who'd been observing her every move. Beyond thoughtful paw licking, Magic didn't respond.

"Have it your way," Louise said and awakened the laptop to peruse the manuscript. She'd barely found her last edit and proceeded to the next paragraph when the drywall scraping started again.

Mindful of her back, Louise swiveled slowly but didn't bother to comment. Paws braced against the wall, the cat's head turned to face her. Amber eyes flashed uncannily.

"I give up," Louise muttered. "For now, mind you. Once the drawer units are in place, you won't have a wall there to sharpen your claws."

The idea appealed and gave the impetus to check in with her contractor, who'd promised to come back soon to add the much-needed storage. There'd been a boarded-up under-eaves space that might once have been some sort of closet. Worried mice might get into the loft bedroom from the wall cavities, Louise agreed to temporary measures, replacing the ill-fitting plywood sheet with drywall. She needed to recheck the pre-purchase photos she'd taken to make sure this was the spot they'd marked for the storage units.

Her concentration broken, Louise decided on a coffee break. In truth, she admitted to herself she wanted to flip through the photos on her iPad. Armed with a mug and the device, she soon resettled at the desk. The cat perched behind the open laptop lid.

Louise scrolled the iPad's photo library until she found the ones she'd shown to Raymond. He'd been right. Images of the kitchen, bath, and living room bore witness to the marvelous transformation job her contractor accomplished. The family photo she'd seen in Zoe's living room must have been taken against the wall downstairs. Though, the presale photo didn't show the same furniture. She swiped on to the photos of the loft, zoomed in on some pics, and smiled when she recognized some artwork.

'Ew! What an ugly wall-to-wall carpet.' Even now, her mind reproduced a fleeting whiff of the musty odor. Maybe age had impaired Carol's sense of smell. She certainly hadn't been too hard up to invest in regular house and carpet cleaning. If she could afford to lend the young couple a down-payment, take back a mortgage, and spare $10,000 for her ex-lover in her will, it wasn't stinginess either.

"Make that an ex-friend," Louise said to the kitty. "I doubt your nemesis and Carol ever were lovers. I guess your person simply wasn't house-proud."

Lighter patches on the walls underscored that the entire place hadn't seen a lick of paint in a decade or more. In her mid-eighties, Carol might've disliked the upheaval and mess of floor replacement and paint jobs. It certainly wasn't a lack of good taste. The woman's artistic preference, also evident in the shots of the loft, showed a keen sense of aesthetics.

A couple of the pictures finally showed what she'd been looking for. She shuddered as she zoomed in on one of them. Were those ragged gaps at the bottom of the old plywood sheet mouse holes? The idea of rodents having once invaded her serene bedroom and might again roam the under-eaves space next winter was the stuff of nightmares. Serious mouse-proofing must come first on the contractor's to-do list.

As she glanced up from the iPad's screen, her eyes met the kitty's stare. A slow blink veiled the yellow irises.

Louise laughed and tickled the white spot below Magic's chin.

"I know what you're thinking, kitty. Only a trusty cat mouse-proofs a home. Nice try," she added as the pink tongue reached for her finger. Impatient now to get the storage affair done, she shot her contractor a quick email. Better not disturb his working hours with a text or call, she figured.

From below came a faint knocking, followed by Shadow's sharp bark. Magic leaped off the desk and scuttled under the bed.

Less excitable than her companions, Louise ambled downstairs.

Forewarned by the pooch's low growl, she hung on to his collar while easing the door open. A large pot of luscious greenery, dotted with violet and blue blooms, swung to and fro in her line of vision. A masculine hand suspended the massive planter aloft.

The bearer's face craned around. "Peace offering. Will you forgive me?"

"Goodness, Dennis. Were we at war? There's nothing to forgive." Beside her, Shadow strained to get out.

Though the dog no longer growled, Dennis stepped off the front stoop onto the walkway, making room for Louise to join him outside.

"You have every reason to be angry with me, Louise. When the police spoke to me this morning, they asked about the miserable supermarket flower. I felt thoroughly ashamed of myself." A contrite grimace accompanied the words.

"No big deal," Louise said mechanically, her mind wondering if Raymond took the foxglove incident far more seriously than she did.

"First, I thought, why didn't Louise just toss the darn plant into the rubbish bin instead of involving the police? But then I was so glad I found out about it. Even the hard way." He mustered what she assumed to be his version of a frank smile. It bore traces of a well-honed sales pitch.

"If anything, the police involved themselves," she said. "The sergeant literally stumbled upon the little pot at my door. When he recognized the foxglove, he worried this pooch here might nibble it. The leaves are extremely toxic. But the whole plant is. So, he offered to take it off my hands. His wife's a keen gardener."

Such an elaborate explanation should lull him into a confiding mood. Dennis, however, carried on with his own agenda, she thought, suppressing a wry smile.

"So, here I am," he said, swinging the planter aloft again, "bringing a safe offering. The florist included a hook if you'd like me to hang it here." He pointed to the portico's support beam.

"How thoughtful and kind of you, Dennis. A perfect spot out of my pooch's and little Daniel's reach." Though to her own mind, such solicitude seemed overkill. Perhaps it was in keeping with his purveyor mentality.

"Rest assured, these lovelies are absolutely safe." He dug into his shirt pocket and handed her a slip of paper. "I insisted the florist list the names of the plants so you can google them."

"My, you went out of your way, Dennis. No need at all, but it's so sweet to take such trouble."

"Not at all, Louise. I'll just pop in downstairs if you don't mind. There ought to be a ladder."

"Er, my ladder isn't in the crawlspace. Give me a second. I'll get it from the closet." She waved vaguely at the entrance behind her. Did he go through all this rigmarole for an excuse to invade the bowels of her home again?

"Splendid," he said unabashed and lowered the planter. "Let me help you."

When the odious man stepped off the walkway onto the front stoop as if to follow her inside, Shadow rose with a growl. The pooch's instinctive reaction suited Louise.

"Sorry, Dennis, my guard dog can be inhospitable. But thanks anyway." No way, she'd invite the number one suspect into her house.

When she returned with the folding step stool, Shadow hugging her side, Dennis was pacing the driveway, whistling a toneless tune.

He rushed to relieve her of her light burden and elaborately tried for just the right spot to suspend the large pot, asking repeatedly, "How about here? Take a step back. Maybe a little to the left?" and so on, until she insisted it was perfect.

The operation completed, Louise admitted the luscious planter made the portico even more charming. She thanked Dennis and praised his sense of aesthetics.

"Your mother and I," she added, "had something in common, I discovered."

The preening at her praise gave way to wary interest. "Eh? What's that?"

"We both like the same painters. If you plan on selling some of her watercolors, let me know. Depends on the asking price, of course."

His frown deepened as she spoke. Now, he shook his head. "You've lost me, Louise. I've no clue what paintings you're talking about." A cunning expression narrowed his eyes. "When did you see my mother's stuff? Was it still here? I mean, you must have viewed the house before you bought it."

"Er. No. Not quite." Louise hedged. "Some artwork was still in the house. Didn't your lawyer provide an inventory? As Carol's son and her heir, I presume." She left it dangling.

Puce blotches darkened his tanned face. His cynical bark didn't sound amused. It made Shadow jump to attentiveness.

"So did I. What a joke." The sour moue spoke more than the words.

"Oh?"

Her gentle interjection worked.

"Mind you," he said, recovering his boisterous demeanor, "my lawyers are on to it. Undue influence. Old women are easily swayed by wheedling youngsters and nostalgic to boot." His arm swept the neighboring properties on both sides.

"Wills can hold such unpleasant surprises, don't they?" Louise said soothingly while her mind registered Dennis's lawyers must have apprised him of the terms of Carol's last testimony. Otherwise, he wouldn't glare so vindictively toward Mr. Simpson's place.

Lawyers of the heir presumptive would request immediate access to the will, regardless of Carol's stipulations against a reading until after probate. As she'd suspected, if he knew of Gilbert Simpson's legacy, the same held for the treasure clause, as she called the codicil in her mind. Hence his eagerness to search her place. Carol's lawyer apparently denied him access to it during probate.

With a start, she realized the man watched her intensely without speaking.

To cover her interest, she composed her features into an empathetic expression and said, "It's so upsetting when family disputes overshadow grief."

He blustered. "None of my doing. I won't have them swindle me out of what's mine."

"Ay. What a tough situation. Money trouble never goes alone, does it? The start-up you mentioned didn't pan out, I was so sorry to see. A business going belly-up is awful. Believe me, I'm well aware from my ex-husband's business efforts going awry." Only her ex, she thought, had cunningly secured his assets offshore to save them both from his creditors and the divorce negotiations.

"What?" An ugly red marred the tan again. "What do you know about my business?"

"My, I'm so sorry. The idea of start-ups intrigues me now that I'm self-employed. When I googled the business you mentioned, a bankruptcy notice popped up. What a disappointment for you." As her rambling didn't soothe the entrepreneurial feathers, Louise stopped.

With a delayed guffaw, he assured her, "Losses are write-offs. Part of the game, dear lady." The grin puffing out his cheeks didn't affect the calculating stare. "Didn't you say you freelance? Better get ready for loss. Got to roll with the punches."

"My recent divorce prepared me well." Her tone remained conversational as if they were businesspeople trading experience. "It taught me all about recovery, too. As the man said, I feel your pain."

"Oops. Put my foot in. Sorry about reviving memories. Geez, I wondered about a lady like you living alone. A dog isn't much company." He leaned toward her, prompting her to step back.

"Dogs are the best companions, I'd say. Plus, the cat—" She broke off, regretting mentioning the kitty. Was Magic part of the estate? Would the son inherit her? But no. Zoe said Auntie entrusted them with the cat. Might the will override the oral agreement? Why hadn't Carol made provisions for the kitty? Maybe Estelle forgot to mention it.

Louise pulled up short. What was she thinking? She merely was the kitty's foster mom. Sadness washed over her.

"Is something wrong? Aren't you feeling well? You've gone all pale. Should I help you inside?"

The man's concerned yet insinuating voice brought her back to her senses. Shadow's snout nudging her hand restored her equilibrium.

"I'm quite alright, Dennis. Thanks. Something came to mind that I need to check. It disconcerted me for a moment." Her hand stroked the pooch's silky head and neck. The warmth bucked her up.

"Goodness," she added, "I've kept you standing here far too long, Dennis. Again, thank you kindly for this gorgeous gift. Lovely of you to beautify my entranceway."

"My pleasure. Least I could do." He stepped back and shook a playful finger in parting. "Now, don't you go tale-telling to your police cronies again. Keep your nose clean, is what I always say."

Taken aback, Louise watched him stride whistling along her drive until the trees hiding the lane swallowed him.

Surely, he wasn't threatening her, was he?

Chapter Twenty-Seven

Just after 4:30 that afternoon, a text came in from a number Louise didn't recognize. She frowned at the snippet '5 pm ok? Can...' on the home screen.

Whatever was that all about? Her thumbprint already unlocked and opened the app.

> 5 pm ok? Can spare 30 min for your junk. Kendra

Louise sighed. With so many distractions, Cascade proved a trial for her work ethic. Still, she was keen on chatting with the antique lady, who'd been thick as thieves with the victim. Wasn't that what Owen had said?

She sped off a thumbs-up. The timing coincided with Shadow's needs. If Kendra was okay with dogs, she thought, an off-leash outing would please the pooch who loved bouncing along free as a bird.

When a slightly battered delivery van drove up, its white paint bleeding brown tears from rust spots, Louise clipped on Shadow's leash just in case. Last minute, she remembered to lock the front door. Mr. Simpson's sneaking and Dennis Benson's impromptu visits taught her caution.

"Hello, Kendra," she called when the shopkeeper slid out of the driver's seat, clad in well-worn pull-on pants with a crumpled blouse tucked in haphazardly. The waistband's elastic strained over her ample stomach. A woman perfectly at ease with her spreading middle and galloping middle age, Louise acknowledged. With a pang of envy, she thought of her self-imposed guilt trip whenever she indulged in rich cakes or fast food.

As Kendra banged the vehicle door shut, Louise considered the woman's fluffy strawberry hair. "Did you bring a hat?" she asked. "Would you like to borrow one of mine? The blackflies are out in droves."

"Don't bother. I've got this." Kendra whipped a small bottle from her pants pocket.

Both Louise and the pooch jumped back when the antique lady pushed the trigger, and a cloud of noxious insecticide fumes fouled the air. A low, rumbling growl vibrated in Shadow's barrel chest as he pressed against Louise's leg.

"Want some?" Their visitor proffered the bottle.

"No thanks. We stick with natural bug repellents," Louise said. "If you're ready, we'll go this way." She pointed down the slope, along the fence on Mr. Simpson's side. "My dog discovered the easiest route."

"Lead on," said Kendra.

They passed the end of the fence without encountering her unpredictable neighbor.

Louise asked, "Do you mind my dog running free? He's used to it."

"Just keep him away from me," her companion said gruffly. "Never could abide their slobbering."

Mildly offended, Louise lied for the pooch. "Shadow doesn't drool." At least not as bad as some, her mind added.

"They all do," the woman claimed, dismissing the entire species with a wave of her pudgy hand.

Yet, when Louise unclipped the leash, her setter-lab cross didn't take advantage of his freedom but heeled voluntarily. Against his usual easygoing nature, he flattened his ears back in wariness, she noticed.

Pesky, tiny flies encircled them, out to suck their lifeblood. Swatting left and right, Louise trudged through the budding foliage with Kendra in her wake. Rain and sun worked wonders for speeding up nature. Another week, Louise guessed, and the last traces of a long and hard winter would be erased.

Birds sang jubilantly, chipmunks chirped, and squirrels chattered. A chorus of tadpoles joined in. 'There's a pond close by,' Louise thought, enjoying the spring symphony.

Now that she knew the way, the distance to the lower part of her property felt much shorter. Still, emerging from the dense woods into the open field had Louise exclaim in delight.

"How lovely! What an amazing view." She turned to the woman sidling up on her other side, well out of the pooch's reach. "Isn't it just made for a gazebo?"

The view across the river gorge dazzled in its green finery. Clouds in shades from white to deep inky pewter at the far horizon threw the cliffs on the opposite side into stark relief. One villa perched atop sparkled in blinding white.

"A folly," Kendra's flat voice remarked.

"Eh?"

"Your gazebo. Folks called them follies."

"Oh, that. Yes, I know," said Louise.

Her companion's shrewd glance swept the field and came to rest on the distant vista.

"Storm's moving in." The icy-blue gaze returned to Louise. "Let's sort this before the weather breaks."

"Goodness, you're right." Out in the open, the wind picked up, weaving last year's brittle stalks and this spring's delicate grass and fluffy dandelions. With every gust, zillions of spores sailed forth.

Louise readjusted to the task at hand. "The heap's over there."

"So I see," commented the antique dealer dryly and led the way down the sloping field.

Casually, Louise introduced the topic foremost on her mind. "Dennis came by again this afternoon."

From the corner of her eye, she caught Kendra's piercing glance. Habitual, she decided, when no response followed.

Without emphasis, she went on, "He brought a lovely hanging planter for out front. Kind of him, wasn't it?"

"If you say so."

Louise laughed. "Do I detect a touch of sarcasm? You aren't a fan of the man from down yonder, I take it."

Her companion heaved an exaggerated sigh. "Didn't I tell you? His own mother thought him a loser. Wouldn't trust him as far as I can throw him."

They reached the junk pile, and the dealer prodded some rusty implements with her foot. "Garbage," she commented. Without meeting Louise's gaze, she muttered, "Watch who you get friendly with."

"No danger of making friends with Dennis Benson," Louise said, and catching Shadow's attention, gave a quick signal with her finger for him to sit and wait off to the side. "Some paintings from Carol's collection caught my interest. Purely business, you might say."

As expected, the dealer's ears pricked up. Cheeks puffed and red from the exertion of bending to extract a wheeled seed roller, Kendra swung around, eyes narrowed against the sun breaking through the darkening clouds.

"How come you know of Carol's collection?"

"I caught sight of one or the other and recognized the painters," Louise said. "If Dennis—or Trevor, for that matter—inherits the artwork, I might bid for those. If the paintings are still there."

With surprising muscle strength in such a rotund person, the antique lady pulled the seeder free and examined it intently.

"Worth keeping," she said. "Give me a hand."

Together, they dragged the roller a few yards off to the side.

"Pass me that chunk of wood there," the dealer ordered.

When Louise handed her the weathered end of a four-by-four, Kendra wedged it against the rusted cast iron roller and lifted the ornamental push bar. Its upper end resembled an old-fashioned bicycle handlebar.

"With a bit of elbow grease, it'll be quite attractive," she said, still puffing. "Might not fetch a lot but adds charm to your old place. Or I can find you a buyer."

'Thus speaks the clever dealer.' Louise suppressed a smile. Aloud, she said, "Must weigh a ton. How would we haul it back?" Her glance traveled from the woods to the vista. A genuine smile tugged at her lips. "Maybe it'll grace my folly."

Her eyes swept the surrounding area. She shivered, recalling the sheer drop to the river below. Didn't bear thinking of if Shadow or one of her new friends would wander toward the end of the field. The overhang would continue to erode and wasn't safe to be stepped on. Fence off the perimeter? Would ruin the view.

But how would they bring in equipment and lumber to build her gazebo? The reality check sobered her and made her shoulders sag in disappointment.

Behind her, Kendra said in a bored tone, "Up to you." Then, more urgently, "Hear it?"

Deflated, her writer's bower dream dissolving, Louise said without interest, "What? The wind?"

"Hm, no. Sounded like a cat's shriek."

Louise whirled around. "Where? I didn't hear a thing," but realized thoughts of the folly had tuned out the now.

"Came from over there." Kendra pointed.

Louise froze. "From the ledge?" Not waiting for an answer, she stepped forward. The wind gusted and brought with it the rushing rumble of the cascades below.

Surely, Magic couldn't have found an escape route from the house and followed? Were all the windows closed? The sharp claws could shred mosquito screens in seconds. What if the silly kitty strayed too far and tumbled over the brink?

Twice the cat had done it when stretching on the edge of the mattress. The cartoonish flaying of paws seemed comical. Not the least bit funny when the drop was a hundred feet rather than one.

Mental images of disaster spurred Louise to investigate. Even if it were someone else's cat in peril, save it she must.

By a trick of her ears, the rumbling now came from behind. Disoriented, Louise glanced over her shoulder.

And screamed.

A sharp bark answered.

Hurdling toward her came the lawn roller, its handlebar bouncing uselessly off the rough ground. In its wake stumbled Kendra in an unsteady jog, arms stretched in vain for the handle.

As she threw herself sideways out of the runaway roller's path, Louise saw Shadow take a giant leap right against Kendra's back, flattening the dealer facedown into the weeds.

The woman shrieked like the furies.

With barely a yard to spare to the prone Louise, the lawn roller spun over the edge.

Louise scrambled to her feet, yelling, "No! Shadow. Off!"

Her own outcry mingled with the shrieking of metal crashing over rocks, reverberating in ripples through the valley's echo chamber.

'That could've been me.' The phrase ricocheted in Louise's brain as she scampered up the slope. Her hand gripping the collar, she yanked the growling dog off the woman, who'd gone stock-still.

"Oh, my God! I'm so sorry, Kendra. Are you alright?" Louise dragged Shadow a few yards, fished for the leash, and tied him to the axle of a plow stuck fast in the junk pile. "Wait," she ordered and hastened back to aid Kendra.

Much shaken, face beet-red, the woman sat in the grass.

When Louise offered both hands to haul her up, the dealer found her voice. "Is that all he gets for attacking me? I'd give him a sound beating."

"I'm terribly sorry, Kendra. Please—"

"That dog is vicious!"

"Shadow never did anything like this before. Hitting is pointless or worse. He won't connect it with what happened before." Louise glanced at the pooch, who whined anxiously. His behavior seriously worried her. Thank God the woman appeared outraged rather than harmed.

"I'd kick the living daylight out of the mutt." Swatting at the proffered hands, the antique lady scrambled to her feet.

Thunder rolled in the gathering clouds.

"We'd better head back if you feel recovered from the scare," Louise said, glancing at the darkening sky.

Her eyes fell on the soil-stained pants of her still-incensed companion. Bits and pieces of weeds and grit stuck to the shirt, no longer tucked into the waistband.

"Sorry your clothes got all dirty. I'll pay for the cleaning," Louise offered.

The antique lady brushed traces of rust and soil off her hands and wiped them on the pants legs. With a venomous stare at the dog, she said, "I'd worry about your mutt, not the clothes, if I were you. Could get sued for a stunt like that."

Chastised, Louise untied the pooch, who eyed her guiltily. Of course, he only reacted to the atmosphere, she realized, but muttered to him under her breath, "Now we're both in the doghouse."

As they hurried through the woods toward the house, Louise silently thanked heavens, or her insurance company, for a generous liability provision.

To Kendra trudging ahead, she repeated her apologies, adding, "We've got some serious retraining to do. Back to dog school. Still, the incident is completely out of character for my dog."

"Pshaw. That's what all dog owners claim when their beasts attack someone or even kill a kid."

"Goodness. Shadow has no murderous intentions. He somehow got the wrong impression. Or, most likely, misunderstood my cry when the roller came at me. Plus, the brewing thunderstorm affects him. Dogs are so sensitive to atmospheric pressure."

As if he understood her desperate defense of him, the pooch pressed close and nudged her hand.

Without bothering to look back at her, the dealer assumed a hectoring tone. "You know, Louise, our municipality takes reports of dog attacks extremely seriously. Vicious dogs get destroyed."

Louise blanched. Her hand gripped the leash tightly. Such cases hit the news in Toronto on rare occasions. Before she could speak, she cleared her throat but still sounded hoarse. "Come on, Kendra. This pooch never hurt a fly. Like I said—" The dealer's icy glare stopped Louise.

"I'm not saying I'll report it. This time." A stubby finger jabbed toward the dog, making his chest rumble in a growl. "Get him a muzzle. He could have bitten me."

A loud clap of thunder cut off Louise's protest.

"Run for cover," yelled Kendra and fell into a waddling trot. "Lightning's dangerous in the woods."

With no death wish, Louise hastened after the dealer. Shadow stuck to her side as though he didn't understand the sudden commotion yet sensed trouble.

Chapter Twenty-Eight

The next day, Louise felt on edge as she sat by the living room window, staring unseeingly at the laptop. Lines of her client's urban fantasy seemed to dance on the screen.

As if disturbed by her unrest, the kitty's head peeked over the rim of the Mac's lid. Amber irises fixing Louise, the black cheek rubbed against the laptop's rounded corner. Only Shadow slumbered peacefully, sprawled on the floor, rear end under the table.

Yet, a sense of time running out pervaded.

Last night, sleep had deserted her for long stretches. Jittery from her near escape at the cliff and a nagging worry the antique lady might still report Shadow, Louise had tossed under the duvet and pounded her pillows.

"You weren't happy with me at all, keeping you awake," she now told the kitty. "Blame it on this dratted case. It's getting me down."

For whenever she'd dozed off, she'd come to with a start certain the answers hovered at the precipice of consciousness. In her attempts to grasp them, they tumbled back into the unfathomable recesses of the mind.

Impatient with her flights of fancy, Louise forked her fingers through her short hair as if brushing away the cobwebs of the night, muttering,

"Count your lucky stars." Unthinkable how yesterday's incident might have ended.

"Attack of the runaway roller. Sounds like a catchy title," she told the kitty with a wry attempt to see the funny side. "Our friend down there just misunderstood." She pointed at the pooch by her feet, letting sleeping dogs lie. "Nothing vicious about him. He's so gentle with you, kitty."

The cat blinked in response.

A knocking from out front invaded the stillness of the moment.

Shadow raised his snout, sniffed, and yipped. Nails scrabbling on the hard floor, he bounded to the door.

Resigned, Louise followed and grabbed the excited dog by the collar before checking who came knocking.

It was the gardener who stood well back from the portico as if not to crowd her. Baseball cap sideways, wisps of longish hair escaping the haphazard ponytail, his extended arm proffered sheets of none too clean paper.

"Well, hello, Alfred," Louise greeted him.

"Hey, Louise. My notes for planting. Sorry, got a bit of soil on it." An almost shy smile creased his lean features.

As Louise let go of the collar to accept the sheets, Shadow pushed past her in exuberant canine greeting. The head nurse-cum-gardener, crouched in obedience to the pooch's demand for a belly rub.

From below, Alfred grinned at Louise. "My cell number's at the bottom. Text me when you've decided. I'll pick up the plants you like at the nursery."

With her eyes on the carefully labeled sketches he'd drawn of flower beds and borders, Louise said, "What a great job, Alfred. I need to google some of the plant names. Did you estimate the costs?" This didn't look cheap, and she hadn't budgeted for gardening supplies yet.

"Ah, not to worry. We're good for this spring. Carol paid ahead for the material. Plus, there ought to be fertilizer and stuff in the old cellar left from last year. Or did it get thrown out?"

"In the crawlspace, you mean? Not sure. I noticed some gardening things."

With a final pat on the dog's back, Alfred rose. "If it's okay by you, I'll inventory what's there and list anything needed. Need to update the account book I kept for Carol."

"My, that's thorough." The man was full of surprises, Louise acknowledged, impressed by his honesty about the advance payment.

He shrugged. "Goes with the territory. In my job, record keeping is second nature." His chin jutted toward the hanging planter. "Looks nice. If you want more, it'll be cheaper getting pots and order extra plants from the nursery. Easy do-it-yourself job, those planters."

"Oh, this one was a gift." She watched Alfred closely, continuing, "From Dennis. Carol's son, you know. So thoughtful of him."

When his lip curled, she added, "Not a favorite with you, is he?"

Alfred picked at his thumbnail with that of his other hand. He didn't look up when he admitted, "Don't know the guy well. Lots of people stress when a parent is in care."

"Not in front of the parent, though," Louise said gently. "I heard Dennis lost his temper while visiting his mom."

Instead of a direct response, Alfred crouched and patted the dog, murmuring, "Can't have folks upsetting my patients. Or else they've got to leave."

"A sensible policy. Did you have to step in?"

His frown reminded her of his professional standing at Rosewood. It must require confidentiality.

"Let me reword," she said. "If I were to start an argument with a patient, say my dad, and even yelled at him, what would happen?"

The head nurse rose and cracked a smile. "We'd compliment you right out of the front door and tell you not to come back if you can't behave yourself."

"Fair enough." Louise grinned back. Soberly, she added, "When Dennis staged his big entrance at Carol's birthday party, you had to remind him to behave, I heard. Sorry, Alfred, there I go again."

Without meeting her eyes, he moved away. For a second, she thought he'd walk off. But he only bent to rummage among the dead leaves under a huge maple tree near her front door, muttering, "Needs sweeping."

When he turned, he held a club-size stick.

Louise's eyes widened. As his arm rose, she ducked behind the portico post in reflex.

"Here, buddy. Fetch!"

Shadow leaped up as if he'd been waiting for the invitation. Tail flying high, he pounded after the projectile when Alfred let loose.

A gleam in the man's eye told Louise he'd cottoned on to her momentary fright.

"Can't trust anyone, can you?" His forefinger wiped below his nose and left a streak of dirt on his upper lip. "How do you think it feels, folks giving me side-eyes? Suspicion written all over their faces. Took a leave of absence. Matron refused to fire me. But I can't be on duty with this going on."

The pooch came between them, nudging his new friend with the stick. Alfred held out his hand, saying, "Give," and threw again.

"For everyone's sake, we must find Carol's killer," Louise said firmly. "Will you help and tell me about the night she died? I understand about confidentiality." She left it dangling.

A fleeting smile hovered around his lips and crinkled the corners of his eyes. "Are you and Nora playing sleuths, Louise? Too serious—"

"Let's leave Nora out of this," Louise cut in.

"Try if you can. Nora is a force to be reckoned with." He shook his head with a low chuckle.

"All the more reason to clear this up before mischief happens."

Though his gaze followed the dog, who was exploring fresh scents in the yard, Louise felt encouraged by Alfred's nod to say, "By the end of Carol's birthday party, did she still seem normal? Were there signs of illness?"

He frowned at her. "If she'd seemed ill, we'd have reacted appropriately. There was nothing you'd not expect after an event like that. Matron and I tried to discourage the whole party idea. But she insisted. Somehow, she got hold of a bottle of her favorite tipple. No surprise, she was flushed and woozy. Mildly intoxicated and overexcited, we assumed."

Glad Alfred appeared willing to share, Louise ventured, "You didn't see who brought the absinthe? Or was it her own bottle?"

"No way she could have sneaked in a bottle," he said without hesitation. "I wheeled her in myself. Picked her up from her room with a wheelchair. I'd have noticed a bottle."

"We know who made the birthday cake and who delivered it," Louise said. "Any guest could slip a bottle in a gift bag."

"So could staff or Matron or I, for that matter," Alfred said wryly. "No need to spare us. My money's on the booze. Much easier to tamper with. Everyone knew how fond Carol was of the vile stuff. I took the glass away when someone had refilled it."

"What did you do with it?"

"Hid it behind the huge vase on the fireplace mantle. Piece of luck that. Next morning, when we found her, I remembered, and it was still there. What with going off duty when the last guests left, I'd forgotten to chuck it. Uma and I sent it to the lab with the other samples."

"Oh? Uma didn't mention it."

"Got her to sign for all we did. Pointless, but still. Uma was rattled after finding Carol. It's only human, and she's just out of nursing school." His hand reached up to scratch his ear, tilting the baseball cap farther down the other side. "Poor girl worried we'd blame her for neglecting the patient during the night. The log for her rounds showed nothing unusual or amiss. She'd done her job alright."

Louise pounced on this. "Of course! You keep records. Do the entries narrow the time of death? And record symptoms observed?"

Alfred heaved a sigh. "Not really. The nurse, who helped her to bed after the party, also assumed Carol was tipsy and a bit disoriented. Nothing unusual in someone of that age to feel drained after an event and wanting to sleep. Carol didn't want to bother with dinner. Said she felt nauseous after the fatty cake. None of that was good for her to begin with. But she told us you only live once."

"A sad irony for sure," said Louise. "When did Uma's shift start?"

"She was on from 9 p.m. until 5 a.m. Last nighttime check was at 11 p.m. Patient was breathing heavily but no more than common in her condition. By the next round, just before Uma was to go off duty at 5, Carol was dead."

"My God. What a shock for the young nurse to have a patient die on her watch."

"You never grow used to it. Or better quit if death no longer affects you. Just my opinion. Take no notice. Reality is, in a place like Rosewood, there's only one way residents leave. Few move on to other facilities. Unless it's the hospice. Means same thing."

The creases in his rugged face seemed to deepen as he spoke. 'Tough to live with.' Shaking off the thought, she asked, "What happened to the bottle?"

"No idea. When I took away Carol's glass, I did a quick check to move the bottle out of Carol's reach. Didn't see it and assumed Uma removed it. Next day, we did a proper search but didn't find it. The cleaning staff stored the leftover wine bottles in a locker with Carol's name. No absinthe bottle. The champagne was empty. Carol loathed the stuff anyway."

Louise watched Alfred scuff the flagstone path with the toe of his heavy work boot, his hands buried deep in his frayed jeans pockets.

"I see," she said deliberately. "At a guess, Alfred, what poison killed Carol?"

He didn't flinch at the blunt question but pushed the cap far back to scratch the hairline. "The cops asked that. Told them I won't hazard a guess unless they show me the lab reports."

"So, you never received the report, did you? Why did the lab take so long, anyway? Doesn't that vitiate the results?" Surprised, Louise realized she hadn't considered this until now that the questions had formed of their own accord.

"They did the testing right away but had a backlog in paperwork. Someone slipped up if you ask me." His boot scuffed faster as he spoke. "Since Covid, lab staff feels totally overworked. I didn't harp on it. Felt uneasy about having sent it to begin with. Once the cops got involved, they put a freeze on things."

"Makes sense. So, no guess at what poison it was? Based on the symptoms, and so on?" Louise felt sure the head nurse would have a good idea, even if he didn't know for certain.

Shadow chose that moment to sidle up. After a perfunctory lick at Louise's hand, he sat next to Alfred, leaning heavily against the man's leg. She could have sworn the pooch was grinning at her, lopsided tongue lolling.

"So much for your reputation as vicious attacker."

"Eh? What's that?" Alfred asked. "Who? Me?"

"Hah, no. We had a situation yesterday. Shadow jumped at Kendra from behind and threw her over. She believes he was attacking her and called him a vicious dog."

Shadow's champion laughed with genuine amusement. "Handsome here, did that? Good for you, buddy." He patted the pooch's head. "Seriously, that woman just loathes dogs, and they sense it, I'd say."

"As long as she doesn't report the incident to the town. Shadow's never done anything like that before." The dog gazed at her with what she hoped was adoration.

"Nah, don't worry." Alfred stood, hands in his pockets again. His face grew somber. "Back to your question. You can figure out the answer for yourself, Louise. Whatever it was acted like alcohol. Other symptoms, like vomiting, occurred about 8 to 12 hours later. Else, Uma would've noticed already on her last nighttime round at 11."

He eyed her to make sure she followed his reasoning. Louise nodded.

"When I saw her shortly before 5 a.m., she hadn't been dead for long. The doctor confirmed that and put her death down to gastrointestinal causes. Blamed us for allowing her to eat rich food and consume alcohol. But the old guy was Carol's GP for ages and knew no one could stop her if she decided about something. The whole village knows that. Or at least the ones on the village committee."

"Her physician passed it off as natural causes?"

"Jeez, Louise. The woman was 86. I don't even know why my guts told me there was something wrong. I just thought a piece of cake and a bit of booze wouldn't kill off someone so strong-willed like Carol, I guess." He shook his head ruefully. "When I told the doc, he got sharp and yelled at me, 'Mind your nursing business and watch what patients get to eat. Leave doctoring to me.'"

With a mumbled, "Excuse me," he took a few steps into the driveway and coughed. Shadow's velvety doggy eyes followed the man as if concerned.

Louise held out her hand, and the dog crossed to her side, tail wagging just the teeniest bit.

"No worries," she whispered to the dog. "You'd be hoarse too if you'd bark as much as humans talk."

Alfred joined them. "Sorry, Louise. Frog in my throat."

"Ew. I should hope not," she joked. "Okay, Alfred. Now give me the answer. What noxious substance fits the case?"

"Don't take my word for it. Without seeing the lab report, it's mere guesswork. I'd say any alcohol like isopropyl or methanol would kill."

"But who would think of using something like that? I mean, one knows not to drink it, but still." Definitely something worth researching, she figured.

"Lots of folks know what such stuff does to you. Homeless alcoholics down just anything when they've hit rock bottom. Addicts no longer care. Jeez, no one would become an addict if they cared about the effects of stuff like heroin or fentanyl." He gazed into the trees' canopy.

"But we aren't talking addiction," Louise reminded him mildly.

"Addicts are not the only ones. Ever read about home distilleries? Amateurs produce some deadly stuff. Worst thing if kids get into stuff like glue-sniffing or drink rubbing alcohol."

Shivers crawled along Louise's arms despite the mild weather and the cardigan she wore. Her mind worked feverishly. The man across from her knew all about addiction. He had the medical knowledge of the modus operandi.

But would he talk so freely if he had done it?

Chapter Twenty-Nine

When Nora's text came in late afternoon, Louise had put in a solid day's labor at the laptop.

The bolded message jumped out at her and made her blanch.

Friends of the late Carol Benson
You are cordially invited
Tonight at 8:00 p.m.
Rosewood Manor — Events room
Light refreshments will be served

Frantically, Louise thumbed a response.

> Nora! You promised not to. Please cancel the invitation. I'll be right over.

The reply came in seconds.

NORA

> I promised to let you know, and I did. Sorry, no, I'm at my physio. Come at 7:15 for a quick dress rehearsal. Signing off now – no phones allowed.

In helpless frustration, Louise pounded the table with her palm.

Magic jumped, either at the slapping sound or Louise's "Ouch!"

"Sorry, kitty, to wake you and your brother. It's okay, Shadow. I'm mad at Nora, not you guys." She stroked ruffled cat and dog fur. The silky warm feeling calmed her just as much as the pets.

How could a woman of Nora's mature years do something so fool-hardy? For a moment, Louise considered calling Raymond but balked at such betrayal. She would, however, urge Nora to do so when she got to Rosewood. Not that Nora would listen.

Louise went in search of her purse, dug out Sgt. Marpel's card, and added his number to speed dial on her mobile.

Over the next two hours, she prepared for the evening's showdown. For the wily actress, she felt sure, planned to trap a killer among the friends of Carol Benson. If any of them showed up.

Such a last-minute invitation, Louise reasoned, would find few takers. Or was only hers last minute? "Don't fret about that," she admonished herself. "Figure out what Poirot would do and take charge."

The kitty and the pooch, who sat awaiting their dinner bowls, meowed and yipped at her monolog. "I take this for agreement rather than a complaint about the slow service."

It was five minutes to eight when Louise descended the elegant staircase at Rosewood Manor, her right arm linked with Mrs. Norton's. Nora, she noticed, trailed her other hand lightly along the smooth wood of the gleaming railing.

Louise's mouth felt dry, not merely from the tense talk in Mrs. Norton's room. Would her sleuthing partner stick to the script or veer into improv?

Uneasily, she glanced at the petite figure by her side. Silvery-white hair immaculately coiffured accentuated the deceptively simple midnight-blue shift. No jiggling bracelets today. A single strand of pearls and a silk scarf in potent shades of blue adorned the classy outfit.

Despite her nervousness, a little smile tugged at Louise's lips. She, too, had opted for power dressing. Conscious it would boost her confidence for the evening, she'd donned a light gray silk blouse matched with tailored black linen trousers. Its sophisticated hidden placket gave her a clean, no-nonsense, authoritative appearance. She'd even spent five minutes styling her short auburn hair with some silky mousse.

Her mind's escapist digression ended abruptly when they reached the foyer. The parlor's double French doors stood wide open. Cast in brilliant light from an antique chandelier and wall sconces, Rosewood's events room appeared too festive for the somber occasion.

As they entered, only one guest awaited. The café proprietor turned around from contemplating the fireplace mantel. Owen's presence gave Louise a twinge in her stomach. So awkward after their last encounter.

"Well, well. The lady of Charlotte. Were you a friend of Carol Benson?" His eyes mocked her.

"Don't be silly, Owen," Nora chided him playfully. "I insisted on Louise joining us. After all, she lives with Carol's restless spirit."

"What?" cried Owen and guffawed. "News to me. Carol haunts the old place on Charlotte?"

Now, he eyed Louise with a mixture of disbelief and mirth. "C'mon, Louise. You don't buy such bunkum. Or do you ladies propose a séance tonight? Ouija board and all?"

Nora's delighted titter forestalled Louise's response. "There's an idea, Louise. Why didn't we think of that?"

Still standing wide-legged in front of the ornamental fireplace screen that guarded a lavish dried flower arrangement rather than logs, Owen drawled, "What's the plan, then?"

"Plan?" asked Nora and fluttered her hands as if dismissing the notion. "Why, it's an impromptu gathering to honor Carol's life and accomplishments. Wherever she is now," the former actress added with a pious gaze at the ceiling, "She'll be pleased."

A phlegmy cough, preceding the familiar cackle, came from a circle of voluminous wing chairs behind them. Louise swiveled to see the wizened visage of her erratic neighbor peek around a chair's backrest. Tonight, a brocaded nightcap crowned the yellowing hair.

"Goodness. Mr. Simpson. I didn't hear you come in." Though she felt sure he'd been there all along. They'd have noticed anyone entering. The sneaky fellow was eavesdropping again.

"Good evening," said Mrs. Norton, slipping into her hostess role. "So kind of you to join us."

Two Rosewood staff members wheeled in a trolley with refreshments and distracted Louise's attention. Amused, she noticed Nora wasn't taking any chances. Commercially wrapped single-portion snacks and beverages in cans and bottles made for boring, albeit presumably safe, choices. Not tamper-proof for a devious killer, Louise thought, but the best one could do.

While the staff sat out their offerings, the other guests arrived. Most entered quietly and subdued.

From the sidelines, Louise watched. The hostess greeted each newcomer graciously with somber affability. Owen kept his alpha stance in front of the grate. Mr. Simpson remained hidden unless one stepped around to face his cushiony lair.

"I'm so glad you're here, Louise." Arms stretched out, Zoe bore down on her but stopped short of an embrace. "I didn't want to come, but Trevor said we must."

The anxious expression spoke volumes. Though lovely, the deep forest green of Zoe's calf-length dress emphasized her pointed features and the hollows of her pale cheeks.

"Good to see you both," said Louise, but felt like a traitor. "A get-together in honor of your aunt wouldn't be the same without her loved ones." Eager for a pleasant topic, she asked, "How's little Daniel?"

The dad grinned as he joined them. "Up to his monstrous tricks, I'd say. He's at a sleepover with his playmate." Despite the casual jeans and T-shirt, he didn't appear laid back. Louise detected worry lines around the wide mouth.

"Daniel's just adorable," she said.

"Try living with him," joked Trevor. "Hey, by the way, how's the cat?"

"The kitty's no trouble at all." No way she would betray her foster pet and mention the irritating wall scratching.

"Don't think we forgot about finding a home for her," Zoe said, all anxious again.

"Actually," Louise began, unsure if this was a good time to raise the topic, "I meant to talk to you about—"

A commotion caused by a loud voice cut her off and drew everyone's attention.

"My dear Mrs. Norton, as the son, I should have been consulted." Dennis loomed over Nora, making her look frail and diminutive. "It's inconsiderate to invite my mother's friends behind my back."

Though Nora stood her ground, Louise excused herself from her neighbors but heard Trevor shush Zoe's hiss, "The creep!"

As she crossed the room without conspicuous haste, Louise caught sight of Jessie from the patisserie in conversation with the antique lady. The shopkeepers resembled each other not only in their stocky, ample figures, magnified by clingy flower-pattered dresses, but in the redness of their fleshy faces. Neither one looked pleased.

Next to Jessie hovered a scrawny, middle-aged man. When he laid a timid hand on Jessie's arm, Louise assumed him to be Jeremy, the baker from Petit Four You.

By the time she'd crossed the large room to join Nora Norton, another man had subdued the irate Dennis. If she'd seen the man spruced up like this on the street, Louise thought, she might have done a double take before recognizing Alfred.

The short-sleeved, white button-down cotton shirt worn over equally spotless dark blue denim pants looked casually dressy. No cap hid the longish hair caught in a tidy ponytail. Freshly washed, it turned out to be silky blond.

Scrubbed like this, he'd shed several years. Early forties, Louise guessed.

"Hey, Louise," he greeted her as Nora steered a scowling Dennis toward the refreshments.

"Alfred. Good to see you. You look nice and relaxed," Louise said. Somehow, the head nurse off-duty appeared more at home in Rosewood's parlor than any of those present. Certainly far more than Uma, who stood transfixed by the French doors as if of two minds to enter. The girl twisted her long black braid nervously between her capable hands. A wine-colored tunic over wide-cut beige cotton pants was faintly reminiscent of her professional wear, if only in shape.

Following Louise's glance, Alfred's eyes rested kindly on the young nurse. No resentment showed against the employee who'd ratted on him to the police.

Surprised, Louise said, "I hope you don't mind my saying so, but your leave of absence does you a world of good. You seem so much more at ease. Funny, you look perfectly at home off-duty at the manor."

For the first time, she heard him laugh, albeit softly.

"It kind of makes sense," he said, laughter still in his voice. "In a round-about way, I am at home."

"You mean because you spend most of your days here?"

"More because my ancestors built this place. Rosewood is our family name. Instead of bequeathing the manor to my dad, my grandparents formed a trust dedicated to a seniors' living facility."

"Goodness, I'd no idea." As she spoke, Louise cringed at having stereo-typed Alfred.

"Few people know." Alfred eyed her keenly. "Nothing to do with my job here."

Though the thought had crossed her mind, Louise assured him, "Of course not. Were your parents and you okay with the trust idea?" In today's real estate market, the manor must represent a significant value.

"My dad wasn't interested," said Alfred. His gaze swept the room. "As a kid, I resented losing my favorite playground." A regretful expression flitted over his features. He brushed his cheek with the back of his hand. "Resentment was my middle name as a teenager. Took a while to grow out of."

He hooked his thumbs into the pockets of his jeans and grinned ruefully. "Hey, I'm still working on it. Don't get me wrong. My grandparents did the right thing."

"I agree," said Louise. "In its present function, the manor brings happiness to so many people." 'Except to Carol,' her mind added unasked.

"Alfred?" came Nora's voice from a few steps away. "Would you and Owen bring over some chairs? I thought it would be so nice to sit together and share our memories of Carol's life."

'And death,' Louise added to herself. 'Here we go.'

"Jeez, is she serious?" muttered Alfred under his breath. "Are you in on this?"

Louise was spared an answer as Owen sauntered up. "Okay, man. You heard the lady. Let's get the show on the road." Leaning close to Louise, he whispered, "Is this your doing?"

In righteous indignation, Louise retorted louder than intended, "It is not! Believe me, I had nothing to do with this."

Mrs. Norton interrupted, rounding up her guests. "Leave Louise alone, Owen. I've got a mind of my own and take full credit for our little gathering here."

The head nurse, who'd followed the exchange with narrowed eyes, murmured, "Right. Don't we know it?" And to Owen, "Let's shift those chairs."

"Louise, would you shut the French doors, dear? I think everyone's here now." Nora propelled Louise forward with a gentle but determined hand to the elbow.

Glancing over her shoulder, Louise scanned the room. Counting herself and Gilbert Simpson, whose hunched figure lurked behind the broad wing of his chair, there were a dozen people in the room. She saw Dennis Benson grab another of the bulky armchairs in front of the draped bay window. Uma had pulled up the smallest chair right next to Mr. Simpson's. The patisserie owners, Jessie and Jeremy, waited with the antique dealer, Kendra, for Alfred to position chairs. Trevor lent Owen a hand, watched anxiously by Zoe.

"I don't see Matron. Isn't she joining us?" Louise whispered to Nora.

"She's had prior commitments in Toronto. I'm sure she'll pop by if she gets back before we're finished," Nora said sweetly.

Offended, Louise eyed her hostess. "You didn't tell me." During their colloquium upstairs, the cunning lady had already admitted to misleading Matron Juniper. Allegedly, not wanting to complicate matters, Nora claimed to organize a meeting of book club aficionados.

"Promise to stick to the script," Louise hissed. "This is not a solo performance. If things go awry, we call Raymond. Don't you forget that."

"Trust me, dear," murmured Nora, then tittered coyly as if she and Louise had shared a naughty joke.

When Louise turned after closing the doors to the deserted entrance foyer, the seating was arranged in an orderly oval. Across from the French doors, three wing chairs stood in front of the bay window, with Dennis in the center, flanked by Nora to the left and Owen to the right. Mr. Simpson's now faced Jeremy and Jessie on the far right.

Louise made for the empty chair next to Jessie, glad to have Zoe and spouse on her other side. Beside Trevor loafed Alfred, legs stretched out, feet crossed at the ankles. He'd opted for a straight chair that backed on the French doors. The antique dealer on his left scowled at Uma, who listened amiably to Mr. Simpson. He peered at the girl with what must pass in his books for a smile.

Though Louise expected the hostess to address the friends of Carol Benson, it was Owen who took charge. Fingers braced on the knees of his black jeans, sleeves of the sand-colored soft shirt rolled up, he leaned forward.

His gaze swept the assembly and rested for a moment with a frown on Louise before addressing their hostess.

"Now, spill, Nora. What's the real point of all this?"

Chapter Thirty

The actress rose to the occasion. Her delighted, trilling laugh caught everyone's attention.

"That's telling." She mimed a slap on Owen's arm.

Distracted, Louise pictured Nora in a Regency play equipped with a lacy fan for such playful gestures. Rosewood's elegant parlor was a tailor-made setting.

Dennis, on Nora's other side, lost his patience, if he'd ever had any. He harrumphed and blustered. "I wish you would tell us. Really, Mrs. Norton, I don't like it one bit. What is this all about?"

"Can't you guess?" Poised and stern, Nora's tiny figure exuded authority. "As her son, you ought to be the first to ask: Who killed Carol?"

A collective gasp ran through the audience, carefully watched by Louise. Next to her, Zoe uttered a soft cry, causing Trevor to cover his wife's hand with his own.

Mr. Simpson cackled belatedly. As though it were the overture to a comedy, he waggled a talon-like finger in Dennis's direction, whose face crimsoned in response.

"I knew it." Owen's sarcastic tone held an accusatory note. His eyes fixed on Louise across the expanse of the oriental rug. "The lady of Charlotte is behind this. She as much as accused me of being a killer."

"I did not!" The outcry hardly escaped her lips when Louise's mind admitted he might well feel suspected.

"Give me some credit, Owen," Nora cut in. "This is all my idea." With a dramatic sweep of her hand, she included the assembly. "Except for Louise, each one of us could have murdered Carol. The question is, who brought the means?"

The gray-blue eyes went from face to face. Silence descended on the room like a paralyzing fog.

'No one's going to speak,' thought Louise, 'for fear of seeming guilty.'

When the suspense reached its height, the actress's thrilling voice continued, "Who had a motive?"

This time, restlessness gripped her listeners. Low murmurs arose to be drowned by Dennis's noisy protest. "What utter rot! I'm not staying for this. If you are suggesting, I— My dear mother must be turning in her grave—"

Nora's "I don't think so" fell together with Owen's "Feeling guilty, Dennis?"

"The bugger's a nail in her coffin," Mr. Simpson rasped.

Zoe, Louise noticed, slumped in relief, perhaps glad Dennis took center stage. Alfred's attentive gaze never wavered. Was it concern that brought on his frown? Louise couldn't tell.

Jeremy appeared lost, while Jessie repeated indignantly, "Well, I never—"

Lips pursed, the antique lady sat back, pudgy hands crossed over the stomach rolls that the clingy dress exaggerated.

Nora's voice filled the room. "Except for the guilty party, no one has anything to fear."

"Leave it to the cops," Owen interrupted. "The fuzz is slow, but like the Mounties say, they always get their man." He gazed around, "Pardon me, ladies. Or woman, I should add."

"As you all know, my godchild, Sergeant Marpel, is on the case." Mrs. Norton twinkled but couldn't hide her pride. "Of course, he's an excellent detective. But we have an unbeatable advantage. We were here when Carol was poisoned."

The blunt statement caused some sharp breath intakes.

"How do you know my aunt was poisoned at her party, Mrs. Norton?" Trevor asked in a quiet and reasonable tone.

A fair question, Louise's mind admitted.

The actress fluttered her hand, bare of rings today. "Let's say a little bird told me."

Louise kept a stony face. Sgt. Marpel wouldn't be amused if he'd heard his godmother insinuate insider information.

"Ridiculous!" boomed Dennis. "How could you poison someone at a party and not everyone get sick? The food was free for all. We ate the same stuff."

"Not quite," Nora said and paused a fraction too long for effect.

Owen stole her thunder. "If you think her birthday cake was poisoned, it sure wasn't me—"

"Nothing wrong with my Jeremy's cake," Jessie put in with conviction. She patted her husband's skinny knee.

The baker paled and shook his head, apparently dreading the attention. Louise felt quite sorry for him.

"C'mon, Nora. Don't be a fool. You know us village folks." Owen leaned forward to pin their hostess with a stare.

Dennis, wedged in between the two, inched his chair back out of the line of fire.

"Unlike some people," the café proprietor's glance shifted briefly to Louise before continuing, "you can't think we'd go offing old ladies. Jeremy and me had no reason in the world to be shot of Carol."

"He's right, dearie." One hand still on her husband's knee, either to reassure him or brace herself, Jessie scuttled to the edge of her seat. "Nora, dear, you've patronized our business from the get-go. It's spick-and-span. Nothing goes bad at Petit Four You."

"*Er...* Jessie, I think Nora's not talking about food poisoning." Trevor's gentle words voiced the general astonishment at the patisserie owner's misconception.

"Well, I'd never," muttered Jessie, her cheeks aflame.

Without undue dramatics, their hostess said, "I've lived in Cascade longer than any of you. Don't forget, I've witnessed Carol's fights with the local business community. You fought tooth and nail to keep main-street parking."

"And won," Owen commented with a smug grin.

"Would you have succeeded if Carol had mobilized the municipal council?" Mrs. Norton glanced meaningfully from the café owner to the bakers and to the antique lady.

Kendra, engrossed by something on her mobile's screen, said without looking up. "My business doesn't rely on random street customers."

This seemed to trigger Dennis's entrepreneurial vein. He scooted his chair forward. "Do you sell online? I can connect you with some key players—"

"Thanks, but no thanks." The antique dealer sounded scornful. "My trusted clients come through word of mouth."

'So, trustworthy clientele rather than dealer? One way of looking at it,' thought Louise.

But there was no time to ponder the implications. For Owen, who'd been jabbing at Nora behind Dennis's back, now burst out, "You've got to be kidding, Nora. Carol was a toothless tiger. Isn't that right, eh Jeremy?" he appealed to the baker, who looked nonplussed.

"Even if she'd regained her health," he continued, "she was long beyond running the village committee. Never mind having any clout with the municipal council."

At this, Gilbert Simpson treated them to his insane laughter. Uma eyed him with professional detachment.

Next to Louise, Zoe fidgeted. Pulling at a loose thread in her beautiful dress, she asked fretfully. "What are they talking about?"

"Nothing to worry about, honey." Trevor tried to soothe her.

Louise wanted to signal Nora to regain the reins, but Dennis already boomed, "What I want to know, who tipped off the police? Was that you, Louise? Like with the miserable little plant?"

Suspicious glances from several guests made Louise want to squirm. "Me? How could I?" It came out far less assertive than intended.

"Louise didn't even live here when your mother died," Alfred said in his authoritative head nurse voice. "Blame it on me. I collected specimen and requested a toxicity test."

With few exceptions, the others must have been unaware of Alfred's actions and now looked scandalized. Louise gave him kudos for not throwing Uma to the wolves.

Dennis puffed up his cheeks. "Then why was I not notified? If staff suspected funny business, it was their duty to inform me. Were you afraid I'd sue you for negligence?" He pinned Alfred with a scathing glance. "I've got a mind to sue you now."

"Be my guest." Alfred didn't seem frazzled by the prospect.

"Rosewood and its staff did not neglect your mother." Nora's thrilling actress voice recaptured everyone's attention. "If it hadn't been for the nurses' vigilance, your mother's murderer would get away with the cowardly killing of a helpless invalid."

"Hear, hear," said Owen.

"That poor woman. Gives you a bad turn, it does." Jessie nodded. "So wicked. And on her birthday."

She squeezed the petrified baker's arm. "Nothing wrong with my Jeremy's cake. Handcrafted, as we say now. My Jeremy used the finest absinthe. Didn't you, dear? Just like Carol loved it."

The baker continued staring at his reddish hands.

"What you've got to ask yourself," said Owen to no one in particular, "*cui bono?* Me, I had nothing to gain by poor Carol's death. I kind of enjoyed our squabbles, and she thrived on them. Us here from the village knew her bark was worse than her bite."

"Are you insinuating I'd kill my dear mother for my inheritance?" Dennis sputtered. His finger pointed at Trevor and Zoe. "For money grabbers—look no further. This precious pair benefits the most. Weaseled their way into my mother's confidence and took her to the cleaners. Cheated me out of what is mine!"

"That's so not true!" shouted Zoe.

Though spoken softly, Louise heard Trevor say, "Don't let him bait you, honey."

Not heeding the caution, Zoe pushed aside her spouse's restraining hand. Her body tensed forward. "You only came back because you thought Auntie might change her will. And she would have, too!"

"Zoe!" Trevor's sharp hiss fell into the stunned hush.

Dennis's face lost its color and crimsoned with a vengeance right after. The veins on his temples bulged. "You little viper. So that was your game." His voice grew shrill. "My mother would never disinherit her only son."

"She would so!" Zoe half rose, shaking off Trevor's arm. Disregarding the "Honey, don't!" she glared at Dennis. "If Auntie had lived another week, she'd have cut you off without a penny."

Gilbert Simpson wriggled in his seat. Gleefully rubbing his hands in the air, he shouted, "You show them, girl. Only one here with some spunk."

Though Nora's idea of goading the suspects to incriminate each other clearly panned out, Louise feared it getting out of hand. Mrs. Norton deigned not to see her signals to rein things in but watched the players with keen absorption.

Just when Louise decided to take charge, Zoe yelled at the swearing Dennis. "You killed Auntie. 'Cause you were afraid she'd change the will."

"That's enough, Zoe." Trevor pulled his wife back onto her chair and hugged her close to his side, his eyes blazing at his cousin. The young woman slumped against her spouse and broke into tears.

Fists clenched and feet planted apart, Dennis outstared his cousin. "Manipulated the old woman to split my inheritance with your little brat."

At this, Mr. Simpson bounced in his seat and distracted everyone with a wild cackle. Still, Louise heard Zoe ask Trevor, "What's he talking about?" Louise knew only too well what Carol's son meant and what that implied.

"Stop that!" Dennis hollered at Simpson. "You evil dwarf. Wormed your way back into my mother's good graces. 10,000 bucks! Left to you, of all people? Proves she'd lost her marbles."

Abruptly, Gilbert Simpson's hee-hawing broke off. Open-mouthed, he went still and seemed to shrink before their eyes. The whisper was almost too soft for Louise to catch the words. "She couldn't have."

The clawlike fingers gripped the armrests. He pulled himself upright and coughed.

His voice was firm when he said, "I'll refuse. I won't accept a cent of her money." He eyed Dennis with a calculating stare.

"No," he added and giggled. "Then it'll go back in the pot. Got a better idea. I'll donate it to the dog rescue."

The decision seemed to restore him to his usual self. He shrieked and fist-bumped Uma's arm. The nurse grinned at him.

Louise figured Uma must be used to all kinds of idiosyncratic behaviors from her nursing charges. Bonding with Simpson appeared to destress the girl.

"Looks to me like you've got the strongest motive, Dennis," Owen said.

"To kill your own mom," said Jessie, clearly shocked. "Such a well-spoken lady, too." Her chin wobbled as she shook her head, tut-tutting.

The accused rose. Puce faced, he glared at them.

"I don't need to listen to this. I did not kill my mother!"

Chapter Thirty-One

"Feeling the heat, Benson?" Owen taunted.

When Carol's son swung around to face the café proprietor, Louise expected the men to come to blows.

But Owen just laughed.

"You just shut your big mouth!" cried Dennis. "I hate this damn town. Nothing but interfering snoops. Gawd, I can't wait to get away."

Owen pushed himself up, and Dennis took a step back. "Far be it from me to speak ill of the dead," Owen drawled. "But when it comes to interfering folks, your mom took the cake."

Louise winced at the ill-chosen idiom, but no one else seemed to notice.

A quick move brought Owen between Dennis and the path to the door. "If you hate us interfering village folks," he said, "maybe you hated Carol, too."

With an impotent growl, Dennis took a swing at his tormentor but was no match for the other's nimble dodge.

"Gentlemen," cried Mrs. Norton. "Please. No fighting."

Alfred was on his feet, ready to chuck the combatants out.

Assuming authority, Louise cleared her throat and spoke loudly, "May I say a word?"

To her own surprise, silence ensued.

In measured tones, she addressed the assembled friends of Carol Benson. "As an outsider, I might see the situation less emotional. On the danger of you calling me interfering, I'd like to give you my five-cent worth."

"Please do," her sleuthing partner said on cue.

Zoe wriggled out of Trevor's protective embrace and reached over to Louise. "Yes, please, Louise. Tell them we didn't hurt Auntie."

Against grumbling from Kendra, who muttered she'd heard enough for one night, and tongue-clicking from Jessie, Mr. Simpson's rasping voice urged, "Go for it. Let the lady speak."

Reluctantly, Dennis scurried back to his armchair. Owen waited until the other showed no sign of planning an escape before taking his own seat, saying, "Okay, lady of Charlotte. Solve our little mystery."

"Well, it's up to you to judge. I can only submit the facts and my deductions." Louise warned.

"We're short a juror if you're the prosecutor. By my counts, we've got eleven," Owen pointed out.

"Ten," Alfred said. "If the killer is among us."

Uneasy glances cast at neighbors told Louise there was no time to lose stating her case. Yet, there was so much to puzzle out.

"You're in for a lengthy session," she said. "Bear with me. Let's agree, for argument's sake, only someone at Carol's party could have poisoned her. Everyone was gathered in this room, and Carol sat just where Nora sits now. I'm told guests were milling about and came up to congratulate or sit with her. Is that right?"

Nods from various people accompanied Nora's, "Quite correct."

"Hence, we can infer everyone had opportunity," continued Louise. "Before I get to the means, let's recap the motives we heard about. You might say they all relate to gain. Nora mentioned the local businesses. Carol's parking prohibition scheme would have interfered with maximizing commercial gain."

"I've said so before," interrupted Owen, "and repeat, Carol failed. Plus, several of the local commercial big shots are on the municipal council."

"Kill for parking? How naïve can you get?" The antique dealer chortled.

"Oh, I agree." Louise smiled at the proprietors. "People might fight over parking spots downtown Toronto. Presumably, things don't get so heated at village committee meetings."

Mr. Simpson snorted. Owen grinned at him. "Yeah, Gilbert, you rattled the committee in your day. We miss your spats with Carol. What a spirited old gal she was, eh?"

"That's no way to speak of my mother," piped up Dennis. He inched closer to the edge of his seat, legs wide apart and hands on his knees, perhaps preparing to jump up at short notice.

Doggedly, Louise carried on, "Direct financial gain, of course, counts as the strongest motive. Carol's heirs stood to benefit considerably. Again, 10,000 dollars might tempt someone to drastic measures."

Instead of protesting, Simpson craned his neck as far as it would go and nodded in little spurts like a pecking hen.

Louise regarded him with interest. "But you didn't know about the bequest, did you, Gilbert? Nor did you want your former friend's money."

Mr. Simpson wriggled sideways and leaned toward Uma. "Smart lady. She's my neighbor."

He waggled a gnarled finger at Louise, who went on unperturbed. "The stakes were far higher for Carol's family. Financial losses through a bankruptcy or loans called in prematurely can drive one to desperate means."

Next to her, Zoe whimpered while Dennis scowled. Louise figured their silence avoided a public admission of financial woes. The business owners, she noticed, relaxed, or in Kendra's case, looked bored. Nora perched on her seat in rapt attention.

"Zoe told us," Louise reminded her listeners, "if Carol had lived another week, a new will might have changed everything."

"That's rubbish," cried Dennis.

Ignoring the outburst, Louise asked, "Did Carol plan to disinherit her only son? Or did she change her mind about willing half of her estate to little Daniel?"

"Hang on, Louise," Trevor cut in. "Where do you get that from?" He let go of Zoe's hand, who wrinkled her forehead in a puzzled frown. It slowly turned into a tentative smile.

Trevor leaned past Zoe to capture Louise's full attention, saying, "My cousin inherits the estate. Don't you, Dennis?"

"As if you didn't know." Dennis sneered across. "You sucked up to her. Don't tell me you didn't see the will."

"How could we? The reading is after probate," said Trevor. "Did my aunt's lawyer show it to you already?"

His cousin sniggered. "What ninnies. Your lawyer's a fool if he didn't demand a copy."

"We don't sue people," cried Zoe. "What would we have a lawyer for?"

"It's okay, honey." Trevor stroked his wife's agitated hands and, ignoring Dennis, explained to Louise, "Mr. Fox, my aunt's lawyer, took care of the legal stuff for the house and mortgage."

"Fools," muttered Dennis.

Zoe touched Louise's arm and whispered, "Is it true? Auntie put Danny in her will?"

When Louise nodded, the young woman's face transformed into a rapturous smile. "Bless her," she whispered.

Pleased to have her assumption confirmed, Louise summed up, "So, Trevor, you and Zoe weren't told of Daniel's inheritance. But Dennis, you saw a copy of the will."

"What's that supposed to mean?" Truculent, Carol's son clutched the arms of his chair and pushed his chest out. His forehead glistened in the bright light of the chandelier.

"It all depends on when you received the copy." Louise watched him closely.

"What difference does that make?"

"Do you recall the date you received the copy?" she asked quickly. Either he was very dense or playacting.

Frowning, he patted the sides of his marine-style blazer and extracted his mobile. Eyes on the screen, he told her, "For all it matters, it was on the

Tuesday after my mother passed away. The lawyers took their sweet time getting it from old man Fox."

"I see," said Louise.

The patisserie owner's gentle throat clearing drew Louise's attention.

"Dearie, me and Jeremy don't get your drift. Do you want our alibis? Like on the Telly?"

"*Er*, not quite," Louise said and heard Kendra guffaw.

"Wouldn't work, sweetheart," said Owen with a hint of amusement. "We're all in the same boat—or parlor, I should say—as far as alibis go."

"So, why the heck is she asking dates?" grumbled Dennis.

Owen rolled his eyes. "Use your brain, man. Or what passes for gray matter in your thick skull."

Mr. Simpson rocked in his chair, giggling between snorts.

"Gentlemen, please," chided Nora.

Alfred uncrossed his legs and spoke calmly. "Louise wanted to find out if you knew the terms of Carol's will before her death or found out after. Makes a difference, Dennis."

"Don't be daft," Dennis retorted. "My mother sharing what's in her will? What a joke." He didn't look amused. Peevishly, he added, "By rights, I'm the heir. Geez, I'm her son."

"Didn't suit you she called for the lawyer to come see her," Alfred said quietly.

"Well, of course, I wouldn't want her to make a new will. Or—" Dennis's brow puckered as if grappling with a mental challenge. "I mean, if I'd known the brat was to get half, I'd want her to change the will. But she never mentioned old Fox was coming."

Seeing Nora's growing restlessness, Louise gave her a tiny sign to take over.

Incredulity colored the actress's speech when she accosted Dennis, "Are you asking us to believe your mother never told you about the will? Not even when you argued with her before she died?"

"She did not!" When Dennis pivoted toward Nora, Louise saw his face distorting like a puce mask and wished she hadn't put Nora into his crosshairs.

He shouted, "Don't you get it? If she'd told me about the will— She didn't say a word about it." His venom turned on Trevor. "Ask my precious cousin how much he got out of her death. As if he didn't know they'd get the house for free, plus her investments. My lawyers are on to it. We'll contest the will."

"Shucks. There goes the motive if Dennis didn't know," said Owen and gave Louise a thumbs down.

"Depends on how badly he needs money," Louise said. "After all, he assumed—"

"Kill my own mother to get at cash?" Dennis sputtered. "What rotter do you think I am?" He gave Louise a cunning look. "A flopped venture never worries me. Got more irons in the fire."

"Oh, I'm sure you do." Louise glanced around the circle of suspects. Time to move in for the kill. "I don't think your mother was murdered for the inheritance. The killer had a different motive."

"Avenging a past wrong." The actress's voice carried an impressive note of vengeance.

All eyes followed Nora's piercing stare at the hunched figure almost lost in the commodious wing chair.

Gilbert Simpson rasped, "Vultures! Found your scapegoat?"

"Carol hurt your feelings," Nora persisted. "And you believed she killed your dog—"

"Outrageous. Typical of the paranoid nutcase," Dennis interrupted.

"Auntie wouldn't harm a dog." Zoe sounded offended. "She loved animals."

"My poor Peek-a-boo." The elderly voice cracked on the last syllable. Louise could only see his curved back when he twisted to peer at their hostess. "Think I poisoned her in revenge?"

When Nora inclined her head, he broke out into his cackle and swiveled to Uma's side. His crooked finger pointed at Mrs. Norton, but he spoke to the young nurse. "Hear that? They think I laced the birthday cake." His head jerked forward. "I might have."

"You rat," yelled Dennis and prepared to lunge. To Louise's relief, Owen's muscular arm stopped him.

Over the noise of shocked exclamations, Simpson slapped his knobby legs and crowed surprisingly loud, "Hee-hee. But I didn't."

Alfred's firm voice quelled the expressions of disbelief. "One day, you'll go too far, Gilbert. If you pretend to be mental, people will believe you are."

"Yeah. Told you enough times," said Owen. "Stop acting the village loony, Gilbert. Something will stick."

'Too late for that,' thought Louise.

"Gilbert just gets a kick out of winding people up," Alfred said. "He wouldn't harm a fly."

"I wasn't thinking of revenge as a motive," Louise said and heard the antique lady groan.

"Well, are you going to tell us?" Owen got up to grab a can of beer from the cooler bucket. "Anyone wants one?" As the others shook their heads, he scoffed. "Hey, relax. The stuff is sealed." He proved his point by letting the ring pop.

"I'd rather go home and put my feet up with a decent glass of wine," said Kendra. "Are you coming, Jessie?" She scrambled to the edge of her chair, readying to get up.

"Please bear with me a little longer," said Louise. "I think you can help me figure things out. Tell me if I'm wrong."

The dealer crossed her arms and sat back. "What's that supposed to mean?"

"Let me ask those of you who knew Carol well. I got the impression she was a passionate collector." Louise gazed encouragingly from Zoe to Trevor and Dennis. "Are you familiar with her collection?"

Zoe looked blank. But then she grabbed Trevor's arm. "Auntie had a lot of old stuff when we visited last summer."

Trevor's cheeks pulled down, clearly at a loss. "I guess so. Sorry, Louise, not a thing I pay attention to. But, yeah, I had to keep the monster from grabbing things."

Louise smiled and turned to Carol's son. "How about you, Dennis?"

He crossed his arms and shrugged his shoulders. "How would I know? Hadn't seen my mother the last few years."

Kendra snorted. "Decades."

"Hey, wait." Trevor's arm shot up. "Wasn't there that coin collection? Remember, Dennis?"

When the cousin shook his head, shrugging, Trevor said to Louise, "The great-great grandparents started it. Dad used to talk of it when I was obsessed with collecting pennies as a kid. He told me Aunt Carol had it in safekeeping." Ruefully he added, "Probably so Dad couldn't sell it."

Louise gazed steadily at Dennis. Angry dark patches glowed on his cheeks. Slowly she said, "So that's what you hoped to find in my crawl-space. The treasure codicil in the will reminded you of it."

Chapter Thirty-Two

Stone-faced despite her heart's thudding, Louise observed the effect of her words.

Nora, of course, knew what she was talking about. So did Dennis, never mind his bluster and half-hearted, "You're mistaken."

But Zoe's puzzled "What treasure?" sounded genuine.

"How come you know my aunt's will?" asked Trevor.

Owen's triumphant outcry, "I knew it. A treasure hunt! Did you find it, Louise?" had Kendra perk up. Jessie said all agog to her dazed-looking husband, "Like them reality shows, isn't it?"

Only Alfred appeared unfazed. Hands slung around his crossed knee, he observed the excited company with clinical interest. As did Uma. Mr. Simpson, it seemed, had dozed off.

Louise raised her palms to get everyone's attention. "Goodness. I'm so sorry to get your hopes up."

She smiled apologetically at Trevor and Zoe. "No old coin treasure found during my renovations to Carol's place. But the family portrait in your living room made me wonder about Carol's art collection."

"You've lost me," said Trevor. "You mean the one of us with Daniel?"

A sharp fold gathered above Zoe's nose. "It's just a photo of us Auntie took with Trevor's phone last summer."

"Sure wouldn't call that art." Trevor grinned at Louise. "Hey, but it's a great photo. Nothing wrong with it, is there?"

"Nothing at all," said Louise. "The watercolor paintings in the background caught my eye. I recognized the work of a well-known Canadian painter."

"You mean my mother's paintings are valuable?" Dennis cut in. "Where are they now?"

"That I can't say for sure, Dennis. But I can tell you where one of them was the other day. Incidentally, so was the antique cupboard partially shown in your family photo, Zoe."

"The ugly thing with some paint still on it? I wanted to crop it before we got the photo enlarged. But it would have cut off Trevor's arm."

"Glad you didn't, Zoe," said Louise with a smile.

"Where did you see my aunt's stuff?"

Though Dennis echoed Trevor's question, Louise turned to her other side.

Alfred, she noticed, inched his chair closer to the French doors leading into the foyer, its lights dimmed now for the night. Kendra sat with her eyes half shut.

Restless murmurs from some of her listeners hastened Louise on. Yet, she kept her voice casual. "Kendra? Remember, I came to your workshop?"

A glacial stare accompanied the antique dealer's curt reply. "Where you had no business to be."

"So you said," admitted Louise. "Still, it was an interesting glimpse into antique business practice."

Owen guffawed. "Caught you prettifying your junk, Kendra?"

The dealer bristled. "Restoring objects to their natural state is an essential part of my line of business." Her piercing glance shifted from Owen to Louise. "Come to the point. I haven't got all night."

"Put bluntly," Louise replied, "one watercolor from Zoe and Trevor's photo was in your workshop. You stored it in a crate when you caught me staring at it."

"I may have protected a painting from sawdust. What of it?"

Despite Kendra's bored tone, Louise saw her dig plump fingers into the biceps of the crossed arms.

"You claimed it was merely a cheap print copy you were framing for a friend. So, why go to such length *protecting* it?"

To Louise's annoyance, Dennis interrupted already, "Do I get this right? My mother's property was in this woman's workshop?" His chin jutted at the antique lady.

"It certainly was," Louise confirmed. "Plus, the same antique cupboard from Zoe's family photo stood in the showroom. A so-called jam cupboard. Easily recognized by its unique fretwork and coloring."

While addressing Dennis, she saw Mrs. Norton slink from the wing chair and exit through a side door she hadn't noticed before. Louise registered the opening mimicked the white paneling and was virtually invisible. Nora, she thought, must desperately need the loo to desert her at this critical stage.

"What are you getting at?" The dealer's gruff voice recaptured Louise's momentary abstraction. The woman's ample bosom heaved and strained the confines of the flowery dress.

"I'm simply stating facts," said Louise. "But I suspect there are more of Carol's paintings and antiques on the premise. If anyone were to search."

"You suspect?" hissed the dealer. "Are you imputing I stole from Carol? Laughable!" The forced chortle didn't convince.

"Oh, you needn't resort to open theft," Louise said. "I imagine, when Carol prepared her move to Rosewood, she asked you to sell the valuable antiques and art collection."

Since Alfred had slid his chair back and Uma now jiggled hers closer to Simpson's wing chair, it left the dealer in an isolated position. When Louise bent forward, nothing obstructed her scrutiny of Kendra's face. It showed no reaction.

So, Louise went on, "You probably did business together over the years, and Carol trusted you with this major consignment."

"What if she did?" Kendra shrugged. "I source pieces for many clients and help sell where I can. Carol's no exception. I even sold Owen a piece or two for the Witch's Brew."

"You sure did," said the café owner. "And dear they were."

Louise smiled at him. "Remember when we chatted on my first visit, Owen? You said Kendra and Carol were as thick as thieves."

Owen puffed out his cheeks. Then grinned. "Did I say that? Not a bad characterization." He laughed when Dennis swung around. "Oops. Of Kendra, I mean. No offense."

"Insults come natural to you, Owen," retorted Kendra. But the icy-blue glare fixed on Louise. "Nothing wrong with helping Carol make a few pennies. Old folks hoard useless junk. When they end in a nursing home, someone must declutter their house. Precious little thanks I got for helping," she added acidly.

Though the stare was intimidating, Louise persisted in her course. "An intent to help perhaps motivated you. But I imagine the consignment proved far more profitable than expected."

Kendra's lips popped in a derisive *pscha*. "What nonsense. Stick to things you know about instead of letting your imagination run riot, Louise. Don't bore us to death. You've put that old man to sleep already," she added when a snore from Simpson underscored her claim. "Let's call it a night. I've had enough of this drivel."

"Oh, c'mon, Kendra," said Owen. "Don't be a spoilsport. Let the lady sleuth have her fun."

Dennis braced both hands on his knees. "I want to hear this. If this woman defrauded my mother, my lawyers will sue. Can you prove she did, Louise?"

"Preposterous!" The antique lady spat out the word like a rotten nut.

"I couldn't agree more," said Louise. "Taking advantage of an elderly person's failing health to defraud them is indeed preposterous. It started already with a postcard aimed to frighten Carol and speed up her move to Rosewood."

"What?" cried Owen. "Carol wasn't easily scared."

"She never received the card. I did," explained Louise. "A condolence card with praying hands addressed to the resident of 49 Charlotte Lane. On the back, it read, *In the midst of life, death awaits. Thinking of you.*"

"Excuse me, Louise," said Trevor, "but wouldn't that be someone condoling my aunt's death?"

"It's postmarked a few weeks earlier and went awry because of a wrong postal code. Plus, the town's name was difficult to make out," said Louise. "You slipped up there, Kendra. The postal code matches the one on your old store receipt before you moved Precious Treasures to Cascade."

"What utter nonsense!" fumed the dealer.

"Absolutely not," Louise countered. "But the card doesn't matter. It just triggered my unease. Do you deny removing all valuable items from Carol's home shortly after she was hospitalized and unable to oversee the removal?"

"I can answer that," said Alfred. "Carol asked me to tidy things around the house when it went on the market. Kendra came with the stager and some guys who loaded the truck."

"And yet have to get paid for my troubles." As if vying for support, Kendra's gaze zoomed in on the bakers. "Jessie, you know how cheap Carol was. Always wanting favors and making you wait for your money."

"Well, dearie, me and Jeremy didn't—"

"Are you saying my mother owes—"

But Owen cut them both off. "Could we let Louise finish?" Over Jessie's "Well, I never," he urged Louise, "Get on with it. I'm dying to hear the end."

Spurred on by this ambiguous encouragement, Louise focused on the antique dealer. "I assume you sold the most valuable items privately to your trusted customers. A few things went to your store, either for temporary storage or public sale to show some revenue from the consignment."

"There's absolutely nothing sinister in this," huffed the dealer. "Old folks downsize or move into care, and I deal with the disposal of their stuff as a special favor. It's more pain than profit. The old dears are so deluded after treasuring things for donkey days. Their junk is worthless in a competitive market."

"My aunt was not deluded but completely with it," said Trevor and turned to Zoe. "Didn't we say last summer how sharp she was?" When Zoe eagerly agreed, he told Louise, "She still was like this about buying the house from her. Really smart at business."

"Always has been." For once, Dennis echoed his cousin's opinion.

Louise sent them a grateful look. She felt like a skater testing the pond after the first serious frost. The edifice of evidence might tumble around her ears any minute. A tiny smile tugged at her lips at the mixed metaphor.

Aloud, she said with faked confidence, "Such an astute, albeit physically weakened, woman would soon grow suspicious when her antiques and art collection did not yield a profit. Of course, she would ask questions."

Louise drew on Owen. "Didn't you tell us Carol was quite a fighter, like on the committee?"

He laughed. "Was she ever."

"So, we can expect Carol argued about the lack of real profit or sales." As she spoke, Louise saw Uma raise a hesitant hand, just like a student would in class. Encouragingly, she asked, "Yes, Uma?"

With a quick glance at Alfred, the young nurse said, "I heard this lady argue with Mrs. Benson about money."

"Oh? When was that?" Louise couldn't believe her luck.

But Uma's apprehensive eyes were on Alfred. Only when he nodded did she say, "The afternoon before the birthday."

"Did you hear any of the conversation?" asked Louise, and mentally crossed her fingers the girl wouldn't clam up.

Immediately, Uma defended herself to Alfred. "I swear I wasn't listening. This lady has a loud voice and was going on about e-transing money." When the head nurse made no move to stop her, she added, "I followed the rules. They didn't hear me knock. Mrs. Benson was so angry. I would have asked this lady to leave, but they were all smiles when they saw me."

"Did you catch what Mrs. Benson said?" Louise asked quickly in case Alfred might rebuke the young nurse.

"Only a bit," said Uma. "Like, 'the painting is worth 5000.'"

"Chickenfeed," interrupted the dealer. "Like I said, the old have no sense of true value. They think 5000 when it's 50 or 500 tops. There's a record of my e-transfers. All accounted for and above board."

'Yeah, right,' thought Louise, barely suppressing an eye roll. The image of Kendra hunting for the outdated receipt pad was too vivid to forget.

She commented, "Let's not forget the cash sales. You offered the option to me, and I'm sure it's standard practice in your business." Despite her firm tone, she felt defeated at the prospect of proving any of her claims. Did anyone even know what Carol had owned?

"I resent these outrageous accusations," cried the dealer. "I'm respected in the antique community and in this town!"

"Er, Kendra," said Owen, stroking his chin. "Was just thinking. Carol's insurance might have an inventory of any valuable pieces. I know mine has of the more expensive equipment at the café. If Trevor or Dennis gets Carol's lawyer to request a copy, you could prove what sold or is still kicking around your store."

Arms akimbo, the antique lady snorted. "Thanks, Owen. Another of your brilliant ideas. People constantly buy and sell things. You don't seriously think anyone updates their insurance for whatever they own? That's laughable."

'She's probably right,' thought Louise, getting despondent.

"We took tons of photos and videos of Auntie with Daniel last summer, didn't we, Trev?" Zoe clutched Trevor's arm.

"We sure did, honey. Are you thinking..." When his wife nodded eagerly, he said to Louise, "That should show some of what my aunt had last summer."

Though Kendra hooted derisively, Louise thanked the young couple. Unsure how to proceed, she noticed Alfred scratching his head.

"If you show me your shots of Carol's place," he said, "I can tell you what was there before the stager's truck came."

"Who were the stagers?" Louise asked. "It didn't look staged when I saw it." Far from staged, it had looked like a dump.

"Yeah, remove all the nice pieces and replace them with trashy stuff, and a place looks like sh—" Alfred grinned and added, "I told Carol it needed sprucing up and a paint job. But she was in a hurry selling. Anyway, the stager's your buddy, Kendra, isn't she?"

The dealer ignored him. Instead, the frigid stare sought to intimidate Louise. "Why are we talking about my business contacts?" The glare shifted to Dennis. "God, I wish I'd never got involved with your mother's affairs. What kind of son are you not to have pitched in? I wasted my time organizing everything for her—realtor and all."

When Dennis colored and blustered, she hissed, "Couldn't trust you, could she? The way you treated her. Not a word for years on end. Shameful!"

"What? What?" croaked Mr. Simpson. Nightcap jauntily over one eye, he scrambled to semi-consciousness.

Distracted, everyone watched while Uma murmured soothing noises like calming a baby and tucked a wool throw around the elderly gent's legs. His chin sank back toward his chest.

The dealer, it seemed, had used the interruption to muster her resources. For with renewed vigor, she swiveled to face Alfred and launched an attack. "If anything is missing from Carol's stuff, we know who spent his sweet time in her place. Unobserved, I may add."

The head nurse drawled, "I don't take other people's stuff."

"Alfred is not a thief!" Uma burst out with unexpected vehemence. "He's the most honest person I know."

"Can't trust a dope head. Once an addict, always an addict." Kendra recrossed her arms and sat back. Satisfied, she smirked at Alfred's pained expression.

Louise saw the man's fists clench and his jaw muscles tighten under the collective scrutiny.

"Nah, you've got that wrong, Kendra." Owen gave a slight headshake as if disagreeing with a minor point. "Alfred's clean and as honest as—" Perhaps lost for an example of honesty, he added, "You know what I mean."

"That he is," piped up Jessie, who'd been whispering to her husband. "Tells you if you forget to charge for an extra bun, that he does." Her face reddened. "Me and Jeremy are a wee bit lost with all them art things. But my Jeremy got a bee in his bonnet about the bottle," she patted the skinny knee.

Louise pounced. "What bottle, Jeremy?" But the baker shrunk back, head shaking and the scraggy body atremble.

Jessie reached a motherly hand to cover his. "He means the absinthe Kendra brought specially for Carol. Such a pretty bag—"

The lights suddenly dimmed to a weird brown glimmer.

'Oh, my God. Not a power failure?' Louise's mind raced. An outage at this critical moment—

In the murky darkness, Zoe's scream made them jump. All eyes were on the young woman.

"Zoe. It's okay. Only a brown-out." Louise half rose to take charge of the situation.

But Zoe pointed frantically.

Trevor's "Honey?" got lost in Zoe's agonized cry.

"Auntie! She's come back!"

Chapter Thirty-Three

There, in the doorway, framed by irradiating paneling, stood an eerie figure. Bluish light backlit long strands of silvery hair spilling from a black lace mantilla. Eyes blazed in charcoal hollows of an unearthly white face. It contorted in rage when the apparition's arm rose.

"Mother!" Dennis's cry broke the stunned silence.

Zoe's keening and frightened gasps from Jessie sounded unnaturally loud. Far from calm herself, Louise reached over to clasp Zoe's shaking hand.

Like Banquo's ghost, a luminescent finger pointed straight at Kendra.

"You poisoned me."

The apparition's choked rasping as if in the throes of death was so real it sent shivers over Louise's body.

"What the heck—" Trevor muttered and pulled his crying wife close.

Louise let go of Zoe's hand and focused on the accused. In the weak light, Kendra's features morphed from incredulity into fear. The chair screeched on the hardwood when she cringed and shrunk back to scurry out of reach.

With a horrible wheezing, the specter stabbed its clawlike finger at the dealer.

"You robbed me! Your hand poisoned the drink."

"I didn't mean to," croaked Kendra. The pudgy hands flew to cover her quavering mouth. Horror-stricken eyes gulped in the graying face.

"Confess to save your soul!"

Under the spell of the moment, the dealer crumbled. With a tormented animal squeal, she appealed to the others. "I swear—only meant to make her sick. Until things got sorted." Beseechingly, she extended a hand to Dennis, who looked traumatized.

"Honest to God," she pleaded, "I meant to pay her back."

From the corner of her eye, Louise saw the ghostly figure melt into the background, leaving behind a faint reek of camphor. The panel opening closed but didn't quite shut behind the retreating figure. No light penetrated the gap.

Time to drive home the advantage.

"You murdered Carol Benson. Methanol fit your evil purpose," Louise accused the dealer. In a prosecutor's tone, she stated, "Fatality occurs only after 8 to 12 hours. The lethal amount can easily be administered in a drink rather than the cake's icing and filling. Carol drank absinthe. Its intense flavor would mask the taste of methanol. Jeremy saw you bring the bottle."

With an outraged cry, the dealer turned on Louise. "A lie! I didn't mean the stuff to harm her."

"Using potent poisons shows intent to kill," Louise retorted. Her mind boggled at Kendra's denying intent to harm. "If the methanol didn't kill Carol, she'd wake up totally blind, never again to recognize her art collection. Either way, Kendra, you felt safe from detection."

"You killed my mother." Recovered from the first shock, Dennis jumped to his feet, just as Kendra did.

"Whoa, cool it, buddy." Owen grabbed the struggling man from behind.

Louise saw Alfred block the French doors. She fumbled for her mobile, fearing the situation was out of control. As she pressed the key for Raymond's number, the enraged dealer made a lunge for her.

Alfred intercepted the move and pinned the woman's arms.

The crystal chandeliers and wall sconces suddenly blazed at full brilliance, blinding after the dimness.

"Freeze! Everyone. Police," shouted a voice over the general mayhem.

"Goodness," muttered Louise and disconnected the call. She'd never felt so relieved in her life but marveled at Sgt. Marpel's timing.

The sergeant strode in from the side entrance. Just as Louise expected, the actress followed, looking pleased with the performance. She had discarded the mantilla and witch's wig. The fragile features and knobby hands still shone faintly in luminescent white.

Stage makeup was hard to remove in a hurry, Louise noted before the dealer's screech again absorbed her attention.

"Let go of me!" the woman shouted, struggling against Alfred.

The sergeant was a few steps away when the double doors flew open, and two uniformed officers entered.

"Thanks, Mr. Rosewood. We take it from here," Louise heard Raymond say quietly.

He issued his order for all to hear. "Take her in for questioning."

The dealer protested, "Outrageous! This man attacked me. You have no right to detain me."

In unemotional, official tones, the sergeant said, "We have reasonable and probable grounds and can detain a person for twenty-four hours without laying charges. You have the right to call your solicitor. Once we are at the station," he added.

To the officers, he said, "Let's go."

Seconds later, the police and their suspect were gone, leaving behind a benumbed assembly.

"I need a drink," said Nora. The jittery titter showed frayed nerves, after all, Louise thought.

"Not so fast," commanded a voice from behind Louise.

Sgt. Marpel was back. He closed the double doors. "My constables will be here in a moment to take everyone's statement."

"But Raymond, dear," said his godmother and fluttered her hands. "Can't it wait until tomorrow? It's been a long evening, and we're worn out."

Dennis brushed Nora's diminutive figure to the side. "I've nothing to do with this, officer. These women took it upon themselves—"

The sergeant lifted a hand, demanding silence. "Not an option. I must request you to stay and wait your turn." His stern glance fixed on Louise rather than Mrs. Norton.

Zoe's tear-stained face emerged from Trevor's solicitous embrace. "Please, can't we go home? I feel sick."

"We'll take Mr. Simpson back to his place when you're done with us," offered Trevor, motioning to the huddled figure whose head rose.

The wrinkled grimace looked dazed and disoriented. Louise couldn't make out his mutterings when Simpson peered around with bloodshot eyes.

"It's past my Jeremy's bedtime, isn't it, dearie?"

At Jessie's comment, Louise stifled a hysterical giggle. The baker's wife clearly knew their priorities. Louise didn't envy the sergeant's job of gaining control. She only hoped all present remembered Jeremy's vital piece of evidence. She certainly would tell Raymond. The baker observing Kendra gifting the deadly absinthe was a clincher.

Suddenly, the room seemed full of police. There were only three newcomers, Louise realized. But their bulky dark blue uniforms with bulletproof vests and heavy belts made them appear larger than life.

No one spoke as the sergeant assigned two constables to interview the young couple and Mr. Simpson, who were led toward the foyer.

"Mrs. Norton?"

"Yes, Raymond?" fluted the godmother, fumbling for the string of pearls she must have hidden under her dress's neckline for the performance.

"I'll speak with you first. In the anteroom," he said and ushered a contrite looking Nora to the side entrance. Before he closed the door, he addressed the subdued assembly. "No talking, please. Wait your turn, and do not use your phones. The constable will remain with you."

The stoic gaze of the third officer hovered over them. Thumbs tucked into the armholes of his vest, feet wide apart, he seemed a monument to authority.

For a few minutes, Louise covertly observed the others' fidgeting. Crossing and recrossing of legs and arms, shifting in their seats, they waited. Jessie made little smacking sounds with her lips while Dennis stared at Louise and huffed in pointed annoyance.

After a glance at Alfred, who'd moved to Zoe's vacated chair, Louise followed his example and closed her eyes. Time for pondering what to say when it was her turn with Sgt. Marpel.

Epilogue

Two days later, on a dreary Monday, Louise sat at the living room window, laptop open and Shadow by her feet. From above, sounds of sawing alternated with thumps and knocks.

She took a swig from her tea mug but shuddered when the tepid brew hit her taste buds. Frustrated by her lack of focus, she stared out into the dripping foliage. A light ground fog wafted, shrouding the ravine. Gnarled tree trunks grew from a sea of graying gauze like the dyads of old.

Louise shook off the fanciful imagery. She'd lost too many working hours over the past week already. Yet reigning in her wandering mind proved elusive today.

On the weekend, she'd visited Nora twice to hash over 'their case,' as her partner in sleuthing loved to call it.

Nora admitted planning the Carol impersonation beforehand, with props at the ready in the anteroom which really was a butler's pantry wedged between the parlor and formal dining room. As Louise had refused to disclose the suspected culprit, Nora simply waited where the fingers of evidence would point. By sticking her head in the pantry's dumbwaiter's opening, the wily lady eavesdropped after her sneaky departure from the parlor.

238

With a complacent smile, the actress confessed to timing her SOS text to Raymond. As he'd rushed into Rosewood, she'd beckoned to him from the pantry's inner doorway. Before he could stop her, she slipped out the other end to make her big entrance.

Louise could well imagine the sergeant's frustration. From the dress-up, he'd guess his godmother was up to some trick. Yet he remained hidden and listened to what transpired. Was it the fascination with her performance? Or did he recognize its potential of triggering a confession?

Raymond Marpel gave nothing away. Nor did he thank them for unmasking the killer. Earlier this morning, Louise had met him and his team at the antique shop to identify the items she'd mentioned during the interview. When she'd told him about the crate with artwork, he'd interrupted the questioning to arrange the antique shop's sealing and surveillance.

Everything was still there today, causing Louise to marvel at the dealer's audacity. Or stupidity. Even the copper home distillery still sat on the shelf. No telling if Kendra had used woodchips to produce methanol unless forensics found trace evidence. But Alfred's mentioning and the recollection of the copper contraption had triggered Louise's intuition and prompted her to research the toxic alcohol.

On Saturday, Zoe had texted before breakfast to say they'd submitted videos and images taken at Auntie's place last summer, and a constable had collected the family photo.

With a deep sigh, Louise wondered if the young couple realized what a narrow escape they'd had. If Kendra hadn't confessed to a roomful of witnesses, not to mention the lurking sergeant, they'd still top the suspect list neck to neck with the son.

Yesterday, when Louise said to Alfred the police might keep him busy for days wading through the footage to pick out whatever he recognized as Carol's property, he'd laughed. Matron had turned his leave of absence into a paid vacation for another week. There'd be lots of time working in Louise's garden. She looked forward to the transformation of her yard into a blooming wonderland.

Alfred also assured her everyone at Rosewood could testify to Carol being compos mentis to the very last. Dennis's lawyers might find it difficult to dispute the will and the allocation of beneficiaries. She'd put Trevor in contact with Estelle to sort the legal and urgent loan shark issues.

Louise sighed. Maybe her neighborhood and the village community would soon be the peaceful oasis she'd dreamed of.

A loud bang from above followed by an oath rudely interrupted Louise's musing.

Shadow jumped to attention and scrabbled across the laminate when heavy footsteps tramped down the stairs.

Louise rose to meet the contractor descending from the loft bedroom.

"That cat of yours is some tiger!" he said, rubbing the back of his hand.

"Oh, my! Did she scratch you, Earl?" Louise had wondered at Magic's refusal to leave the loft but assumed the inscrutable kitty had taken a fancy to the noisy workman.

Garbed in his tan coverall, muscular, hairy arms crossed over his chest, the contractor wriggled his head as though suffering from a kinked neck.

"Soon as I removed that piece of drywall, your cat pounced into the cavity. It's an old closet alright. The puss won't let me get near it." He raised his hand and sucked at its back. "My mistake. Should of not grabbed her."

"Goodness. I'm so sorry. Here, let me get some hydrogen peroxide for the scratch." She should have crated Magic before the man arrived. But the kitty refused to come out from under the bed.

"Nah, no big deal. I've got a kit in the truck. Good excuse for my lunch break. I'll pop in at the café for half an hour." Unfazed, the contractor left with a "cheerio."

Without delay, Louise called the Witch's Brew and asked Owen to put Earl's lunch on her tab. Owen laughed, saying she'd have to come by soon to straighten her bill and have coffee with him.

Armed with the cat crate from the closet, Louise went upstairs to corner the tiger.

Her conscientious contractor had partitioned off the workspace with plastic drop sheets tacked to the ceiling and trailing the floor. Behind the translucent barrier, a cavity awaited enlargement.

Louise ducked under the makeshift curtain and peered into the dimness of the disused closet. She switched on her mobile's flashlight. In its beam, Magic approached with a curt meow but darted back into the recess when Louise made to grab her.

"Silly of me, kitty. Should mind my manners and ask politely. Hang in there while I get some tempting treats."

An angry hiss answered. Magic scratched furiously at the rickety floorboards.

Louise eyed her curiously. "So, you think she hid it there?"

The scratching grew frantic.

"Okay, I get it." Louise crawled back into the loft and rummaged in Earl's voluminous toolbox. With a crowbar and hammer, she rejoined Magic.

The cat purred as Louise attacked the floorboards. Under the grime masking the seams, she discovered short pieces patching up the original plank floor. Gently, she inserted the crowbar to loosen the inserts from all sides. With the hammer's claw, she eased up one by one.

As soon as she removed the last piece, Magic pounced into the hole. And reemerged victoriously, clutching a limp furry creature in her fangs.

Louise screeched. "A rat!"

Seeking to escape, she toppled backward from her crouch.

A rubbery squeak brought her to her senses.

"Goodness! Magic. You'll give me a heart attack." Sure the kitty would laugh at her if laughter were in the feline's repertoire, Louise felt rather foolish.

"Back to business," she said briskly and inched closer.

Magic remained poised by the hole. Play rat held tightly, the yellow irises glittered as she watched.

Louise pointed the flash into the cavity about a foot square. Inside sat a case. She lifted it gingerly, still worried about discovering real rodents. She couldn't wait to get out of the musty-smelling claustrophobic enclosure.

Once in the loft space, she heaved a sigh and ducked into the safety of her bedroom, just stopping long enough to hold up the plastic for the kitty to follow with her furry favorite.

In daylight, the case proved to be a cracked leather case with two rusty locks. Louise lowered it onto the plastic-covered bed.

"Okay, Magic. We need witnesses. You'll guard the fort while I'll go for reinforcement."

Five minutes later, she was back with Zoe, Daniel, and Trevor in tow. A black shape dashed under the bed when Louise reached the top of the loft stairs.

"Oh, is that your surprise, Louise?" Zoe sounded rather disappointed and frowned at the plastic-shrouded gaping hole in the drywall.

Daniel gurgled from his vantage point on Trevor's shoulders. "Down, down," he demanded. The little fists let go of the dad's ears and stretched toward Louise.

"Er, later," said Louise. She pointed at the old leather case on the bed. "Trevor, could you try to pick the locks, please? Daniel, you help Daddy."

"Sure, no problem." Trevor let Daniel slide right onto the bed. "Let's have a look, bud."

After a cursory examination, he said, "Got a screwdriver? I think they're just stuck."

Louise fetched one from Earl's tool kit.

A satisfying pair of clicks answered Trevor's cautious manipulations. "Should work now," he said and stepped back.

The glance he gave her told Louise, like her, he suspected what the case might hold.

"Sweetie?" Louise bent to the child and tapped the side of the case's lid. "Grab this. Are you strong enough to lift it up?"

With a shout, "Me, me," the kid bounced onto his knees and used both hands.

The lid flew up before the dad's "Easy does it" was quite out.

A dazzling array of gold and silver coins, stuck in black velvety slots, blinked and winked at them. Judged by the depth of the case, it contained several rows of them, Louise figured.

Aloud, she said, "Well done, Daniel. Seems to me you've discovered a treasure. Finders keepers."

Find my books and follow me on me for New Release Alerts
amazon.com/author/evabernhard
and on bookbub.com/authors/eva-bernhard

Book Club Questions for Death at Rosewood Manor

Whether you're reading on your own, with friends, or in your book club, these questions are designed to spark reflection and conversation about Louise Penfold's first mystery.

1. Louise Penfold comes to Cascade seeking peace after a divorce. How do you think her move shapes her outlook and choices in the story?

2. Rosewood Manor itself is a striking setting. In what ways does the building's atmosphere influence the story's mood?

3. Louise works as an editor for true-crime writer Odette Verité. How do you see her editorial skills informing her detective instincts?

4. Condolence cards appear at a key moment. What do you think they symbolize within the story?

5. Animals — Shadow and Magic — appear throughout the book. What role do they play in shaping tone, comfort, or tension?

6. Cascade is a village full of watchful neighbors and quiet secrets. How does community gossip both help and hinder the search for truth?

7. Were there any moments where you thought you had solved the mystery, only to be surprised later?

8. Did you feel justice was reached? Why, or why not?

9. If Louise were a friend or member of your book club, what advice would you give her before her next investigation?

Feel free to pick and choose, or adapt the questions to suit the way you or your group likes to read.

Don't go yet...

Dear Reader,

With your reading pleasure in mind, I'm having a ball, creating Louise's wonderful world. Surrounded by loving animals, new friends, and foes:), who knows what might happen next to Louise?

Find out **Death at Eagle Roost** – *Louise Penfold Mystery* – Book 2

amazon.com/dp/B0DJ5RS77L

Get to know my other Canadian sleuth, Agnes Taylor in the

Agnes Taylor Mystery series

The books are available in standard font, as eBooks, and as

Large Print – Agnes Taylor Mysteries

May I ask a big favor? Please tell your friends about my books and recommend them to your local library. Thanks!

Warm wishes,

Eva

P.S. Amazon sets much store (no pun intended) by customer reviews. As self-publishing (Indie) authors, we don't have the clout and funds of a large publishing house. We depend on readers like you to root for us and spread the word.

Would you be very sweet and post a review of my book, please? Thanks for your kindness!

Don't miss the next
Louise Penfold Mystery

Death
at Eagle Roost

**Behind the grandeur of Eagle Roost
lurks a household at war with itself.**

Mysteries by Eva Bernhard

My sincere thanks for your support.

Gift the LOUISE PENFOLD MYSTERY SERIES to your loved ones.

amazon.com/dp/B0DJ5RS77L

Also by Eva Bernhard

AGNES TAYLOR MYSTERIES

Also available in Paperback and Hardcover editions on your Amazon Marketplace

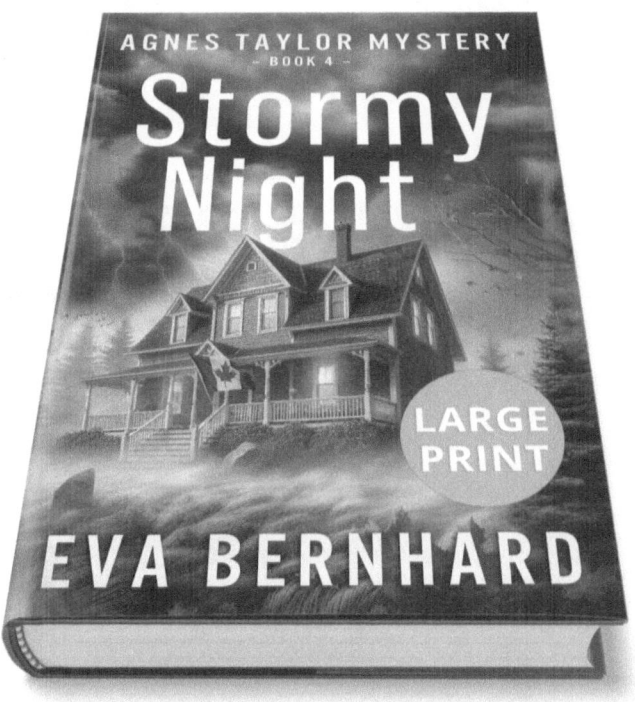

Acknowledgments

Conceiving and writing this first book of the **Louise Penfold Mystery** series was the greatest fun.

Though my writing days are spent in the sole company of my beloved (very elderly) pooch, I count myself fortunate to have so many helpers along the way to publishing my books. For every bit of help I'm truly grateful!

My critique partner, author Rebecca Markus, from Critique Match helped tremendously with feedback on an early draft. Her astute and encouraging comments keep me grounded and often put a smile on my face. ER physician, Dr. JP, known for her *Pick Your Poison Podcast*, answered some crucial questions for me. Once the final draft was ready, my awesome beta reader, Naomi, gave tons of great feedback from a reader's perspective. Thank you all so much!

Before my books ever see the light of Amazon, they are carefully scrutinized by my editor, Pam Clinton. She hunts the error devil, who roams my manuscripts. I can't thank Pam enough for her conscientious and patient help. Though, by and large, we abide by CMOS, we take some editorial liberties. Any linguistic, grammatical, stylistic, and typographic idiosyncrasies are solely my doing.

Last, not least, a big thanks to my virtual writer friends, Carly and Kristal. Our messaging is not only fun but keeps tabs on my writing progress.

May you, my Reader, enjoy this book in the loving spirit it was created!

Warmest wishes for everyone's happiness!

P.S. Early on in the life of this book, fictional Dennis's Australian address was given as Christchurch, which proved confusing. He now lives in the equally fictitious Christurn.

Eva Bernhard is a member of Crime Writers of Canada.